Amanda Brunker is a *Sunday World* journalist and a former Miss Ireland. Glamorous and outspoken, she's rarely out of the public eye.

www.rbooks.co.uk

CHAMPAGNE KISSES

Amanda Brunker

TRANSWORLD IRELAND

TRANSWORLD IRELAND
an imprint of The Random House Group Limited
20 Vauxhall Bridge Road, London SW1V 2SA
www.rbooks.co.uk

CHAMPAGNE KISSES
A TRANSWORLD IRELAND BOOK: 9781848270688

First published in Great Britain
in 2008 by Transworld Ireland
Transworld Ireland paperback edition published 2009

Copyright © Amanda Brunker 2008

Amanda Brunker has asserted her right under the Copyright, Designs
and Patents Act 1988 to be identified as the author of this work.

This book is a work of fiction and, except in the case of historical fact,
any resemblance to actual pesons, living or dead, is purely coincidental.

Addresses for Random House Group Ltd companies outside the UK
can be found at: www.randomhouse.co.uk
The Random House Group Ltd Reg. No. 954009

The Random House Group Limited supports The Forest Stewardship
Council (FSC), the leading international forest certification organization.
All our titles that are printed on Greenpeace approved FSC certified paper
carry the FSC logo. Our paper procurement policy can be found at
www.rbooks.co.uk/environment

Typeset in 12/14pt Bembo by
Kestrel Data, Exeter, Devon.
Printed in the UK by
CPI Cox & Wyman, Reading, RG1 8EX.

2 4 6 8 10 9 7 5 3 1

For my family.
Without you all I am nothing.

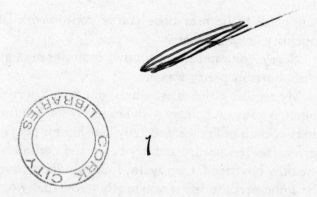

1

Why did I have a full-Irish for breakfast? It's as if I am mechanically programmed to make the wrong decision at every available opportunity.

Why is it that I always seem to order a dirty big greasy fry-up with extra beans the morning before a Hollywood wax? Yes, Saturdays are meant to be my pamper me day, starting with a long brekkie reading the papers, while eyeing up the far-too-young but oh so cute and very do-able waiters at Coffee Cups. OK, so I don't necessarily educate myself with the day's politics and the like; the only current affairs I'm interested in are those of pop stars and reality heads.

Ask me who's shagging who and I'm a grade A student, but ask me who's in charge of the country's finances and I couldn't pick them out of a line-up.

Enough about my shallow pleasures though: I'm stripped and dipped, and as anyone who's had hot wax around their middly bits will know, it's never a safe place to be near once you've consumed a large quantity of gastro fuel.

'Sorry, you can turn over now,' indicates my super-slim, horribly pretty waxer.

My regular girl Ashley, who is just such a gorgeous bitch, is away on holiday with her rugby star boyfriend in the South of France. I secretly hate her for her God-given flawless beauty and her beefy and considerably wealthy boyfriend; then again, I suppose there have to be some perks to life if you're a heterosexual woman who has to stare at other women's naked crotches all day. Yuck! And double yuck!

Over the last year I have become more comfortable in Ashley's hands. Let's be honest – stripping off your jeans and pants to lie on a bed with a bright light shining above you, no matter what soothing music is playing in the background, is traumatic. Especially without a couple of drinks involved.

But today I don't feel comfortable. 'Trish-aaah', obviously named for her gentle touch, is just too squeaky clean looking. To say her appearance is immaculate is an understatement. Her skin is to die for and I can see her frowning at my bruised and painfully white stubbly legs and, worse still, my chipped toenail polish.

'I'm getting them done later,' I lie, feeling the pressure to explain. When I'm the one paying through the nose for the privilege here, I shouldn't really need to.

But, before I get the chance to sound convincing

she blurts 'That's nice', in a sickly, patronizing tone that says: spare me the details, love, I've seen it all before.

As Trish-aaah changes the pan pipes CD to whale tones, I quickly flip over under the facecloth of a towel on to my belly, while trying to hide my dignity. As if.

Now my new pal directs me to get on all fours and pull back my left butt cheek with my hand. Cringe.

Despite the fact that I know this is coming, I never seem to be able to mentally prepare for the moment. While I keep telling myself that I'm looking for something under the bed – because that's the position you assume – the fact that someone is smoothing hot wax around your asshole quickly jolts you into reality. As I crouch in mortification, puce in the face, I make the ultimate *faux pas* – I fart.

Oh, God. World open up and swallow me whole.

As I knelt there face down and gormless, with my mouth open praying that some words of sense, or even humour, would come to rescue me, I was given a lucky escape when the CD suddenly jammed. Maybe I had a guardian angel looking over me.

Thank you, thank you, thank you, whoever you are!

Trisha with the tender touch made her apologies (if only I could have uttered mine) and left the room no doubt to get some air and officially change 'the stupid CD'.

It's January, time for new resolutions. Hell, we're

Europeans now, it's continental breakfasts for me from now on in. The thought of warm chocolate croissants is making me feel better already.

Or it was until Trish strides back into our fragrant room, grinning like she's the most popular girl at school. Obviously her story of Miss Eva – or should that be Scarlett O'Valentine – in Room 5 has amused the rest of the team.

I slowly count to ten as I visualize leaping off the table and smacking her smug face. Funny how my Saturday stars never warned me of any pending violence today. Damn Mystic Meg for not forecasting this fiasco. Who knew that an exciting brief first acquaintance with a tall, dark stranger was really a debriefing nightmare with tango Trish?

Thankfully the ordeal soon ended. Drained and somewhat wounded, I gathered my belongings and braced myself for the most distressing bit – the escape.

It wasn't over until this fat lady passed all the snooty bitches at the till. And just as I had feared, there were four smiley, happy, giggly women camped out at the counter.

Feeling like I had every staff member's eyes burrowing into the side of my brain, I handed over €140 for my full leg and Brazilian smooth-finish and fled the building. Cursing Trisha, Tina, Julie and Sam and their sad little identical and clinical smocks.

My new pal called out, 'Eva, your change.' But I had to get out.

In a fleeting moment of remorse I shrugged back, 'It's only ten euros, keep the money.'

Let's be honest, she earned it.

As I strutted down Grafton Street my confidence returned as the Saturday afternoon prize peacocks started to catch my gaze. I may feel like a plucked chicken, but male adoration, whether from low-lifes or desirable hunks, is always a tonic for the soul.

It's one thing to catch your own reflection in the window of Warehouse, while pretending to look at the mannequins and think: Go girl, you ain't lookin' half bad. But as we all know, appreciation from the opposite sex, even someone you wouldn't even sit beside on a bus, is morale-boosting.

When I say prize peacocks I am of course talking about those greasy gobshites who parade themselves around town just so they can eye up unsuspecting girlies – the younger the better – with hopes of pulling a cracker.

Generally speaking, they come in three genres. First we have the older, pot-bellied gentlemen, most likely with leathery skin and gaudy gold jewellery. I call them Daddy Sleaze.

Spot their thinning hair smothered with hair gel in an attempt to keep it all together and coiffed back in an Elvis tribute. You'll find these creeps hanging around cafés, mostly outside smoking even in the cold months like today. Thankfully I don't smoke so I'll never slip into that spider's web of 'Have you got a light?'

Even eye contact is to be avoided at all costs.

Secondly, you have the slimy Type 2 boyfriends: peacocks who don't mind spending the day in town shopping with their girlfriends, just so they can stand around female changing cubicles in the hope of spotting other half-naked girlies.

Ahhh! These guys really irk me. It's because those fools remind me of my ex-boyfriend, Trevor. What a bastard.

He was your quintessential gentleman, oh so witty and flirty with my mother. Would talk endless drivel with my dad and, generously enough I thought, buy all of my friends drinks. Yes, temporarily Trev was the real deal in my eyes. Although he was not as spectacular in the bedroom as I would have hoped; hey, you can't have it all. But he was a fairly enviable beau to have on my arm when mixing around town.

It wasn't until three months into the relationship that I found him snogging my so-called mate – at one of *my* house parties, the cheeky pup – and I realized what a slimeball he really was. Apparently Deirdre wasn't the first to fall for his charms and open wallet during our short union.

According to Reuters (that's my friend Anna who knows everything about everybody), there had been a Louise, a brunette beautician-type from Galway. And a blonde one who always seems to worm her way into parties, but nobody can work out who brought her or where she's from.

Anyway, before I start to get myself worked up

again, I'll think of all the positives. He gave me that fabulous Gucci watch, that trip to Madrid, and there was the €1,300 he gave me to pay off my Visa bill. Jaysus, maybe he wasn't that bad after all.

Speaking of plastic, that brings me nicely on to the pretty-boy peacocks. Or the Southside €300-a-week gang. They're the spoilt brats who refuse to grow up and pretend to themselves and everyone else that they're Alan Sugar's next apprentice. Most of these little cuties live at home, have meagre jobs, and spend all their cash on their designer labels and boy band haircuts.

In my eyes they're all gay but don't know it – or possibly do, and refuse to admit it. And after spending all day Saturday (every Saturday) trailing Grafton Street with oversized branded shopping bags, not forgetting the hour or two spent outside the city centre pubs proudly displaying their purchases while knocking back a couple of pints of Heino, their Saturday nights are also ritual.

This normally constitutes scoring a blonde dolly bird complete with miniskirt and loose morals. And she always brings with her at least three or four not so good-looking mates, also in miniskirts, who pray that some day they'll get noticed and get the chance to be just as big a slag as their good-looking mate.

While these guys will pretend to be big men about town, they probably won't even get a table or booth in either of Dublin's top nightclubs, Sophie's Choice or Val's, on a quiet night, but that still won't stop them flashing their credit cards and buying everyone tequila shots.

As the saying goes, champagne lifestyles on lemonade salaries. Sadly, that's probably why half of these kids end up dealing drugs. Reality is a bitch when you can't pay your bills, or when Mummy and Daddy decide to cut you off.

Either way they're not the kind of boys you like to play with; well, not any more.

Sure I've kissed a few of them. I'm only human. But from now on I'm going for gold. I'll be shooting for the stars – literally.

And hopefully somewhere along the road much travelled I might just reach the moon. Though, with my luck, I'll discover a bloke called Alfie, who has a penchant for dropping his trousers and flashing his rear, while screaming loudly 'Olé, Olé, Olé, Olé!'

At this stage of the game, most of the faces around town have become all too familiar to me; Dublin is a small enough city, after all. Still, bizarrely enough, I remain optimistic. Hey, if I keep telling myself that, I might just believe it.

When my mother suspects I'm about to take a long walk off a short pier she tries to comfort me. 'You need to concentrate on *you*, dear. Mr Right will turn up when you least expect it,' she tells me. I say I need to wear a T-shirt stating 'Unsuspecting Singleton Comin' Round The Corner'. Who knows? It might just help speed things up.

★   ★   ★

After reaching the milestone age of twenty-nine I've heard that inner clock that the glossy magazines threaten will start ticking loudly when our fertile years start to run out.

My older sister Ruth drives me mad with nasty comments like, 'Eva. I love you, but if you want a man to love you, you better grab one quick.'

'Women over thirty stink of desperation – and you're already starting to whiff. But you'll only end up with the dregs if you don't hurry up.'

And I kind of believe her. But what really annoys me is that she has been with her hubby since she was sixteen and hasn't the slightest clue what it's like trying to meet a man in the big bad world.

In a way I envy how she fell in love, literally with the boy next door. But the idea of just being with one bloke for the rest of my life is a tad scary in my book.

I mean, OK, like a pair of shoes she tried him on, and he fitted. But what if there was a better fit? What if her perfect fit lived down the road and around the corner? Was Joe just a pair of comfy slippers? Or could it be my sis got it right first time?

I'm glad for her 'cause she's a born mammy. She'd have topped herself if she was still looking for a man to impregnate her. But I'm the stronger of the two. And worryingly, it seems, too bloody fussy.

Thankfully I'm not alone on the road to spinster-hood. I've got a few desperado pals to accompany me along the way.

First, there's my model mate Maddie, my most

beloved sister in crime. Her full name is Maddie Lord, and the boys cry 'Oh my Lord' 'cause she's so bloody beautiful. Needless to say she's the better-looking version of me. She's even wittier – which kills me, but I never let her know that, and strangely enough she hasn't figured it out.

At thirty-three (though her Hollywood age is twenty-nine) she's had her fair share of lovers and heartache; in fact she's a bit of a slapper. Whoever said models were easy spoke the truth.

For example her phone reads Tony 1, Tony 2, Tony Mechanic, Tony Big Foot! Previously there had been a Tony Tiddler, but understandably he got deleted from her memory. She's had some close calls down through the years when she's arranged bootie calls with a Brian P instead of Brian B, but if there's one thing our Maddie can do well, it's juggle men.

Saying 'Hello Tasty' to everyone usually saves embarrassing mistakes. Except for that time when we had a ridiculously hilarious encounter with a priest in Wicklow.

Father Eugene, I think was his name. Sadly for us he wandered into our path while we were celebrating pulling a sickie from work. Maddie did her usual 'Hello Tasty', and a rather frisky Father Eugene thought he was on to a winner.

With several glasses of Sex on the Beach in our bloodstream we thought a lecherous man of the cloth highly entertaining.

Maddie teased him: 'I've always had a thing for men

in uniform' and he scared the pants off us by removing his collar and declaring, 'I don't think we'll be needing this now', while eyeing up our cleavage. It was when he uttered, 'God can't watch me all the time' and 'I've dreamt of worshipping girls like you' that we sobered up and decided we *definitely* didn't want sex on the beach with him.

Being my best bud I can call her the 'Tart with a Heart', but that privilege is reserved for me, and me alone. If anyone else dared to slander her slightly tarnished name they'd be nursing a burst lip and fifty stitches. Thankfully it's never come to that, but it's been handbags at dawn on many an occasion.

We've been mates since I moved out of home at 18 and broke my mother's heart. As I was the baby of the family she never wanted me to grow up. Of course I did the opposite: I grew up to be an adult far too fast.

There was never much money; Mother didn't believe in spoiling us. Her money was much better spent on new curtains or carpets, which seemed to be changed as often as Angelina Jolie's lovers. But just like Brad, my mum's last makeover curtains have hung in for a lot longer than everyone thought, and she's now turned her attention to collecting ceramic pigs.

Anyway, back to Maddie. She lived in the digs next door to mine in dingy Rathmines flat-land, and we became firm friends after she lost her key one night and ended up knocking into me with a bottle of vodka and three DJs she'd picked up on the night bus.

lovin' is this good, it'd be
around. No wonder really the
Southside suburbia look down
aight noses at us.

ot doing too bad myself in the figure
it, I'm five foot five, got a Katie Holmes
bob crop, though I'm a tad big bummed
– or should I say bootylicious – compared to Maddie.
Effortlessly she fits into a size 10 Diesel jean, and
bounces on top with a luscious 34D bust.

To this minute I'm still stunned she hasn't been
whisked off her dainty fake Manolos by some hunky
Brad Pitt type. On drunken nights we tell each other
that if we don't find our knights in white Porsches by
the time we're forty, we'll become lesbians and adopt
Chinese babies. A notion that is secretly starting to
scare Maddie big time, as she's convinced herself that
she's running out of fresh playmates.

Third in command – after Maddie and me – is
Parker. As I'm a girl who loves to accessorize he's my
must-have pink pal. Although he'll declare, 'The HO-
MO's in the house', he thinks he's straight. Though
still fancies men. Go figure?

Disillusioned with the gay scene, he prefers to trawl
the straight bars with me as it's 'more of a challenge'.
Yes, we often fancy the same guys, though I tend to
lose interest when Parker pipes up, 'He's definitely
gay. I could *so* have him!' Although he doesn't like
to admit it, he's a total star-fucker, and if ever there
was a man who wanted to use his gaydar to discover

big Hollywood name stars, it's him. He's forever in waiting for the right moment to pounce. Bless. And yes, occasionally he does get lucky. It's just as well Ireland has a thriving film industry.

It's because of his predatory intentions that he pretentiously titled himself the Pink Panther. Because he's always dressed in black, he's kinda tall and slim and he fancies himself as a serious mover, he thinks it suits him.

Maddie lets him get away with it because he's such a lovable cartoon, and so do I; well, most of the time. Some of his unplanned hissy fits can be hard to forget in a hurry.

We do tend to have diva meltdowns regularly. '*No* – it's all about *me*!' is our usual rant. Other people can't understand how we're still pals. But through the huffs and his puffs, it works. I think it's our common spoilt gene that is the cement for our relationship. When Maddie, Parker and yours truly get together we're more like the Bitches of Eastwick: Maddie plays Susan Sarandon, I'm Michelle Pfeiffer and, quite aptly, Parker is Cher.

Thursday night is our favourite night out. Being an art director, Parker has plenty of uber-cool media pals he loves to schmooze, but never before we have a bottle of Laurent Perrier rosé in his Docklands apartment, and scream 'Mirror mirror on the wall, who could be the biggest diva of them all?' Then we descend to the city to cause mayhem.

The fun we share could be classed as bold, bordering

sometimes on immoral or illegal. It's a dangerous friendship at times. But Parker is my addiction.

Speaking of addicts – well, of a fashion and Dior addict – Parker is closely followed by Princess Lisa Tiswell. And she does very well. But although she's tall and blonde, she's no Elle MacPherson. Never fazed by a minor detail like manly features, she does her best with what she's got; which it turns out, is Daddy's flexible friend.

While the rest of us save up for shoes and other essentials, Lisa's rich ole man proves a constant source of finance for Botox, collagen and monthly flush-outs of colonic hydrotherapy. 'What's good enough for Princess Diana is good enough for Princess Lis-za,' it seems.

By chance I found out through her mother over a few G&Ts one lazy bank holiday Monday that Lisa had had rhinoplasty aged sixteen. That's a nose job, to us mere mortals. And it didn't stop there.

At seventeen she increased her measly bee stings to a 36B. Then for her eighteenth she got her boobs pumped up again to a more generous 36C. Her mother even produced before and after photos, slur-ring, 'She was a bit of a mongrel back then!'

While I avoid places like the dentist because I'm terrified of needles, I support Lisa in most of her outrageous beauty enhancements. After all, what fun is an Amazonian woman without a decent pair of knockers?

But what she lacks in natural femininity, she makes

up for in balls. Unlike yours truly, who plays the stupid Cupid waiting game, Lisa is not backward about coming forward, and has no problem approaching men and making her sexual intentions known.

But all credit to her, she has a knack of pulling gorgeous men, and often hanging on to them until she is bored. Literally, she'll say 'I'm done with him' and move on. No obsessing, no deliberating . . . she'll just coldly change gear and not look back. I call it her 'man-itude'. An enviable trait.

With the confidence of a female Simon Cowell, she says she has great pheromones that no man can resist. I say it's her short skirts and Brigitte Nielsen appeal that draws the boys to her lucky charms. Lisa is only ever single by choice, and thankfully for my selfish ego, she's currently flying solo.

It's awful, I know, but unless I'm in a loved-up state myself, I much prefer my mates to myself.

Today we're hooking up for lunch with herself and her somewhat nauseating sister Joy. These days she insists on being called Mrs Joy Deltour, which Maddie and I choose to abbreviate to a worthy Mrs Brain Detour.

Apparently, Lisa mentioned talk of winter holiday brochures for herself and the sis. Thankfully Maddie is joining us, so I don't have to be embarrassed about the Tiswell family wealth and my relative poverty alone.

Of course I'd never begrudge Lisa anything – even that Swedish waiter guy Sven I'd hinted I fancied. He worked at the local Mexican restaurant, Tequila

Sunrise, we all loved, and after three consecutive Tuesday nights eating there, Lisa did a Lisa on it and left the place early without us. But with him. It was an empowering Samantha Jones moment, straight out of *Sex and the City*.

Anyways, Lisa jetting off to St Moritz to pick up loose ski instructors is not a problem. But listening to the less Joy-ous sis moan on about how her hubby Tristan doesn't respect her enough, and how being a modern stay-at-home mom isn't all it's cracked up to be, I'd certainly need back-up.

Even though she had all the money in the world, and then married more, Joy always leaves me feeling drained. She should *pay* people to listen to her problems, not insist on dividing up the lunch bill. Although prettier by far than Lisa, not to mention more married than her (or any of us for that matter), she still obviously covets her younger sibling's carefree lifestyle.

All our lives revolve around the Dublin social scene. We couldn't live without it. In the past, it defined who we were. We all enjoyed being liggers and turning up to the opening of an envelope. It was a shallow existence of freebie drinks that came with the bonus of seeing our photograph in a glossy magazine or an evening newspaper. If celebrity was a disease, then Ireland was dying of a vanity plague. We all wanted to be famous. Children no longer dreamt of being firemen or zoo keepers; modern kids craved *X-Factor* or *Big Brother* success.

If we couldn't achieve fame in our own right, shagging someone worthy of column inches was a very close second. That was sort of Parker's hobby, though he'd never admit it.

I had not become a WAG myself so I was still trapped in a singleton vortex of insincerity. When the post arrived I still got a buzz about opening the invites and imagining the mayhem that could be caused at them. First I'd envisage the setting, then I'd place in it the usual suspects, those I admired, liked, and those I couldn't bear standing close to, and then I'd place myself in the middle of them all, wearing the sexiest outfit possible, holding whatever the branded cocktail might be, flirting, joking, posing for photographers and of course being the centre of attention.

Once you were in the coveted clique, you were made. You could eat canapés, drink alcohol and retain a certain level of minor celebrity all year round, once the PR companies deemed you fit. It was cheap fun, and we all truly loved it. We never wanted to be stranded on the wrong side of the velvet rope.

Sure I wanted more out of life, like a lucrative career, a caring husband and the white picket fence with the 2.4 kids. Not to mention matching Range Rovers in the driveway, and holiday getaways in Brittas Bay, Cannes and Dubai.

Was this fantasy life unattainable? Never. I was a Celtic Cub, and self-belief was everything in this town. Talking yourself up was what us Dubs did the best. No one had to know the real truth – that your mortgage was interest only, the Jeeps would take five years to pay off, and the holiday homes were studio dives kitted with bunk beds and padlocks on the doors. I didn't know why I wanted to mix in such social circles, living beyond my means, spending more money on hair-care products than on my nutrition. My job as a journalist, which included celebrity interviews and other features for a glossy mag, paid well enough, but it's almost impossible ever to make enough money to survive in this town. I knew this socializing of ours was a sickness, but I didn't care. I was always afraid I'd miss the best bashes. There would always be more parties, but I still hated to miss one, just in case it ended up being the best party of the year.

Your friends would laugh and recall stories of the arguments, the unsuitable public displays of affection, the drug busts and the giant bottles of vodka that were being drunk by the neck, and then tut, 'Ah, it's just one of those location stories, you really had to be there . . .'

I'm hoping I'll outgrow this social-climbing obsession before I completely lose my soul. But not yet. There's far too much trouble to be had for this Valentine.

As I walk through the doors of Le Café I spot the gang already tucking into a bottle of white. It's only twelve noon but that's why I love them.

As always, the cute manager escorts me through

the heaving Saturday throng of lunchers and stressed-out staff trying to negotiate their way with hot plates and cappuccinos past the tightly packed seats. As we approach the back of the room, I notice the girls looking extremely animated.

Surprisingly enough, Lisa, Maddie, and even Joy, are laughing hysterically. I'm greeted with a boisterous, 'Eva da Diva!' with enough volume for the entire café to turn to view.

'There's the woman herself,' announces Lisa, leaving me a tad suspicious.

'What's the craic, girls? What's the celebration?'

'We're toasting you, Miss Eva. And your Lizzy Jagger, Calum Best moment.'

'What?'

'Yeah, Paris Hilton eat your heart out, girl. If only you were famous we could make a million from your CCTV footage.'

'Oh, dear God. What are you talking about?' All the while knowing damn well what they were talking about.

'Well, sweetie,' pipes up Joy, 'you've been acting like a slut. Everyone's seen the e-mail pictures of you cavorting with your boss, or your boss's colleague or whatever at some industry lunch.'

Speechless, I throw a fake smile as the manager steals a chair from another table and winks at me as he places it between Lisa and Joy. His niceness distracts me only for a moment; already I'm totally stressed. Taking a giant gulp of Maddie's wine, I wave at the empty bottle on the table in front of us and give him the nod.

'Right then,' demands Maddie, clearing her throat, 'You've Been Framed. Spill the beans on your adulterous affair.'

'Oh, girls, I had a moment of weakness. Please tell me this is just between us?'

'Sorry, hon. I better review this for you. You kissed David Barron . . . Yuck . . . Your boss's close golfing mate. He's also publisher of *Dubliners View*, AND Mrs Barron's husband.'

'Excuse *me* – he kissed me.'

'Speak to the boob, sista. You kissed him in the not-so-private stairwell at the Haven on Wednesday night. By Friday morning I'd received video footage of the hot and steamy affair, and so had everyone else on Speedy PR's mailing list.'

'Oh, my God. Why didn't you tell me?'

'Sorry. I was hoping someone else would. Officially you're a slut, whore mistress and everyone you know in the world has received the proof. Hey, it could be worse – it could have been some Daddy Sleaze. He is sort of cute. Very much married, but cute. Sorry, have I mentioned already that he is *married*?'

'Yes, yes. So what exactly does it show?'

'Well, you were there, you should know . . . OK, well, the quality wasn't great, but there was a lot of tonsil tennis, with hair-ruffling. And I reckon he's worked out that your mammary glands are totally real.'

While the girls nearly spat up their vino with the laughter, and I apologized to the middle-aged couple sitting next to us – not that I think I needed to, as our illicit tale seemed to tickle their fancy too – Joy interrupted with the statement of the day: 'You're a bit of a guzzler, aren't you?'

'Excuse me?'

'Yes, I've often thought if you were chocolate you'd eat yourself. Turns out you're a man-eater too – it looked like you were going to swallow the face off him!'

Coming from such a snotty bitch, I kinda took that as a compliment. Hell, I've been called a lot worse in my day.

Somewhat embarrassed by her caustic sister, Lisa dragged me to the toilets to grill me on my extra-curricular activities.

'Well, was it fantastic? Are you going to see him again? Did you wear a condom?'

'Whoah! slow down, sister. It never got that far.'

'You're a liar!'

'I'm not, I swear. But if I tell you what happened you can't go back upstairs and tell that mouthpiece of a sister . . . You promise?'

'I promise.'

'Ah, feck it, it doesn't matter. It was awful. Truth is, he bit my tongue. Then he pinched my nipple so hard I think he drew blood. I mean, did he think that would turn me on? Anyway, and then—'

'What?'

'And then . . . Oh, God . . . No, it doesn't matter.'

'Tell me, you bitch.'

'OK. Two words. P–R–E–MATURE—'

'Noooo . . . Ejaculation!'

'Yep. But look, what am I going to do? If everyone has seen the e-mail, the shit is really going to hit the fan. No wonder my phone hasn't been ringing. People must be avoiding me. Thank God, I took Friday off to work at home.'

'So what happens now?'

'I don't know. I'm too stressed to think. What if his wife finds out?'

'Bold Eva . . . Marriage-wrecker . . . !'

'Ah, stop. Don't make me feel so bad. He pursued me.'

'Tell that to his wife – joke! Only joking!'

Grabbing me by the hand Lisa pulls my lacklustre big ass up the stairs, informing two unsuspecting souls on the way, 'This is my friend, the guzzler. She's a legend.'

By the time we returned to our seats, the wine had obviously gone to Joy's head and poor Maddie was being bored to tears with, 'My Tristan this . . . and my Tristan that.'

'Ya know he really wants me to take this holiday with Lisa,' proclaimed Joy. 'But I bet the bastard just wants me out of the way. I don't believe a word that he says about his new sec-a-tary. Nobody called *Cindy* could be a plain Jane. Ya know, he says my breasts are no longer sexy after the babies. All men cheat.'

Thankfully saving the moment, four plates of yummy strawberry cheesecake arrive at the table. As does another bottle of wine, courtesy of the manager. He always treats us. And he continues to welcome us even when he gets constant complaints from neighbouring tables about our noise levels. I suppose there's *some* nice perks to being a journo.

'Ladies, with my compliments for being my most fabulous customers,' he smiles, darting me another cheeky wink before fleeing in the direction of some smashing plates, screaming, 'P45!'

Oh, I really do love working in the media and having a magazine column where I can easily throw in praise for 'trendy' and 'happening' eateries.

'To the guzzler,' announced Maddie. 'If she can't find her own husband, she'll find someone else's.'

'To the guzzler,' seconds Lisa, 'and to Eva's début as a cover girl for Adulterers' Weekly.'

By 10.30p.m. I'm standing in the sweaty toilet of the Haven.

Currently the *club du jour*, the place is wedged to capacity, and mirror space to check how beautiful one was is at a premium.

I swore blind I'd go home and never look at another man again, married or otherwise, but I'd lied to myself once again.

My guilt and shame had to be subdued by alcohol. If I got myself into another drama in the process, what better way to forget my original headache.

Despite having several bottles of vino and two vodkas inside me, I had convinced myself I was still as sober as a judge, and began applying my make-up so that I looked like Janice Dickinson at Hallowe'en. In true girlie tradition I became best friends with the blonde in the queue in front of me. We didn't swap names, just lip gloss. And while waiting for the cackling women to finish their lengthy chats in the cubicles, I started to explain to her my innermost secrets.

As nonchalant as you like, I started gassing: 'You know, I'm as horny as hell. But I can't have sex. I only got a Hollywood wax done this morning.'

'Yeah, I'm the same the day I get mine done. There's just something about being bald that makes you want to grab a man.'

'God, I haven't been with a guy, properly, in ages. But I so couldn't go there tonight, even if I got the chance . . . I'm like a plucked chicken!'

Feeling my plight, she offered up some sisterly advice. 'You know, tea tree oil is the best for reducing the rash. Oh, and Sudocrem is great.'

'Is that true?'

'Yeah, and a bucket of booze . . . The rash mightn't be gone – but you won't give a fuck till the morning!'

As the two of us curled up with the laughter, one of the toilet doors swung open, stopping me in my tracks. There before me was my arch-enemy Caroline Higgins. Once upon a time we used to be friends, but she betrayed my trust and any friendship we ever shared was long since gone.

In retrospect it was like a John Wayne movie. Or a toilet stand-off. Unfortunately my bessie bud was oblivious to the situation, and quickly brushed past Caroline complaining, 'About time.'

Instantly my mood flipped from jovial to stressed. Caroline was the only person I knew who had the power to upset me by just looking at me.

Several years back I had fallen in love with a suit. Unluckily for me, she was his best friend and some-time occasional shag from college. Though I think leech would have been a more appropriate title.

His name was Kevin Brennan. Looking back, he was pretty dull. But of course, ever the optimist, I overlooked his nerdy ways. Yes, by day he was an IT something-or-other. By night he was a bit of a madman. Like me, he had his moments – loved to party, loved spending money. Most of all he loved the trivial glamour that my job as an ace celeb reporter and columnist in a national magazine brought.

Despite being highly successful in his own field, he revelled in the excitement of being my Eva + 1. Like a fanatical teenage girl he took every opportunity to star-spot and loved the chance to hobnob with our minor local celebs. Once we even bumped into Bono and his mates in Val's nightclub. The poor fella nearly passed out with the enthusiasm.

Now, I know that Kevin didn't really care about me. It was more the life that I could provide for him.

But at the time he had my heart, and thorn-in-my-side Caroline Higgins didn't want me around.

In short, she did everything in her power to split us up in our brief six-month relationship. We had started off as friends, and often did date things together as a threesome – which on reflection, made her a major gooseberry; but at the time we had a laugh, and I dismissed the inconvenience of her being around.

Unfortunately, the happy days were numbered, when Caroline decided three was a crowd, and that I was the unlucky spare.

Extremely cunning, she easily manipulated him into thinking that she was as sweet as pie and I was a nuisance that he needed to get rid of.

Talk about an ego dint. I thought I'd never function again. Eva Brennan certainly had a ring to it. Or so I thought.

I was devastated at losing a possible husband. Though I think I was equally pained because I let her win. I felt like I had failed. And that is something I hate to do. Effortlessly she took her prize after provoking me into being such a frenzied nag. And he walked off into the distance with HER!

Now here we stood, face to face, neither one of us daring to flinch first.

She still looked as hard as I remembered her. Her peroxide hair and her ever-present dark roots to match her black eyeliner. She was rough when she wanted to be, but she didn't scare me. I had booze on my side.

I was going to brazen out this staring match. After all, I'd had a bad day, and I needed to muster up some confidence before depression kicked in.

After what seemed like a week, Lisa, Maddie and Anna fell through the main door, singing and bumping into unsuspecting pedestrians on the way.

'Hey Eva, I was just filling in Anna on Davey-baby's spillage,' shouted Maddie, before realizing that Caroline was standing in front of me.

Now, I'm not one to back down from a confrontation, but even I gasped when I saw Maddie stepping forward, as she was bolstered with the same amount of grog as me. For a second I thought she was going to start a tirade of abuse, but instead she gave Caroline the silent treatment and brushed past her to the mirror.

'You look fabulous tonight, Eva,' mused Maddie, doing her best to ignore Caroline. 'Do you know that?' she continued. 'You look absolutely fabulous.'

Clearly intimidated by our numbers, Caroline lowered her head in submission and just ran straight out the door. Probably just as well, otherwise our mugs could end up on the back page of some gossip newspaper in some Cheryl Tweedy style brawl. So we just avoided the tag lines 'Showbiz hack gives a Higgins a diggins!' or, 'Model gone Mad-die'.

The rest of the night was a bit of a blur. I vaguely remember boring some bloke who knocked half of his pint over me, telling him I was a woman on the edge, and the incensed face of the taxi man who had to shake me awake when we arrived at an address fairly similar to mine.

Thankfully, after much pleading he did drop me at my place, but despite the €8 tip he sped off as soon as I hit the path instead of waiting for me to get inside my door like he'd promised.

Sunday lunchtime I awoke to the sound of my own brain thumping. The distant beat of next door's stereo blasting out Fat Boy Slim was almost soothing compared to my internal drum.

The glass of water beside my bed was coated with a layer of dust, but I still drank it to the bottom. Consuming stale two-day-old water was better than having none.

My body needed fluid.

It also needed another ten hours' sleep.

As I lay in bed, memories of the previous day's events came flooding back.

My mischievous snog with the creepy David Barron exposed. Ouch. This is going to come back and bite me, big time. Without doubt I've created myself seriously bad karma with this situation.

What if his wife finds out? Christ, that's all I need. Barron was *so* not worth the bother.

Kissing a married man is something I said I'd never do. I'm not religious, but it's still a cardinal sin even in the unwritten atheist's book. In moments such as these I wish I were Catholic, just so I could say a few Hail Marys or whatever and have my soul cleansed and my sins forgiven. If only it could be that easy.

'You're such a naughty girl,' he told me, undressing me with his eyes. 'You're very naughty and very sexxxy.'

'And what else?' I asked him, thinking I was oh, so seductive.

'You're mine,' he replied. 'Mine, all mine for the night.'

He hit the nail on the head. I should have heard alarm bells ringing there and then, because he spoke the truth. Just for the night, that's all he wanted me for, like I was some disposable object. One use only, not needed ever again.

How could I have been so indiscreet? Well, I suppose alcohol was a major factor. That and sheer loneliness and frustration. He made me feel like I had butterflies in my belly; well, at least until it all went pear-shaped.

But of course, for all my lectures to Maddie and Lisa, I'm the one who messes up and breaks the rules with an attached bloke. And not just any bloke: I had to tangle with a fella with a public profile.

He may not be an A-list celebrity, but this guy is forever in the Sunday papers and glossy mags with or without his glamorous missus. A circulated e-mail is bound to make column inches in the gossip-mongers' pages. Let's hope he has his celebrity solicitor Alfred whatshisname on speed-dial to get the story quashed.

Then again, what am I worried about? I'm single. I

wasn't the one who did the chasing with classic cheesy lines like 'I love your work. It's edgy, young, and very much of the moment. *Dubliners View* could really benefit from a vibrant talent like yours.'

Desperate for a few compliments I sadly believed his bull.

Just then I noticed next door's blaring out 'Stupid Girls' by Pink. Why is it that music always seems to fit your mood? A stupid girl was exactly how I felt.

Yes, Eva Valentine, ace showbiz hack, was soon to be rebranded a marriage-wrecker. Forget all my years of cutting-edge interviews with celebrities and politicians, forget the features I'd written on Romanian orphanages, or the time I'd spent in Calcutta doing aid work, I was surely destined to become known as the Whore from the Sewer.

I've got a feeling Mr Barron was my worst mistake of the year. It's just depressing, it's only January and it'll probably haunt me for at least the next twelve months.

So much for my New Year's resolution, I must be a good girl.

Men might enjoy playing with bad girls like me. But they only ever marry the annoyingly sweet ones.

Maybe Barron's wife is just as painful as Lisa's sister Joy? Maybe that's why he was playing offside with me? Or maybe he's just a serial cheat like half the married men in Dublin.

A shiver went down my spine as I remembered

my confrontation with Caroline Higgins. Oh God. Will that woman just ever disappear? She's like a bad smell that won't go away. She so brings out my worst emotions.

Minutes passed which seemed like hours. I contemplated getting up and then thought better of it. I thought about reaching to the floor to retrieve the TV remote which had got flung there on my tumble on to the bed, but my body couldn't manage the stretch.

Right now I needed a cure. I needed two Solpadeine and the giant Tupperware stash of home-made ice-cream which I prep for special hangover days like these.

I discovered the recipe not so long ago, on one of those highly informative satellite cookery programmes. The pitch was 'How to make luxury brown bread ice-cream for a tenth of the price of shop-bought brands'. I fell in love instantly. I was wooed by the fact that it contained a healthy dose of Bacardi, on top of lashings of double cream and as much castor and icing sugar as you can get your hands on. Simply toast some breadcrumbs with the castor sugar, mix it all together – and Bob's somebody's uncle.

I personally think it's been my sweetest romance yet. After much soul-searching, head-pounding and tummy-rumbling from the thought of my scrummy yummy feast, I finally raised myself from the bed with my head gently tilted to the right, trying to ease the pain of the ascent. Before I stumble to the bathroom to assess the damage in the mirror, I notice a far from holy shroud on my pillow, and decide a bucket of tea is needed before I brave such a scary vision.

Still obviously smashed I trip over my prized Canal Street Gucci handbag on the way to the door, and kick out its matching purse and my pink crystal encrusted mobile phone.

What a relief.

I've spent many a Sunday afternoon ringing the phone company trying to get my number temporarily blocked, and fretting because I can't even remember my own mother's mobile phone number.

Undoubtedly numbed by the alcohol in my system, I sit in my cold tiled kitchen in just half the clothes I had worn the night before.

Marinated in that bloke's beer and my own boozy sweat which will continue to seep out till I fully detox at some point tomorrow, I hesitantly scan my mobile for evidence of drunken misbehaviour. Right enough, I'd reason to fear.

Sent: Higgins Bitch. 2.30a.m. . . . 'I ahte you!'
Sent: Higgins Bitch. 2.32a.m. . . . 'Whoos man did U rob 2nite?'
Sent: KEVIN BABY. 2.34a.m. . . . 'I hate hate hate ure bitch mate . . .'
Sent: Higgins Bitch. 2.40a.m. . . . 'U make me sic.'

Cringe. Cringe.

Starting to sober up I check my inbox, dreading what I might find.

Surprisingly there's no angry reply from Kevin;

well, not yet. And nothing from Miss Caroline either. I'm sure the sly cow is still plotting some evil comeback. Or maybe I give her too much credit.

Instead there's a lonely text from an unknown number saying, 'We've got to talk.'

After some simple detective work I hacked straight into the voice mail.

I winced in pain: 'You have reached the voice mail service of David Barron. Please leave a message after the tone.'

No thanks. I'd rather stick pins in my eyes.

As I discover the milk in my fridge is two days out of date, the landline phone rings and 'Maddie Home' flashes up.

'Are you sitting down?'

'Why?'

'Are you sitting down?'

'Jeez, yes. Why?'

'Your worst nightmare has come true.'

'What, George Clooney has decided he wants to marry an Irish woman and that woman is you.'

'You're obviously still drunk. Eva, you've made the papers—'

'Shit. Connected with Barron? Is there a picture of me?'

'Yes, Miss Vain. They've used *the* pictures.'

'Oh, God no. Not the CCTV pix?'

'I'm afraid so.'

'Which paper?'

'All of them bar the *Star* . . . Are you OK?'

'My mother is going to kill me.'

'Well it's not exactly the most complimentary, hon. You have been described as a social climbing wannabe It girl.'

'Is that the worst?'

'Eh, no, there's mention that you're a thrill-seeking tart and the possibility that it's been a long-standing affair.'

'That's completely untrue.'

'I think you should go out and buy them yourself. Have you heard from anyone else yet?'

'No, not yet. I better call the family before they call me. What am I going to do? Do you think it'll die down by the time I go to work tomorrow?'

'Ha! Fat chance, I'd say. You'll have to ride the storm. What's your boss going to say? He's best mates with Barron, isn't he?'

'Yeah, golf buddies. Not looking forward to seeing him. I'm sure he'll blame me for the whole thing. Right, I gotta go. Wish me luck.'

Resembling an extra from a bad spy movie, I crept into my local newsagent's, complete with oversized floppy hat and dark glasses on a mission to perform a quick snatch and grab of all the Sunday papers.

Apart from the fact that I was hiding from the shame of being the new Christine Keeler on the block, I was still sporting panda eyes from last night's make-up overkill.

As if picking flowers, I grabbed a bunch of red tops

and some broadsheets and headed straight for the till, head down.

Sneaking a peek I let out a silent scream as I got smacked in the face by the size of the photographs on the first of the back page gossip columns.

It was sort of a fussy haze, but very recognizably yours truly in several grab-shots with the love rat.

'Eva Rises Barron's Stairway To Heaven' read the headline.

'Barron burrows after CCTV scandal.'

'Reputed publisher David Barron's marriage has hit the skids after a raunchy clinch was captured on hidden camera.'

'Today Barron is said to be in crisis talks with his wife of seven years Annette Barron, after he was embarrassingly caught making an X-rated film.'

After being snapped in an erotic embrace with writer Eva Valentine, Barron has issued an official statement.

It is with great remorse that I apologize for the embarrassment I have caused my wife and our families.

I feel that I have been a victim of a smear campaign, and that this young woman targeted me and wants to destroy my good name.

I realize I have been irresponsible, but believe I have been set up for financial gain.

I hope the public will respect my family's privacy at this vulnerable time.

Stunned, I handed over my money for the equatorial rain forest under my arm, and left the shop. I stood outside trying to deal with the magnitude of the situation, until the harsh elements of this January day drove me home.

Somewhat bedraggled I sat back down at my caffeine-stained kitchen table, with a convenience breakfast of tea, a Double Decker and a KitKat.

I simply didn't have the energy to turn the grill on. As if swotting for an exam I spread the papers across the table, but not before carelessly swiping some old breadcrumbs on the floor. As I placed my mobile neatly beside my tea, for easy access, I realized I had left it on silent. I had lots of missed calls. There were five calls from a private number, and the rest of the messages were from Anna, Lisa and Parker.

Beep . . . 'Hey girlfriend, it's Anna here.'

'Brazen Barron beds busty brunette, eh? Can't believe they call you busty. I'm only jokin' with ya.'

'Talk about sex, lies and videotape. Ha! Apparently his wife has kicked him out of the house. I was talking to a friend of mine who goes to the gym with her best mate, and she says she's devastated.'

'I can't believe it made so many papers, you bitch.'

'Call me; I wanna hear all the gories.'

'Oh, my pal Gavin says he thinks you're hot. He says if you want to record a sequel, he's your stud. He wants to be your Martini man, any time, any place, anywhere.'

'Call me now. I need to hear *everything*.'

Beep . . . 'Eva, its Lisa. OH MY GOD. You must be a wreck. Fuck! What are you going to do? I can't believe the weed tried to blame you. He has a cheek.'

'Mother thought it was a hoot. She says she wants to take you for lunch at the Four Seasons. Says she wants to show off her celebrity pal to all her golfing buddies.'

'Hope you're OK.'

'Ring me.'

Beep . . . 'Hey busty, Parker here. You're scandalous. I love it.'

'I presume it's all a pack of lies, don't let them get you down. Half of this town just wishes they were described as a "Toy Girl Temptress".'

'Jeez, that Barron guy could publish my affair any day of the week. I'm getting all hot and bothered just thinking about it.'

'Love you. Call me.'

It was three o'clock and still no word from the folks. I had to bite the bullet and call them.

'Mum . . . have you seen any of the papers?'

'Yes, your father brought them in an hour ago after your gran rang in a distressed state.'

'. . . Do you hate me?'

'We're very disappointed in you, Eva, very disap-pointed.'

'But they're all lies, Mum. The papers are basically

43

saying that I'm one of these kiss 'n' tell tarts. I'm not, I swear.'

'Eva, your father and I are very hurt right now. You've brought a lot of shame on the family name.'

'What's that supposed to mean? We don't exactly have a name to begin with.'

'Don't take that tone of voice with me, young lady. You've caused enough problems already. I don't know how I'll be able to hold my head up at Weight Watchers this week. And your father had promised to paint the pillars out the front today, but of course that plan got scrapped. He couldn't stand the sympathy from all the neighbours.'

'Sorry, Mum, it was a shock to me too, you know.'

'There's nothing really to say here. Your father and I are too upset to talk to you. I think we should let the dust settle for a bit. We don't want to say anything we don't mean. Eva, we'll talk again.'

'But Mum . . .'

'Eva, I said, we'll talk again.'

Decidedly subdued, I crept through the doors of *So Now* magazine.

My usual entrance speech was along the lines of 'SO NOW I've arrived, let the work begin', or 'SO NOW how are the great unwashed today?' 'SO NOW . . . blah blah.' You get my drift.

I'm sure it irritated the hell out of the company receptionist, who always threw me daggers, but after my Starbucks double-strength cappuccino fix *en route*, I thought it highly amusing and witty.

It's scary that I'd worked there over seven years, but apart from that one time I got caught on holiday with some of my gay mates in Ibiza instead of being at a family funeral, I've never felt so bad about showing my face around the office.

Thinking back on it, subtlety was never my strong point. When I mess up, I like to do it spectacularly.

That time, despite buying a T-shirt that read FUCK THE TAN, I arrived back to work after a week's absence several tones darker and with an exact tan-line of my favourite Dior shades etched on my face.

Needless to say, the boss was none too impressed. Further salt in the wound came after he found out I had charged the developing of my mischievous sabbatical to the company photo account.

Jeez, it's hard to remember primitive life before digital cameras.

Anyhow, this morning felt like a first day at a new job.

I wasn't nervous, I was petrified.

So much so, I must have been to the toilet at least six times before I left the house at 7.30. I then arrived at 8.45, approximately fifteen minutes before everyone else, in an attempt to avoid judge and jury at the water cooler.

The women in my place are such bitches. Today will be like all their birthdays and Christmases come together. With this gossip they'll think they've died and truly gone to heaven.

The only person I really get on with is Elizabeth, who sits at my desk. Like me, she doesn't do the after-work drinks and keeps her socializing well away from the department.

Apart from being a features writer, she's a wannabe actress, but has never been cast in anything other than a TV commercial for incontinence pads, and a small stage part where she played Woman who Delivers Pizza, Woman who Complains about Noise and Woman who Asks for Directions.

To be fair, the ad paid her €7,000 which went some way to make up for the embarrassment of having to endure endless slagging over her bowel movements. Jibes such as 'Do you need your nappy changed?' and 'Golden shower girl' will haunt her for ever.

She was also quite brilliant in all three theatrical roles, despite her rather limited script of 'That'll be €25.80', 'Keep the volume down', and 'Could you tell me the way to Love Lane?'

A place both of us were still searching for.

I was feeling totally cursed. Elizabeth was away this week on a freebie lig to Eurodisney, where she texted me to say she was 'Freezing her bits off'. So I was to brave the outcome of my dangerous liaison alone.

So there I sat in an empty office. Dazed and confused; fearful of what the day might hold.

After seven minutes precisely – the TV in the corner was constantly on and I counted on the Sky News clock as I read 'Latest Headlines: 15 dead in fresh car bomb attacks in Baghdad' – I popped to the loo one final time before my critics took their seats. Catching a glimpse of myself in the mirror I got a shock. That wasn't a familiar face staring back at me. My nun-like High Court styled makeover made me look like a condemned woman, not the fresh-faced angel I was going for. Who was I kidding? My no-make-up make-up made me look washed out and ill. With my pale pasty skin I needed a lot more effort than a few smears of Vaseline, a brush of mascara and pinched cheeks.

But with nothing more than Black Cherry lipstick and Charcoal Sparkle eye shadow in my handbag, I thought I'd better stick with my original look.

Let's be honest. In everyone's eyes I was already slutty enough.

By the time I finished fretting over my appearance, I could hear several members of staff starting to buzz about the office. Thankfully they were mostly advertising staff: they were never interested in anything other than their X-Boxes, some Eureka programme, and other nerdy *Star Trek* amusements.

Thinking I was in the clear I made a bolt for my desk. It was only a moderately sized office so I thought I'd make it. Instead I was disturbed by, 'Eva. Can I have a word, please?'

There, skulking behind the printer, was the editor of *So Now* magazine, Josh McKenzie. Towering over me, he looked fierce. I didn't remember him being so tall.

'I've just a few things on at the minute,' I offered weakly.

None too impressed he bellowed back, 'NOW!'

Submissively I followed him into his glass office. I wanted to run in the opposite direction, but I thought it best to get the ear-bashing out of the way.

'So now, what's the problem today, boss man?' I joked.

'You,' he replied.

'Listen Mr Mac, I know David's a good friend and all, but like—'

'No, Eva, *you* listen for a change.'

'But if I could just explain—'

'Eva, I'm not going to drag this out.'

'Drag what out?'

'There's no easy way of saying this, so I'll just come out and say it. Eva, you've violated our agreement by bringing shame on yourself and the company. You were never made staff, so you're still officially a freelancer. I want you to pack up your desk and be out by lunchtime. You're fired!'

2

Surviving on a junk diet of the *E! True Hollywood Story*, *Girls of the Playboy Mansion*, *The Hills* and *America's Next Top Model*, I realized I had become a TV tabloid bulimic.

As if Velcroed to the couch with my thumb superglued to the remote, hours, days, even weeks had passed as I absorbed worthless knowledge on everything from Hugh Hefner's girlfriends and Lara Flynn Boyle's struggle to success to Navan man Pierce Brosnan.

Tacky sayings such as, 'This is where the magic happens' and 'Next on the E! True Hollywood Story', began to penetrate my brain. I started to feel that my mind was about to explode into tiny pieces, which would splatter across my four walls and remain unnoticed for months.

Maybe next door's cat would discover me? Then again, he'd probably turn his nose up at me, and disown me like everyone else.

I then dreamt everyone from Cameron Diaz to the not-so-newly divorced Jessica Simpson had all started laughing at me.

In one dream I was watching the news. A massive tower block was collapsing after a terrorist attack. I was fearful and paranoid. It felt so real, as if I was in a disaster movie. Somehow I started to clamber over the rubble trying to find people I could help. But there was no one left alive.

Then I saw David Beckham. He looked down at me from a ledge and smiled and winked. Exhilarated at such a heavenly vision I made a run for him but I tripped at the feet of my old school headmistress, who strangely looked like Pamela Anderson (in reality she looked more like Judge Judy). But she put her hand out in front of me and told me I wasn't to go after 'Golden Balls'. They were her words.

'You must never have sex with that married man,' she said, then pointed at a football pitch. 'This is your destiny. You must walk around this field for eternity. You must never leave here,' she told me.

As I started to trudge around the goalposts I spotted my mum and dad having a picnic. I tried to wave at them but they refused to acknowledge me and turned their backs.

In floods of tears I looked to the sky to see a plane flying by with a banner. At first I couldn't read what it said, but when I wiped my eyes it became clearer. 'Welcome to your hell,' it read. 'Keep walking.'

Suddenly I woke up, sweating and extremely

shaken. Mentally bruised, I felt I had done ten rounds with Tyson.

It was 4.20p.m. and 'Pink Panther' was flashing on the house phone for the seventh time that afternoon. Knowing that he wouldn't give up, I answered it just to get some peace.

'*Yes?*'

'When are you going to snap out of this depression? It's been nearly two weeks since your halo slipped. Get over it,' complained Parker.

'Eh, excuse me, but I never saw *your* name being dragged through the mud. Can I have a little sympathy please?'

'OK, then. Poor you . . . Now get over yourself. I'm the only person who's Girls Aloud to do drama in this relationship.'

'Charming, you're all heart.'

'Yes, well my suits are too expensive for you to be crying on them, so let's build that bridge and step out of that river of misery you're drowning in.'

'Jeez. I'd hate to hear how you deal with people you don't like. Be nice. I'm a little fragile at the minute.'

'With an arse like that you're hardly fragile, dear . . .' Parker was practically tutting with annoyance.

'PARKER!' I screamed back indignantly. 'Yeah, well the only snap here is between your face and my arse.'

'There she is. Good to have you back. Now, are you coming out tonight? I'm so bored. I need to play.'

'I can't . . .'

'Pray tell why? It's not as if your social diary's full, now is it?'

'Thanks for reminding me.'

'OK, so you'll come out tonight before I die of boredom?'

'Parker, I can't. I'm totally broke.'

'Already? That didn't take long. I know you've been let go, but you'll get another job soon. Money matters can't be that bad.'

'Well they are. Not everyone has amassed your wealth, sweetie.'

'Damn right they haven't. And I'm worth every penny.'

'Parker, the only magazine in this town that isn't owned by either Barron or the Cooper organization is that feckin' teen sex mag *NEU Today*, and they've told me in no uncertain terms to eff off as well.'

'OK, my poverty princess, you don't need money. Well, not tonight. Just put on your glad rags. I presume you still possess nice clothes, or have the bailiffs come for them too?'

'Ha. You're wasted. You belong on the stage.'

'Right then. Be at my apartment for ten o'clock, and bring a smile. They cost nothing.'

By eight o'clock I managed to pull myself off my tiny two-seater couch and away from the TV. My knee joints pained with cramps.

Trying to shut out the nagging voices that kept

screaming at me to go and hide under my duvet and never leave the apartment again, I struggled into my black skinny jeans and donned my lucky pulling top. It was only a black polo that I bought for €20, but it looked great on, and always made me feel sexy.

Surprisingly enough, tonight was no exception.

I had to endure the narkiest taxi driver complaining about 'Foreign lads takin' taxi plates', who then managed to test my patience even more by leaving me a good walk from Parker's apartment block.

'Sorry luv, but I've gotten anudder fare. This traffic ain't movin', I'm gonna have ta leave ya here.'

So I had to immerse myself in the cold night's fresh air.

As I teetered over the complex's designer cobble-stones, my Nine West heels sank in a gap, slightly scraping the leopard-print motif.

Argghhh! Even the outside world was attack-ing me. Maybe this was God's way of telling me I shouldn't have left home at all. This guy sure had a sense of humour.

Dodging the swooping seagulls I breathed a sigh of relief as I reached Parker's intercom. My fate wasn't all bad though, as I was fortunate enough to avoid any hassle from the resident junkies.

And in this neck of the woods, they were hard to dodge. The Docklands is still up and coming, you understand. Millions have been spent giving it a glamorous new century makeover, and while the dotcoms have moved in, not all of the undesirables have moved out.

My neighbour Mrs O'Flaherty had once told me about St Jude, the patron saint of lost causes. She said if I prayed to him, he'd take care of me. In light of recent events I had attempted an occasional chat with the fella.

But I think my waffling had fallen on deaf ears. He must have thought I was beyond lost.

Buzz . . . Buzz . . . Buzz . . . I hammered at the intercom. 'Let me in, it's Eva.'

'Ohh, hello my little marriage-wrecker,' gushed Parker. 'Move it on up, girlfriend.' Buzz.

The lift doors opened and I pulled on a weak mask of a smile. Parker greeted me with his usual pose. The music in the mirrored lift may have been Bach, but Parker quickly changes the tune to totally diva.

He ushered me through to his bachelor-style grey and black living room, giving me the inquisitive, once-over eye. 'Well, tickle *you* pink, you don't look bad for a woman on the edge. A little fleshy around the gills but that's to be expected after your hibernation. But not bad, Miss Valentine, not bad at all I must say.'

'Thank you, Parker. Your support is super-generous and appreciated.'

'OK, enough about you, I'm in the middle of some text flirting. Quick, grab a glass, I need your help.'

Knowing my grievances would fall on deaf ears, I pulled a large John Rocha out of one of the smoked-glass units in his stainless steel kitchen, and filled it to the brim with the ever-ready supply of pink bubbly which Parker keeps in the freezer. Why in the freezer? Well, it's just never left there long enough for it to fully freeze.

'So who are we toying with tonight then?' I asked, strutting back into the room with my glass and the bottle and staring out the large glass patio doors overlooking the city and the River Liffey.

'The builder boy,' he beamed.

'Which one is he?'

'The buff puff with the scar on his chin, that I met a couple of months ago. His family are worth millions, don't you know. Well, he pretends to be straight, but he really loves the boys.'

'Nah, I don't remember him.' I found it hard to keep up with his conquests.

'Who cares, it doesn't matter . . .'

'Hang on a minute, I do remember him. I thought you said his hairy back freaked you out.'

'Ha! Yeah that's the guy. But it was his hands that were hairy. Anyway, I'd forgotten all about him until this evening. But he started texting about half an hour ago asking me to meet him. What should I do?'

'Ignore him. What's the point if you don't like him?'

'Yeah, but he also mentioned that he wanted to fly me – get this – in his own plane to London for the weekend. Apparently there's some society party with loads of celebrity types that his company is sponsoring, and he wants me to go with him. What should I do? I didn't realize he was a pilot as well. How cool is that?'

'I'd say arctic. Need anyone to carry the bags?'

'Maybe, let's ask him . . . So, builder boy. How big is ure – plane?'

Like children we sat giggling around the phone waiting for his reply and swilling on the already half-empty bottle of Laurent Perrier rosé. The bubbles had started to go to my head, and I relaxed into ole Valentine mode.

Beep. Beep. '1 Message Received' flashed up in Parker's phone.

'BUILDER BOY: It's always large with me babe x x.'

Not wanting to let the moment pass, I grabbed the phone and texted back, 'Are you writing cheques you can't cash?'

Thinking I was decidedly witty I refused to let Parker have his phone back, convinced of a great reply, and ordered him to top up my glass.

Beep. Beep. '1 Message Received BUILDER BOY: ????'

'Ah, crap.'

'What did he say?'

'Absolutely nothing. Look, he only sent back question marks. He's no fun.'

'Shut up. Let me have a go.'

'Builder Boy, since ure plane is sooo big, can I bring a fabulous friend?'

'BUILDER BOY: Sure, bring a couple of girlies. The Piper Seneca seats 6.'

At that the two of us jumped off our chairs, spilling a little bubbly over the stone suede sofa, and did our victory dance. Think Joey's jazz hands crossed with a Jack McFarland tap dance.

'He sooo wants me,' cooed Parker. 'I wonder is there a bed on the plane? I've always wanted to join the mile-high club.'

'You can have him and his hairy extremities. Now don't mess it up. I *need* to party in London. I *need* some rich Brit to rescue me from this life of poverty. 'Cause my situation doesn't look like it's gonna mend itself.'

'Well, I can do hairy – especially in London. OK, let's get details. So, builder boy, when is the party and I'll see if I can make it?'

'BUILDER BOY: I'll take care of u and ure friends Pink Panther. Just say YES 4 sat :)))'

'Oh, my God. He wants us to go this Saturday. What'll I wear?'

'Parker, you always wear the same thing. It's always black. What the hell will I wear?'

'Who cares, gorgeous? I've a rich boyfriend.' Then Parker ran out to his balcony which ran about thirty feet alongside the apartment and broke into a diva-style performance of 'Money, Money, Money'.

Obviously, this was not typical behaviour for a man in his early forties, but for my Parker, the words tart and fickle could sum up his personality adequately. The only thing with depth about him was the fact that he liked deep pan pizza. Apart from that, he was as flighty as they come.

Not a great trait, it has to be said, and one that caused us many arguments when we first became friends, but now that we all know him for the Shallow Hal that he is, we work around it and love him regardless.

Caught up in the moment, we started on a second bottle of bubbly, sang our way through 'Cabaret' and 'Sweet Charity' while Parker paraded around the apartment in a pair of silk boxers, a cravat and a vintage Gucci hat he bought on eBay that allegedly was once owned by Madonna.

It was only as he murdered his favourite Shirley MacLaine number 'If they could see me now', that I remembered we hadn't texted our Builder Boy back. By this stage it was 12.30a.m., which was admittedly quite late on a school night for a person with a regular existence.

Trying to think sober, we managed to type back, 'Yes. Sat cd b ure luckkky nite.' But we never got a reply.

Resisting the temptation to text again and annoy the poor bloke into retracting his invitation, we occupied our hands with buttered popcorn and nachos, and finished our evening in front of the TV.

After all, why go into town and risk ruining our happy buzz? Instead we channel-hopped until we found some fairly hard-core American gay porn for Parker, which I sat and watched for ten minutes before

I got totally grossed out and crashed in one of his spare rooms.

I just loved staying over. It felt like a five-star hotel. Slumping in my sumptuous Ciaran Sweeney oasis – Parker just loved his stuff, and had most of his apartment styled in his trademark hand-printed silk velvet – I drifted off to sleep thinking, maybe life's not so bad after all . . .

One o'clock Saturday afternoon I was propping up the Ice Bar @ the Four Seasons Hotel; spray-tanned, plucked, perfumed and preened to within inches of Miss World requirements.

It's one of our favourite hangouts as it's a total gossip factory.

A haven for the rich, the mega-rich and the wannabe-rich, on any afternoon you could end up working through the cocktail menu with A-listers like Colin Farrell or Michael Flatley.

Though most of the time the reality is you end up being caught in a corner by some Daddy Sleaze who's removed his wedding ring, and who pretends to be big in beef. When in reality he works in a camera shop. Trust me, it happens.

Normally, we'd place ourselves at the middle of the long marble bar so we could rubberneck the two entrances. From our regular spot we could gauge what talent was where. Today, though, I couldn't care less about trying to impress anyone. I needed to be focused on London. I was a woman on a mission.

Amanda Brunker

I wanted a man.

I *needed* a man.

Tonight, I was gonna fall in love.

He'll be rich.

He'll be famous.

I'll walk into this party and he'll instantly fall for me. I'll be the most fascinating and captivating person he's ever met. And we'll live happily ever after in a mansion in Chelsea, with weekend apartments in Dublin and New York and a getaway summer retreat in the South of France.

Ahhh! I felt better already. There's nothing like a mini pep talk with myself while sipping on a Bellini at the Four Seasons, surrounded by beautiful people, to give you a boost of confidence.

Looking good and feeling sexy was always half the battle. Today I was going to be militant in my approach to finding my hero. By next week I would be standing on a beach in Cancún wearing nothing but a white bikini like Pamela Anderson. I'd be sipping cocktails once again, while my Tommy Lee says 'I do' in a sexy, gravelly voice.

As I started to drift off into daydream land about the beautiful children we'd make, Anna and Maddie strutted through the door looking like extras from *The Rocky Horror Picture Show* pulling their little trolley-dolly cases.

Parker had text-demanded 'B on 4 seasons 4 court @ 2 on sat EXACTLY.' So of course we arranged to meet at one o'clock to discuss wardrobes and to generally snoop around the hotel to see what stars were hiding out.

'Well, are we hot or wot?' demanded Maddie.

'I think we're FAB-U-LOUS,' declared Anna, before giving me a chance to comment. 'I'd wanna get with us . . . Tonight, Eva, we're going to be every girl's nightmare. Tonight is our night.'

Laughing at their dogmatic self-belief, and their brazen ability to wear Madonna-inspired corsets and miniskirts at lunchtime – in *February*! – I called over one of the cute barmen and flirted. 'Can I have two of your best Bellinis for my shy and retiring friends please, Colin. They need something to elevate their mood.'

When their drinks arrived Maddie proposed a toast. 'OK ladies, cheers to London. Here's to flying in some fella's private jet, fair play to him. Cheers to the Pink Panther for organizing it. And most of all here's to getting the spirits down to get the spirits up, first class all the way, baby.'

'Cheers.'

'Cheers.'

'Cheers. Let the games begin!'

By 1.45 I had started to get worried about Lisa's whereabouts. She wasn't normally late, and strangely her phone was switched off.

I was just leaving my fourth message for her when I lost the power of speech. David Barron's wife, Annette, had entered the bar, and she was charging in my direction.

She was immediately eye-catching because of her trademark blonde bob, but was unusually dressed in a casual tracksuit.

She looked emotional.

She was looking for me.

Despite quickly turning my face and sheltering behind Maddie, I knew that she had spotted me.

'Shit. Shit. Shit.'

Oblivious to the situation a giddy Maddie screamed, 'What's wrong with you?' In such sterile marble surroundings, her voice could be heard by every patron as it pinballed around the room.

With that, a somewhat dishevelled Mrs Barron came storming over to us, put her hand on Maddie's shoulder and pulled her out of the way. Maddie let out a 'Hey?' before she realized who had butted in.

In complete shock the three of us just stared at her, frozen.

Afraid to take a breath we waited for her to speak, but instead she just stood there looking frazzled. Momentarily it felt as if the entire bar had come to a standstill. Everyone was silent. Everyone was fully aware of the situation. But most of all, everyone was waiting for the best gossip to happen in front of their eyes.

Who would triumph? Would it be the spouse or the temptress?

Could the scorned wife kick the muddied journo's ass? Or would the tart take a stand and tell the wife she obviously wasn't taking care of matters at home?

Then a lonely tear rolled down Annette's Botoxed and collagen-enhanced face. The three of us, immobilized, watched as this solitary tear slowly etched its way down her reddened face. Making its way across her high cheekbone, it meandered over her trembling lip and then clung to the bottom of her chin, before dropping off and landing on her baby pink Juicy Couture top.

God knows why Barron cheated on this woman. She still looked stunning even in her most desperate hour.

I couldn't help but feel guilt for causing her pain so I stretched out my hand to her, and with a quiver in my voice said, 'I'm so, so sorry.'

Retaining her composure, Annette took a deep breath, brushed the tear from her face, and with one look at my outstretched hand she shook her head slowly. Almost muttering she whispered the words, 'No way', then turned as if to walk away.

Just as I began to release the stress from my shoulders, Annette quickly swooped back round to face me and WHAM smacked me square across the cheek, leaving me literally gobsmacked.

Physically and emotionally wounded, I grabbed my face in bewilderment. It really hurt, but almost too much to feel it.

I looked to Maddie and Anna for support but they just looked back at me in this vacuous way which said: don't look at us, you were the one who scored her husband.

Paralysed at first, Annette then started screaming at me, '*You bitch. I hate you! You're a slapper. You're nothing but a slapper!*'

It was possibly the most surreal experience I had ever had. No one had ever hit me before. My mother used to chase me around the kitchen with a wooden spoon, but this was a first. I was caught up in one of my nightmares again.

Before I knew it, several members of suited staff had rushed over to intervene, along with some friend of Annette's who grabbed her and ushered her away.

'Come this way, *please*, Mrs Barron,' ordered the manager.

'She's just trash,' I could hear her friend say before she looked back and grimaced at me. 'Nobody will touch her ever again.'

Quickly returning, the dutiful manager asked, 'Are you OK, Eva? Can I get anything for you?'

To which I could only reply, 'Thank you. No. We're leaving now anyway.'

Scanning the room I could see that every pair of eyes was fixed on me. I'd catch their stare and they'd tilt their heads down and put their hands over their mouths to continue delighting.

I felt like being a total fishwife and screaming, 'What are you all looking at?' Thankfully, I thought better of it.

I probably would have ordered another stiff drink if it hadn't been for Annette crying in the corner. Her very disturbing sobs made me feel as if I'd killed her husband, not snogged him.

Then again, a most heinous crime had been committed. Not only had I nationally humiliated her through the papers, I had massacred her marriage in the process. I deserved nothing but to go straight to hell. But as my mother would have said, I deserved nothing.

Feeling it was improper to hang around, Maddie slung her arm around me, giving me a reassuring firm squeeze, and chaperoned me out towards the car park.

'C'mon girl,' she encouraged, but I felt worthless to my very core. I had destroyed that woman's world, and through no fault but my own, torn my own down around me too.

Just before I stepped out through the swinging doors I took one final glance back at Annette, but was obstructed by a ferocious-looking woman, mid-forties, screaming at me: 'Just leave. You're not wanted here!'

Noticing Annette and her cronies huddled in a tight circle in the background I gave the interfering stranger a fake smile and turned on my Gina heels. The woman looked oddly familiar, but I still feared a repeat attack. Knowing damn well I was the afternoon's hate figure, I admitted defeat and left, repressing a retort.

★   ★   ★

Without a moment to catch my breath, Parker was the first image I saw. Garishly hanging out the back of a stretch white limousine Hummer, he was waving, frantically shouting, 'Excuse me? Where's my welcoming committee?'

Mortified, we ran across the cobbled car park, pushed Parker aside and clambered in the back of the Hummer.

'Get in, Parker, quick!' I screamed, but with a look of total disgust he just peered back at me through the doorway, and with the lungs of a sixteen-year-old girl squealed, 'Excuse me?'

As Maddie tried to coax his nibs inside – to complaints of, 'Not everyone has seen us yet. I only got this bloody thing so everyone could be jealous' – I noticed I had ripped yet another heel on the stones. That was the second pair ruined in one week. My karma was screwed. And as I sat surrounded in opulence, glamorized by mood-changing Christmas lights and buckets of ice stuffed with snipes of Moët, I wept. It was only when Maddie managed to find the volume button to turn the stereo down that she realized what a state I was in.

As my mascara stained a road map down my face, Maddie did her best to mop up the mess with a napkin that read 'Get Happy – Get A Hummer!'

Doing a better job of lifting the moment than the purple, to pink, to yellow strip-lighting, Maddie joked, 'Well, I always thought it best to be miserable in comfort, sweetie.' And the two of us laughed.

Well, laughed until I started to cry again.

By the time Anna had dragged Parker away from flirting with the doormen and stuffed our luggage up the aisle of our big bus, I had started to catch my breath.

In hyper form, Parker slammed the door and declared, 'The Princess can't make it, girls, as she's having her arse injected into her crows' feet today.' With that he took one look at me and teased, 'It's not worth getting upset about, hon. Her arse isn't big enough to fill all of her lines. You'll still be considered one of the prettiest.'

All I could manage by way of retaliation was, 'You're so sweet . . .' before Anna stepped in to inform him of the confrontation.

I'm sure his screams of '*Fuck off!* Fuck off! Fuck right off!' echoed in the ears of every guest in the hotel.

With that Parker ordered, 'Driver, take us to Lucan, good man, away from all this riff-raff. Our private plane is waiting for us.' Anna, who was practically salivating with excitement, handed out the snipes of Moët to lubricate the discussion. Always thinking ahead where gossip was concerned, she came close to being booted out of the car several times with stupid tactless comments like, 'I wonder is it too late to make the papers tomorrow?' And, 'She must really hate you, Eva.'

Trying desperately hard not to channel all my anger towards my pretty, but single-minded gossiper friend,

I turned up the volume on the TV which was set on MTV2 and screeched, 'Enough already. Let's get this party started.'

With that the four of us sat kneeling up on the leather seats shaking our champagne bottles in the air and head-banging to Kellis's 'Milkshake'.

Although I was still at a pushing myself to feel happy stage, it felt good to be back to normal. Well, my kind of normality.

I might only have €100, and £28.50 which I found in an old jar in my purse in case of emergencies, but I somehow always managed to surround myself with expensive pleasures.

I was an unemployed celebrity journo; sorry, I was apparently an unemployable celebrity journalist. Yet I was surrounded by champagne, while being driven in a stretch limo to take a private jet to London, to party with some famous celebrities. On the up-side, life wasn't too bad – *yet*!

Born lucky instead of rich, the good life found me, and it scared me to think I could be ousted from my comfort zone.

So I chose not to be.

It was easier to sing, dance, laugh and forget about the real world. Other people lived there.

And just as the energy in the Hummer had started to lull, Britney Spears came on the TV. With her first words 'Baby One More Time' we all jumped to our knees again, shrieking with excitement, singing along. Like sycophants we eyeballed each other as we religiously and meticulously sang her song, taking a line each at a time – until the driver hit the brakes abruptly and the four of us tumbled to the back and then the front of the Hummer like rag dolls.

As our shoes and our drinks flew around, we fell in a heap, screaming with laughter.

It turned out the driver had pulled off the motorway into a petrol station at the last minute to buy cigarettes. Happy to go with the flow, we girls made a run for the smelly toilet around the side of the garage, while Parker rang his date about the exact location of the private airport.

Fifteen minutes later, we were all back safely in the limo, readying ourselves for meeting Parker's rich builder boy.

After hair and make-up had been fixed we managed to gather our belongings and the spare snipes of champagne as we pulled up at Weston Airport.

Like an excitable teenager, Parker was almost pinging off the walls, but like a true pro he reeled it back in as he stepped out of the limo to meet his hairy-handed man.

As butch as you like, he marched over to his new boyfriend, patted him on the back and said, 'Howsigoin', Jeff? Not a bad day for flying, eh?'

Trying desperately hard not to crack up laughing, we lined up like the hired help to greet our new host. In a complete Walter Mitty moment Parker delved for the deepest voice he could find and said, 'Jeff, these are the ladies I was telling you about. Aren't they gorgeous?'

Amanda Brunker

Our new friend Jeff played the charmer, and even gave Maddie a playful wink. Happy to go along with the game, we gushed and cooed as Jeff flirted with each of us individually.

He was a man with manners. And for us to even hint that he wasn't batting for our team would have been improper protocol.

What a waste for us girls, though. Like Parker he was tall, about six foot two, and quite broad. He looked extremely sporty. You could tell he was the kinda guy who would go skiing in the winter and surfing in the summer, and had a subtle mahogany tan as a result. Hairy hands aside, he was a buff puff, who came with a serious reservoir of cash and assets to impress us with.

Laughing, Jeff teased us as he gave us the tour of the airport, joking, 'I hope none of you girls are afraid of flying?'

All pulling startled faces, Maddie shot back, 'No, but we're all afraid of crashing!'

She may have been joking, but it was true. This might have been executive travel, but all of the aircraft looked extremely flimsy.

'Where are you hiding the Boeing?' I asked. 'Or are we flying by Lear Jet today?'

Jeff had clearly heard it all before. 'Oh, it's good to see everyone is in high spirits. Now let's see how you all get on with the weigh-in,' he said with great amusement.

Automatically the four of us looked at each other,

clutched our chests and cried in camp horror, 'Weigh-in?'

'I thought that might wipe the smiles off your faces. I can't let anyone on the plane without weighing you first. I couldn't take the chance that any of you ladies might shave off a few pounds here and there.'

While Maddie, Anna and myself all hated the scales as much as Marmite, Parker looked the most worried of the lot of us. 'Emm, what's the relevance of know-ing our exact weight?' he asked. He looked almost pale with the news.

'It's just a formality, really.' Jeff chuckled. 'We just need to know where to put the heavy people.'

As if claiming a mini-victory Maddie piped up, 'Is there a skinny model VIP section to this plane?' Jeff thought for a moment, then said, 'Yes, skinny models to the back of the plane, fabulously healthy people front and middle.'

Relishing her status Maddie asked in her best pre-cocious voice, 'So, why is it the fat people have to sit up the front?' doing her best to wind up Parker and Anna.

'Well,' said Jeff, 'the plane would never get off the ground if we got the weight wrong. And that goes for your baggage too.'

Looking at the size of Maddie's bulging case I did my best to put a smile back on Parker's face. 'Eh, it looks like you're carrying a few extra pounds yourself there, missus. You might have to leave some of your non-essentials behind.'

'Non-essentials!' screamed Maddie. 'The only thing non-essential about this trip is your bad karma. I wouldn't be worrying about my baggage, hon, but trying to shed some of your own.'

Without giving me time to answer Jeff had ceremoniously ushered us and our luggage on to scales at a nearby Portakabin, throwing his eyes up to heaven at the sight of our bags.

'You're allowed 34 pounds excess weight per person,' he explained.

Still feeling super-skinny, Maddie joked, 'So where are we going to squeeze Parker's ego?'

'Probably on a roof-rack alongside yours, dear,' squealed Parker. Realizing he had let his butch image slip, he straightened his shoulders and declared, 'If any of the girls are over I don't mind leaving some of my stuff behind. I don't mind travelling light.'

The luggage safely on board, we girls peeked our heads back out of the Portakabin to see if we could spot a plane that looked safe enough to travel in.

When the other pair joined us they were happily laughing; no doubt Parker had made some crude comment along the lines that the only package Jeff needed to take was the package between his trousers!

Resuming his headmaster role Jeff led us like sheep to the slaughter, steering us in the direction of the small runway and a tiny plane. Indicating the toy-like trinket, he said, 'OK guys, this is us. Meet Florence.'

In unison we went, 'Huh?'

'This is my plane,' he explained, 'I call her Florence

after my grandmother. She was an exceptional woman. And this is just a beautiful plane.'

Parker leaned into me and whispered, 'You see. I bring out the homo in him.' But I didn't see the humour. I was staring at the smallest plane I'd ever seen. And fear had gripped my body.

Wanting to yell out, 'I want my mammy', I hesitantly pulled Jeff on the arm and asked, 'Are you serious?'

'Of course,' he replied, oblivious to my anxiety. 'OK, everyone, all aboard,' Jeff instructed us. 'We've got a fifteen-minute window. Maddie and Eva in the back, Anna in the middle with Parker.'

With that Maddie rudely blurted out, 'I can't get in that. It's a tin can with propellers.'

'She's never failed me before,' offered Jeff, looking a tad hurt.

'But . . . but, didn't JFK Junior and his missus die in a little plane like this?'

'Yes, well, kind of. Theirs was a smaller make, though,' said Jeff. 'It was only a single propeller plane. If you look at this baby, it's got twin propellers. Plus I don't come from a famous cursed family. So we'll be fine. Now hop in.'

Not wanting to have a fall-out before the weekend even started, Parker took control of the deteriorating situation and with one of his stern looks, motioned to us with his eyes to climb on board.

Unsure if we were more scared of Parker or of the thought of plummeting to our death in an aviation tragedy, we stuffed ourselves and our bags inside the plane, in stony silence.

Far from Concorde, Florence was more like an early Elvis number with its baby blue velvet seats, blue carpet and matching side panels. Parker did his best Austin Powers impersonation with a loud, 'Yeah, baby!' It failed to lift my mood.

After all, I'd already been slapped in the face at the Four Seasons. Oh, how a plane crash would just finish off my decadent disaster of a day.

Settling into our taxi with wings, wedged in like sardines, some young fella looking no more than eighteen hopped in the front beside Jeff and started flicking switches and muttering 'Roger to that.'

Seeing my distress Anna and Maddie each grabbed one of my hands but their touch didn't work. Instead, frustrated by me being difficult, Parker did a Parker and began to sing. I put my fingers in my ears and started to hum. But all I could visualize was this flying coffin, spinning out of control and crash-landing in the sea.

Where were the snooty air hostesses? I wanted lunch with real cutlery. Not a gliding minibus to take me across the Irish Sea. It was a far cry from the John Travolta beast that Parker and I had been expecting. Without letting his disappointment show Parker continued to sing 'Leaving on a Jet Plane'.

'Shut up, Parker,' I screamed, letting my nerves get the better of me. 'John Denver died in one of these planes as well.'

'So did Buddy Holly, Ritchie Valens and the Big Bopper,' laughed Jeff.

'Oh, don't forget Jim Reeves and Patsy Cline,' added Parker. 'Are we making you *crazzzzy* yet?'

'SHUT UP!'

Getting into the spirit of things Anna gave me a reassuring nudge before spurting out, 'Christie Brinkley nearly died in a plane crash. But after six hours of sitting in the snow on the side of a mountain, she was rescued. So that's something positive.'

Baffled at her reasoning I could only moan, 'Do you think?'

It was when Maddie offered, 'And didn't that young singer Aaliyah go down over the Bahamas?' that I finally started to laugh. 'OK, OK, you all win,' I conceded. 'If we're going to hurtle to our death, so be it. Just please try and avoid turbulence. And definitely don't crash, Jeff. We're all too good-looking to die.'

'Will do my best,' smiled Jeff. 'And so will I,' said the very young co-pilot, before he resumed muttering into his headset.

Shortly after our bumpy take-off, Maddie remembered the spare snipes of Moët she had stuffed in her bag, and in true rock 'n' roll style we necked them back while singing Westlife's 'Flying without Wings', along with various other aviation-themed songs for the duration of the journey.

★　　★　　★

75

By five o'clock we were sitting in London traffic, after our thankfully uneventful flight to Heathrow. What a relief.

The little suited man, complete with chauffeur's cap, waiting for us with the sign JEFF'S PARTY PEOPLE, was hilarious.

Resembling Sid James from the *Carry On* movies, Charlie C spread the cockney charm on thick, with cheesy lines like, 'Olright my lovelies. Neva before 'ave I seen such beauties', and, 'Treacle, are you what they call Oirish royalty?'

Loving the attention being showered on us, we hardly noticed that Parker and Jeff had huddled in the back seat of the people carrier, locked in a private chat. Despite previous hesitations, Parker seemed to be uber-keen on his new suitor. It was good to see him so happy. Come to think of it, all complications aside, I was happy too.

London, lock up your sons, I thought, da diva was comin' to get ya.

An hour later we were still stuck in traffic, but Jeff's driver had kindly hopped out of the car and bought us chips, chocolate and Diet Cokes.

'Sorry about this, Jeff, but we're starving,' I said, as I dripped ketchup on my damned shoe and on to the carpet.

'No worries,' said Jeff. 'I'm sure Charlie here is more than happy to have you ladies in the car, even if it does mean it stinks of salt and vinegar.'

76

'So what's the plan tonight then?' I asked, curious about what to expect.

'Whatever you ladies desire,' smiled Jeff. 'Fancy an early night? Maybe get a take-away and watch a DVD?'

'As if!' shrieked Maddie.

'Fine by me.' Parker winked, then remembered he was supposed to be playing butch.

A little thrown off track, a nervous Jeff resumed with, 'Ah, em, well would you like to grab a drink in town before we head out? Or do you just want to go back to Primrose Hill and change first?'

'Aren't we staying in Primrose Hill?' asked an over-excited Anna. 'Isn't that where all the celebrities live?'

'Yeah, there'd be a few heads about all right.'

'Perfect! Take us to that pub that Sadie Frost is always being photographed outside looking shit,' demanded Anna, without having the decency to ask the group first.

Throwing Maddie a definite glare, she shot, 'Trust me, it's cool. All the Primrose Hill set hang out there. Ewan McGregor, Jude Law and Jonny Lee Miller drink there.'

'Yeah, maybe when they're not making movies,' offered Maddie.

'Can we go, can we go?' pleaded Anna as she bounced on her seat like a six-year-old.

The perfect host, Jeff asked Charlie to 'Drive us to Queens, please mate,' in an adopted English accent, as we all started to rummage in our bags for lippie to reapply.

'Are you sure you're not thinking of Billie Piper and Chris Evans looking a little worse for wear sitting outside pubs?' I asked, convinced she'd got it wrong about Sadie.

'Oh, probably,' muttered Anna. 'But she's forever being photographed without her make-up on.'

'OK girls, listen up. I'll give you the quick guided tour,' said Jeff, in an attempt to keep us entertained. Coming up here on the left is Gwyneth Paltrow and Chris Martin's place. Noel Gallagher and Nicole Appleton live just around the corner . . . down there. And then Jamie Oliver and his missus Jools live just up here, well they used to as far as I can remember.'

Overawed, we sat speechless, mouths open, as if ready to catch flies. Staring at these elegant stucco Victorian houses, with their wide tree-lined paths, was like looking at a movie set. Coming into her own, Anna piped up with some of the worthless knowledge she'd absorbed from the gossip mags.

'Doesn't Kate Moss have a pad here too? The paparazzi are always camped outside her place.'

'Yes, very good,' praised Jeff. 'There's also a great vegetarian restaurant here called Manna, and I've heard Moby goes there a lot.'

Trying to be nonchalant Maddie asked, 'Anyone else?'

'Wow, you girls are tough to please. Erm, Helena

Bonham Carter and Tim Burton live around here somewhere, and as far as I know they filmed parts of *The War of the Worlds* here. So I can only presume Tom Cruise would have stayed in the area.'

'OK, we'll give you five out of ten for your tour guide skills,' I joked, 'but I think we need to see some of these stars for ourselves.'

Just then our cheeky Charlie livened up again and said, 'Boys and girls, here we are. This is Queens.' Hopping out, he opened the door for us and offered us each a hand out.

'If you see Katie Moss, tell her to stop calling me,' he teased. 'I've had to change my number three times already.'

Feeling like we were attending a film première, we stood outside the pub, fluffing our hair and plumping up our cleavage as we waited for the boys to follow us. But they didn't.

Sticking my head back in the car door, I asked, 'Are you all right?'

But they looked far too comfortable.

Passing me a handful of sterling, Parker shooed me back out, directing me to 'Go buy the girls drinks. We'll follow you in.'

Happy to oblige I grabbed the money and ran by the girls laughing, 'The last one to the bar gets the ugly mate.'

'Tits out, tummy in.' Anna winked, and with a massive intake of breath she strode through the heavy door.

It hardly looked like a celebrity hangout, just an average English pub, but, with a quick thought to St Jude, I morphed into a cool diva and prepared myself for an entrance.

Several bottles of Coors Light later and there was no sign of Jude Law, Ewan McGregor, Jonny Lee Miller or even one of Sadie Frost's young boyfriends. And the mood started to wane just a little.

'You know it's Valentine's Day in ten days,' mused Anna.

'What's your point?' snapped a disgruntled Maddie.

'Yeah well, you were dateless last year as well Maddie, weren't you?' sniggered Anna in a sarcastic tone that said, don't get stroppy with me.

Just as I was about to butt in and cool the frayed tempers, I noticed a very sexy guy walk towards the bar. He'd been sitting in front of us since we'd come in, but with his back turned the whole time.

Although I didn't recognize him, he had a certain X-factor aura about him. He was gorgeous, a total hottie in a kind of unshaven John Cusack sort of way. Actually, he was better looking than John Cusack, he was a rugged Tom Ford, wearing old jeans, a frayed style T-shirt and an old grey hoodie top. And now he was standing right beside me.

As the girls continued to make bitchy remarks to each other, I used the classic, 'Oh, sorry am I in your way?' line as I pulled at my stool a little.

'Gosh, no,' said my perfect stranger, waving the

remark away. 'No, you're fine,' he smiled. He had a mild New York accent.

'Wow, you're a long way from home,' I blurted, before taking the time to plan my next move.

'For sure,' he cooed, smirking down at me as he rubbed his hand over his designer stubble. 'I like London, but I much prefer Ireland.'

'You're very perceptive,' I flirted back, thrilled by his ability to recognize an Irish accent. 'Next you'll be telling me you're a quarter Irish.'

'Actually I am.' He laughed, barely missing a beat.

'Oh, for shurrrr!' I mocked, as I kicked Maddie in the leg so she'd see my new pal.

'You may be a non-believer but I'm actually half Irish. My mother was from Cavan,' the handsome stranger insisted.

With that a boisterous Maddie swung around on her stool and announced, 'Well, hello tasty. Who are you?'

'Oh, em, hello yourself, I'm Michael,' gushed my handsome stranger. 'Can I buy you girls a drink?'

'Well, come take a big bite outta me!' shrieked Maddie, as I hung my head in my hands with shame. What can of worms had I opened here?

Choosing to ignore my embarrassment, she raved on, 'Oh, *yes*, Michael, we'd love a drink, wouldn't we, Eva? And I'm Maddie, and Michael, this here is Anna. And for the record we're all single.'

Truly mortified, I just shrugged at Michael and expressed my feelings towards Maddie with my eyes.

'Don't mind her,' said Maddie, pulling at his sleeve. 'She's just gone quiet 'cause you're her type. You've got that arty thing going on. You're definitely her type.'

'Thanks for that, Maddie,' I was trying desperately hard to seem pissed off. Of course, I wasn't. I was thrilled. Maddie had done all the groundwork for me. All I had to do now was try and look sweet; well, sweet in a sexy way, and hope that he would fall for it.

Thirty minutes later, I had found out Michael was a fashion photographer who was currently trying to break into making videos and commercials. He had worked with all the big names from Gisele to Naomi Campbell, and apparently she was 'not as temperamental as the media makes her out to be'. Although he had dated many models, and had a small crush on an Irish model, Catriona Balfe, who also lived and worked on the 'Island' (Manhattan, of course), he was currently single – and 'actively looking for a good woman to love'.

As he stared deep into my eyes, as if trying to read my mind or capture my soul, all I could do was gaze back at him.

Was this guy for real? I wasn't a supermodel, so why the hell was he talking to me? Maybe all the drink I had had made me more confident, and so more appealing. Yanks loved confidence, especially New Yorkers, but still . . . I just couldn't understand. Judging by his body language he was true. Leaning into me, his smell of Davidoff Clearwater was filling up my senses, but it was his whole persona that was starting to over-power me.

By now Maddie and Anna had muscled over to his mates' table and seemed happy enough. Occasionally I'd hear a flirtatious yelp or scream from Maddie, so I knew she was coping on her own.

After suppressing the need to pee for about twenty minutes, terrified I'd spoil the moment, I excused my-self from my American dream.

'I'll be right here,' he said, in a smouldering and smooth tone.

Unfortunately I then went and ruined the moment slightly by jumping off my seat and chirping, 'O-K', as if I wasn't bothered.

After a lengthy toilet break and a quick text to Lisa: 'The Princess: Miss U. GR8 nite. Wish U were ere', I gathered my composure and strutted back outside – and found Parker draped all over Michael.

'I've just been acquainted with your new friend, Eva,' gushed Parker. 'Isn't he just the dogs?'

Unfazed by a strapping gay man swinging from his shoulder, Michael explained, 'I hear you're going to some big party tonight. It sounds great.'

'Does it?' I asked, totally clueless.

'Yes, Miss Eva,' interrupted Parker. 'It's going to be totally fabulous – *if* we ever get there. We're already past fashionably late, so get your skates on.'

Panicked, I just stood there looking gormless. I didn't want to leave. I wanted my chat to Michael to go on for ever. Damn Parker for coming in and ruining my moment. Backing away, Michael handed me my jacket and my fake Prada handbag – it looked money even though it wasn't – and threw me a winning smile.

'Well, I guess I'll be seeing you around.' His velvety words melted out of his mouth like chocolate.

'Yeah,' I replied, praying for him to ask for my phone number. But he didn't. He just smiled back at me. Then Parker grabbed my hand, and pretending to use me as a puppet he put on his camp girlie voice and flapped my arm around saying, 'Right then, bye-bye Mr America, lovely to meet you. Byeeee.'

As he pushed me towards the door, Maddie and Anna air-kissed his friends goodbye and then blocked my view of Michael.

'Fuck sake, Parker,' I barked, 'could you not have given me an extra minute? I thought I was getting somewhere with him.'

'Oh, come on Miss Valentine, he's from New York. You'll never see him again. What's the point?'

Devastated I got back in the people carrier. I didn't want to leave so I had to be pushed.

A little emotional from the amount of alcohol in my system, I sat in a mood, and refused to make eye contact with the group. As Charlie drove off, I just cursed them all for crushing my happy-ever-after fantasy.

I felt utterly cheated. He could have been my Mr Right. He was definitely a very hot Mr Maybe.

★　　★　　★

Acting like a spoilt brat I moaned for what seemed like hours.

Eventually we arrived at the bash that Jeff had flown us over for. It was a very stately Victorian home with massive spotlights circling outside the front and an illumination of some model on the wall with the words 'To The Manor Born' written across her naked body.

Unimpressed by the pomp, I huffed past the model waiters offering champagne cocktails, and then returned to them to demand where the toilets were.

Furious, I had to queue behind women who were laughing about how hilarious Gary Lineker was and what a wonderful wealth of knowledge Jeremy Clarkson had. I had to keep my head down and bite my lip so to stop myself crying.

When I returned to the group I then had to endure Maddie rattling on about how beautiful Nicole Appleton was in person. I know I should have shown more of an interest as she gushed, 'She's so down-to-earth. Look, I got a picture with her on my phone.'

But I didn't care about meeting any stars. I still didn't even know why they were all here, other than that Jeff's family's company was sponsoring the event. Tired and emotional, and still wearing the same clothes from that morning, I told Parker I needed a minute to myself. Wandering out to a garden area, I found a space to sit on my own.

It was ten minutes before I realized he wasn't

following me out to cheer me up. I was gutted. Staring at my phone to make it look as if I was doing something, I was at pains to think who I could text or call.

I had texted Lisa earlier but had heard nothing back. So I decided Maddie my supposed best friend should come out and comfort me.

Lacking the energy to submerge myself in the madding crowd again, I texted 'Maddie: I'm out in the garden. Come out with a drink pls.'

Straight away she texted me back: '2mins.'

Somewhat relieved, I relaxed into my concrete chair, and people-watched the smokers.

Although a heavy dew had started to cling to everything, semi-clothed glamorous women frolicked around, puffing bellyfuls of smoke to the sky like old movie stars, while a group of grumpy-looking men pretended not to notice them.

Half choked by their unforgiving starched collars and vast footballer's ties, these men looked so absorbed in their own conversation that if the Marlboro Man's ghost had walked up and asked them for a light they'd have totally ignored him.

Another couple huddled in a corner looked very devious indeed. Both in their forties, they definitely looked like they were having an affair; but one that was coming to an end. Uneasy in each other's company, they seemed on constant lookout, as the woman sobbed into her champagne cocktail, and he remained sullen.

Occasionally she'd pound his chest and shout the word 'Bastard', which only made him look more determined and fierce.

Just as the damp had started to numb my bum, my phone, gripped between my hands like a lifeline, beeped '1 New Message.'

Sure it was Maddie telling me it was too cold outside, and that I was to stop being stupid and get back in and join the group, I got a shock to see the words 'TURN AROUND' from an unrecognizable +191 number. Thinking what the fu—? I quickly looked behind me to find my New Yorker standing beside a rose bush brandishing a bottle of Laurent Perrier rosé and two glasses.

'Pinky said it was your favourite.' Michael smiled, making my heart skip a beat.

'For the record his name is Parker,' I corrected, 'but what are you doing here?'

'Hey, I met the most beautiful woman I've ever seen tonight, and then she ran off on me. What's with that?' His eyes smiled as he spoke.

Not sure if I was daydreaming again, I pinched my leg to make sure. 'Am I imagining things?'

'What do you mean?'

'Well, I'm nearly sure we left you in Queens. How did you find me?'

Ignoring my question, he positioned himself beside me on the icy concrete bench, and started to pour the champagne like a pro.

'You know, that Pinky fella really is a good judge of

character,' mused Michael. 'He invited me when you were in the cloakroom. He said it would be *da craic* and not to tell you.'

'What did he say to you? Did he pressurize you into coming here? Oh, God I'm so embarrassed. I'm so sorry. He can be a bit forceful sometimes.' My mind began to run away with itself.

'Whoah! Slow down there, tiger, everything is just rosé in the garden. Don't you think?' A broad smile rippled across his face as he placed the champagne flute in my hand and clinked his glass against mine.

'I propose a toast,' declared Michael, raising his glass to the stars: 'here's to new beginnings and great friendships.'

'Shock entrances, more like.' My confidence had started to return.

'I've always prided myself on my entrances. Much better than my exits, I feel,' he said and then knocked back the champers.

'Well let's hope you never make one,' I said, tilting my glass towards him. And in two magical mouthfuls, I too made my champagne disappear.

Lifting the glass from my hand, he placed the two empty glasses at our feet, and then asked me, 'Can I kiss you?'

Unable to speak, I gave him my best sexy eyes and tilted my head towards his.

Then we kissed, the perfect kiss. It wasn't like kissing someone for the first time. It was familiar and right. Wow! If he kept kissing me like this I could love this guy for ever.

Obviously as happy as I was, Michael pushed my hair off my shoulder and nuzzled his face against mine. The heat of his breath hummed in my ear. 'Have you ever had a champagne kiss before?' he whispered wickedly.

'Did I not just have one?' I was unsure what he meant.

'No,' he said, smiling, 'but, just like last time I want you to kiss me back.'

Then in Jim Morrison fashion, he lifted the bottle off the ground, took a full mouthful of champagne, and before I knew what to do he had leaned in once again to kiss me.

Like an explosion, I could feel the sweet nectar entering into my mouth, gushing across my taste-buds and rushing down the back of my throat. All the while, Michael choreographed his tongue expertly inside my lips.

This was true fizz. Champagne kisses for ever. Then, as if he had read my mind he gave me an intense, deep look and said, 'Do you believe in love at first sight?'

Doing my best coy act, I replied, 'Maybe . . .'

'Well, I do,' he said, coming over serious, all the while making me feel warm and fuzzy on the inside. Nervous with the intensity of the moment, I let out a little laugh and stuttered, 'Oh, oh, do you now?'

'Yes, I do,' he shot back. 'I'm a big believer in what's meant to be.'

Uncharacteristically stuck for words, I gave a nervous cough, trying to gain time. The best response I could come up with was, 'Oh, yeah?'

Laughing, Michael grabbed my hands, which had started to make an annoying flicking noise with my nails, and pulled them close to his chest. It felt warm and strong, and smelt great.

'What you doin' Valentine's?' he asked, after obviously giving it some thought. 'And don't say you'll have to consult your diary.'

'You tell me,' I said as I slid my right hand up to the back of his neck and started to roll his hair around my finger, the cold of the night just melting away.

'I think we should go to Las Vegas.'

'Sounds like a plan to me.'

'Cool. How does this sound? Fancy getting married?'

3

'Hey beautiful, are you awake yet?' The sound of my New York superhero's voice was now familiar to me. 'I've got fresh bagels and some pastries for you and sweet coffee for my sweet . . . Now are you gonna get up? Or do I have to drag your ass outta bed?' His voice resonated from the kitchen, before he popped his adorable head through the crack in the door.

It was the Monday morning after the weekend before, and I was still happily in London after skipping my cramped return flight on Florence with the gang. It wasn't like I had any work to rush back to after all.

'Morning,' Michael smiled, as I yawned and stretched across the bed cheekily exposing my naked nipples over the top of the crunchy white duvet, accidentally on purpose. We hadn't had sex yet, and I was practically bursting with frustration.

'Morning yourself,' I replied, as I patted the mattress beside me, signalling for him to come in and join me.

'You don't want breakfast?' he challenged, adopting a macho, hands–on–hips pose.

'I think I'm hungry, but, er, I think I fancy some meat to nibble on,' I sniggered, failing desperately to keep a straight face.

'You want *meat*?' he said, as he frantically kicked off his Timberlands and swung his belt across the room, nearly knocking over a bedside lamp. 'You got *meat*!' Before I knew what had hit me, Michael had barged in and swept the duvet from the bed. Tossing it to the floor, he climbed over me on all fours as I screamed and wriggled into the foetal position, trying in vain to hide my modesty.

'You wanna play hard to get?' he teased, as he tickled my bare body from my feet to my neck, haphazardly wriggling out of his Edun T-shirt at the same time.

'NO – NO,' I yelped, unable to speak while laughing so hard.

'Well, pumpkin, I fancy a nibble of something tasty myself.' He smiled, then lunged for my neck and vigorously munched.

Giving up the fight, my body released itself into his arms. Pulling him close to feel his smooth bare chest against mine, I felt I had died and gone to heaven. His smell had become so familiar now as well; that was all I could register as my eyes rolled back while he savaged at my neck, rendering my body weak.

Just as I became aware of his right hand sliding down around my waist, he flipped me over like a rag doll, slapped my backside with force and threw me over his shoulder.

'Right, Miss Eva,' he said, struggling as he tried to rise off the bed, 'you're going to have some breakfast, whether you like it or not!' And he manhandled me into the living room and flung me on to a massive burgundy corduroy couch, sending gold embroidered cushions flying.

'There,' he panted, standing over me like a gladiator. 'Now I shall serve you breakfast. Don't move!'

Like a rescued damsel, I cosied myself on the sofa, pulling a wool shrug over me to keep warm. As Michael returned to the kitchen to fetch our food, I scanned the room and its fabulous paintings and memorabilia. It was an eclectic mix of modern meets classic.

Although it wasn't Michael's home, just a pad that his mate lent him when he was in London, I could visualize a huge amount of his personality from his belongings.

Exuding a relaxed, comfortable style, rips on the sofa arm and burn-holes in the curtains hinted that it had seen the odd party or two; and judging by the mini photo-collage over the black cast iron fireplace, the odd celebrity too.

On the lengthy walls hung massive black and white photographs of models, alongside interesting pieces of modern art. Impressively, two pieces were by Damien Hirst, and there was even a small Chapman Brothers amended Goya etching above an old Regency dresser, which was covered in piles of photographs and papers, and several empty bottles of Jack Daniel's.

'Is that really Kate Moss?' I asked, curious about the beautiful people in the picture frame.

'Yeah, she's hot, ain't she?' enthused Michael on returning with the breakfast goodies. 'Frankie, the guy who owns this place, seriously works the London scene. He's currently in Namibia researching his latest book, though. Hunting hidden treasure, I think.'

'Isn't he just a true life Indiana Jones, eh?'

'He's a bit of dreamer is my boy, but ya just gotta love him. I'm just surprised that trust fund of his hasn't run out. It'll be some wake-up call when it does.'

Sipping my Java blend, which Michael had switched into a very trendy mug designed by Tracey Emin, I pondered how wonderful life could be, and thought that maybe my mother was on to something with that whole 'You never know what's around the corner' lark.

She's going to be so happy for me – that is, when she starts talking to me again.

Gosh, wait till Lisa hears where I am. This is definitely more her speed. I can't wait to bore her with all the details of our whirlwind romance. How Michael reckons he can get me a gig writing for a New York publication, and how his family – who own several bars in the city – are going to 'Eat me up', I'm so 'genuinely Oirish'. What a trip she missed!

Contentment enveloped my being, and I noticed Michael had settled himself with a copy of the

Independent in a large wing-back chair beside a sash window. His profile lit up with the strong lunchtime sun. It was unusually tropical for this time of year; I couldn't see a cloud in the sky as I looked out over the rooftop garden. And I sat there for a time thinking this was a sign. Yes, the future looked bright once again.

Noticing I was looking in his direction, Michael tilted his paper and asked, 'You happy?'

'Very,' I smiled back, to which he returned a wink and then resumed reading.

Bloody right I was, I thought. I was in the middle of a fantasy romance novel.

By Tuesday morning, the euphoric feeling hadn't waned. If anything, it had exploded into a full-on Hollywood love story starring Hugh Grant and Julia Roberts.

We'd spent Monday in romantic clinches, knitting hands and talking fantasies and aspirations, and our thoughts on children – which conveniently, we both saw in our future. Thankfully the politics banter passed without us destructing, as we both had a combined hate for George Bush and shared similar views on why Clinton should never have been forced to step down.

My chronicle of how I queued up at a book signing in Eason's in Dublin, in the freezing cold for three hours to meet hunky Bill, impressed him. The fact that I broke security to plant a kiss on his cheek, only to hear a week later he went into hospital to have heart surgery, sent him into hysterics, and earned me the new nickname 'Heart-breaker'.

OK, so he was doing his utmost to laugh at all my jokes: I didn't care, I was in heaven. In our nirvana in Primrose Hill, he was my Adam, and I was his, well, Eva. Only he was the one offering up an apple, the Big Apple. And I for sure wanted to take a big bite out of that and to hell with the consequences.

Thankfully, nobody interrupted our passage of discovery of each other. I had switched off my mobile so neither Maddie nor Parker could convince me to come home. They'd just freak me out and get me to check the wardrobes for bondage gear, and have me standing on chairs to see if the fire alarms contained hidden cameras.

For peace of mind, I *had* checked the wardrobes, but found nothing but old snorkelling equipment, a water-bong for smoking hash, some Jenna Jameson DVDs and an old well-thumbed copy of *Penthouse* magazine. Satisfied I wasn't going to be imprisoned, to be the victim of a snuff movie, I did my best Eva disappearing act, blocked out the world and let the first man ever to propose to me pamper and adore me.

Monday night he'd excelled himself as the ultimate educated bachelor, by serving me up an authentic 'Oirish Stew'.

'Let me wow you, beautiful,' he urged, as he settled me into a steaming bath with candles, bubbles, a glass of Chablis and an old copy of *Vanity Fair* with Kate Moss on the cover.

'First relax, and when your feast is prepared, I will come for you. Then we shall eat. And then, hopefully, you will come for me.' He rolled his eyebrows in a giddy manner, as he carefully articulated each sentence before disappearing off to the kitchen.

He proved a man of his word. I did relax into the slipper bath with a smell of lavender and rose wafting around the bathroom – though I'm sure it was the Chablis that dangerously aided me off to sleep. Drifting into my sweet slumber I dreamt of Kate holding my hand at the back of a tacky Vegas wedding chapel. 'Go for it, babes,' she told me, as she pushed me up the aisle carrying a posy of plastic white roses.

Surrounded by pensioners in wheelchairs carrying buckets of change, Kate stood at the back like an angel, the epitome of cool dressed in her trademark short-shorts, knee-length boots, a leather waistcoat and Jackie O black shades.

As I walked towards Michael and a Dolly Parton look-alike singing 'Islands in the stream' I questioned whether this was what I really wanted. Turning back to Kate for reassurance, I got a fright when I couldn't see her. The chapel had now become overrun with the pensioners, who were now bickering and flinging dollar coins at one another.

'*Kate, where are you?*' I screamed, frantic for a friend, but she was gone. Instead I woke to Michael standing over me, looking inquisitive.

'Wakey Wakey! Who's Kate, then?' He looked disappointed I hadn't been screaming his name.

'I was dreaming of Kate Moss. She seems to be chasing me. Everywhere I look she's there,' I blurted, only semi-conscious, trying to sit up.

'Now, there is a dream combo,' he smiled, kissing me on the forehead and dropping a towel on the floor. 'You and Kate Moss, eh? I like the sound of that.'

His mind full of dirty thoughts, he trotted off happily in the direction of the kitchen.

By the time I fixed myself up, Michael was waiting for me in the living room with two bowls of piping hot lamb stew. It was so good. The kind mother used to make, evidently, his and mine.

Stew was soon followed by dessert – Belgian chocolate Häagen-Dazs à la Eva. But not before he got the fire going. His stew could only do so much to warm our bones.

After the third attempt he had finally managed to light the coals, using rolled-up paper, small sticks and several splashes of Frankie's sambuca. He was no Crocodile Dundee, but then you can't be good at everything.

Leading me by the hand, he positioned me on the floor, close enough to feel just a slight burning on my skin, and using the tip of his right-hand little finger began slipping off the white towelling bathrobe I'd found on the back of the bathroom door.

Starting at my neck, and working his way down to untie the knot around my waist, he took his time to savour each tender moment. His dark brown eyes dilated with passion. His worn faded jeans swelled. Seeing how horny he had become turned me on even more. God, he was gorgeous.

As he expertly disrobed me, it was as if he was touching more erogenous zones than I knew I had. Panting with wanton desire, my body tingled with excitement.

Twitching with arousal, he then painted some melting ice-cream over my extremely pert nipples, the strokes of the cold spoon sending jolts of pleasure through my body and the pleasure-pain factor heightening the eroticism.

He asked, 'Does that feel good?' His voice was now breathy and heavy.

'*Oh* – so good,' I replied, my spine arching backwards to the couch as my head tilted away from him, leaving my neck and body exposed.

Releasing all inhibitions my body sighed 'Ahhh!' before Michael cupped his lips around my right nipple and started circling his tongue around my breast.

'Oh, God,' I whispered. 'Don't stop,' I pleaded, already on the verge of orgasm just from his slightest touch. 'Yeah – oh, yeah,' I panted, feeling the intensity build up. 'Keep going.' I almost forced his head down lower, my body now grinding in rhythm with Massive Attack's 'Karmacoma', that was playing in the background.

Feeling empowered I helped direct him to the perfect position to caress my clitoris, and as he thrust his spirited tongue up inside me, using both his hands to massage me, teasing my different hot spots, within seconds I was screaming with laughter, begging him to stop, as my body spasmed out of control.

'JE – SUS!' I cried, as I lifted off the ground, my eyes stinging with the stimulation, my ears popping as the muscles of my body contracted.

Without saying anything, Michael stood up, unbuckled his studded leather belt, unbuttoned his jeans and pushed them down with his Calvin Klein boxers in one motion, to reveal his magnificently carved Adonis-impression cock standing tall and looking oh so edible.

Oh my God, I thought. It was perfect, as if a sculptor had designed it.

'You're so beautiful,' he whispered, as he rejoined me on the floor.

Grabbing my rump with the full of his right hand, the back of my shoulders with his left, he firmly positioned me on all fours, in front of the now roaring fire.

As he vigorously wrapped his hand around my hair, pulling it tightly back to gain control of me, he gave my right cheek a violent slap. Screaming with ecstasy, I could feel him enter me, asking, 'Do you like that?'

Knowing that he hadn't put on a condom I collapsed to the floor to get away from him, and as I rolled on my back to face him, I did my best porn star expression trying not to lose the moment and said, 'Sorry, baby, I need a condom.'

Only temporarily thrown off track, he fled to the bedroom. I heard the bedside cabinet being abruptly opened and shut, before he returned moments later peeling a condom down the shaft of his still erect cock.

'*Fuck me,*' I demanded, elated that my definite requirements hadn't spoilt this gorgeous production.

'Oh, I'm gonna *fuck you*, beautiful,' he grinned, resuming his position behind me. He pushed himself energetically inside me again, filling me completely.

An accomplished lover, he steadily built up speed, sending shock waves through my body from my fingertips to my toes. With decisive thrusts he pounded me from behind over and over. God, how I missed sex, I thought. I was so happy to be back in the saddle.

My senses heightened from the orgasm, I felt the fingertips of his left hand slightly imprint the skin of my left shoulder as he grappled to keep a firm grip of my body in motion. His right hand gripped my waist solidly, almost too tightly, but it didn't matter.

By now the side of my face was beginning to burn and my knees were chafing from the wood chips that had spilt out of the fire on to the old antique Persian wool rug beneath me, but I couldn't ruin this moment.

As his groans began to reach a crescendo, I screamed out, '*Harder – harder!*' to help him along, as by now his dick, which was somewhat larger than I was used to, was starting to hurt me.

And then with one enormous lunge, he screamed, *'You're the best!'* as his fingernails dug into my flesh. Following it up with weaker thrusts, his body behind me jerked and twitched as he muttered to himself, 'Oh, fuck – oh, yeah – ohhh, yeah.'

Exhausted, the two of us crumpled to the floor, panting and smiling.

Sunday we had kissed and cuddled like respectful teenagers, but after a build-up, *this* was something to report back to the gang in Dublin.

'You – are – so – *hot!*' Michael's inhalations were deep and precise.

Nuzzling his hair and stubble in his hands, he shook himself off like a dog and turned to me with a silly loved-up grin on his face and asked, 'Anyone ever told you what a great lay you are?'

Pausing for a minute to decide whether to react bolshy, I then decided to do a Britney Spears/ Beyoncé/Jessica Simpson impression and said, 'I'm as sweet as apple pie me, I was just a little ole virgin till I met you.'

'Ha. You better change that to cherry pie, sweet cheeks, as I've just stolen your cherry – again!'

'Ha, for sure,' I teased.

'*Wow!* I feel great,' whooped Michael. He jumped to his feet and walked in the direction of the bathroom. When I heard a flush of the loo I knew he had disposed of the evidence. Thank God he had a condom. I'm mad about the guy, but not mad enough to shag him without a condom. Well, definitely not sober anyway.

*   *   *

With a change in the menu to 'Steak and spuds' and old-fashioned sex in the bedroom, Wednesday night was the fourth night in the Big Smoke when we stayed behind locked doors.

But this morning, Thursday, I could tell that Michael had started to get itchy feet. Although we had enjoyed some very enjoyable honeymoon sex in the shower, which had left my hair difficult and yours truly a little stressed, he needed space, and took himself off to see a man about a dog.

'I gotta catch a guy down in Camden,' he told me abruptly, catching me unawares.

I was still drip-drying and smothering myself in some cocoa butter which I had found in a bathroom cabinet which was like an Aladdin's Cave of nasty addictive prescriptions like Stilnoct, Valium, Librium and Limovan, but Michael had dressed himself fully and looked like he couldn't wait to get away from me.

'There's a spare key on the dresser,' he told me, kissing me on the cheek, 'just in case you wanna go out shopping. I won't be long, I promise.' And within seconds he was gone, the door slamming shut behind him. Wondering if he had already grown bored with me, I wandered into the living room and hugged myself on the couch, staring out at the transitory birds visiting our small and somewhat sparse garden.

Had I put out too early? I deliberated. I didn't think so: we had waited *at least* forty-four hours before consummating the relationship. I thought I showed great restraint, waiting that long. But maybe he was used to more virtuous women?

So much for the shotgun wedding – the four-day engagement looked like it could have fizzled out.

What I found most confusing was that he failed to mention the fact that he had asked me to be his wife on Saturday night. How bizarre was that? Did he make a habit of proposing to strange women? Or was he just a tad forgetful? Either way, he didn't bring it up, and I wasn't going to rock the boat. Well, not yet. It just didn't add up, though. Maybe I just got a bit over-excited at his indecent proposal? Let's be honest, he didn't even know my second name. But I couldn't be to blame for getting anxious, I'm female after all. We take things like offers of marriage very seriously, especially when no one's ever bothered to ask before.

Deciding I'd have to face the outside world at some stage, I hesitantly typed in the PIN to my mobile phone.

So far the only interference from reality was a single e-mail from our invisible host Frankie, to say 'Please water my bonsai and if a prostitute called Astrid knocks over, give the bitch the plastic Harrods bag beside the front door and ask her for the key back . . .'

Now six new messages flashed up on the screen.

Maybe this guy in Camden was just a ruse to escape my overbearing grasp? I thought, opening up a message from Anna asking, 'Ave u fked it up yet?' This did nothing to boost my confidence.

Or had Michael made his getaway to Old Bond Street to purchase a five-carat solitaire for me?

Laughing my way through Parker's three messages – 'Does big Mick have a big Mickie?', 'I want to be your bridesmaid' and 'Did you show him your trick with a ping-pong ball?' – and Maddie's frantic, 'Make sure you check in his wardrobe and in his pockets', I got to my final message, which was from a mystery Dublin number. 'Get a solicitor, whore. I'm going to bring you down,' it read.

Doing my usual trick, I placed 5 in its code to phone straight into the person's mailbox. The sound of 'Hi, you're through to Annette,' sent a shiver down my spine.

Instantly reality hit home and pangs of guilt came flooding over me.

Why had I switched on my phone? What did Annette want, and why did I need a solicitor? Fuck it anyway. More importantly, why did Michael do a runner? What if he didn't come back?

Finding a half-empty bottle of Sancerre in the fridge, I took to the bed to pacify my mind. Too many questions to answer and not enough wine, I thought. Stuffing the phone under my pillow I tasted the wine, which was a tad stale.

As I drifted off into a daydream of how wonderful life could be living here, right here, and waking up in this bed every morning, I noticed a mean-looking magpie staring at me through the window from under the Roman blind.

Being a woman who has always courted superstition, I raced over to the window to see if he had a mate, of course, and scared him off his perch in the process. Thankfully, he only absconded to an adjacent telephone pole to join another magpie. Phew, one for sorrow, and two for joy . . . but hang on, on closer inspection I could see another two: one on the ground and one posing on top of a green Saab convertible.

So, what does that mean? One for sorrow, two for joy, three for a girl and four . . . for a boy? Or was it, one for sorrow, two for mirth, three for a wedding, and four for a birth.

Ah, fuckity, fuck. My head was melted with all of the morning's mixed signals. If only I didn't believe in omens.

I heard a rustle in the lock; Michael had arrived back. My phone said 14:36p.m., which was not bad, considering he had only left about noon.

'Hi honey, I'm home!' he shouted in an elated tone. I was so relieved. But then I heard muttering, followed by laughter and banging, which indicated to me he wasn't home alone.

'I'm in here!' I said nervously from the bedroom, as I realized I had failed to get dressed further more than slipping on one of Michael's T's. Feeling an emotional wreck, I had needed to be close to him and comfort myself with his smell.

Bounding in the door, Michael pounced on the bed and started mauling me like a puppy. 'How's my little heart-breaker? Did she miss me?' His mood was more effervescent than I was used to.

Brushing his slobber off my face, I wrestled him off me and sat up straight in the bed. Like a disapproving wife I demanded, 'Where have you been?' But he just laughed in my face.

'You look so cute when you're angry,' he teased, throwing me one of his winning get-out-of-jail smiles. 'I bumped into an ole friend on the street. I brought him back for a line . . . I hope you don't mind?' And with that he rebounded out the door back to his 'friend' in the living room.

Did he say a *line*? I thought. What does he mean? He's brought him back to do a line? Of coke? He never mentioned anything to me before about doing drugs.

Unsure how to handle the situation, I sat at the end of the bed trying to gather my wits. Act cool, I told myself. I didn't have to be forced into anything I wasn't happy with. After a five-minute pep talk, and two failed attempts to get in contact with Maddie, I rummaged through Michael's bags, which lay strewn across the bedroom floor and by now had vomited clothes everywhere. Pilfering a clean pair of combat shorts to complete my walk of shame, I checked my appearance in the *en suite* loo's antique gilt-edged mirror. It had a tiny crack at the bottom left-hand corner, but I did my best to ignore that.

Legs still shiny from the cocoa butter – check. Hair tossed seductively – check. A smear of clear lip gloss – check. I felt good to go.

I was no Kate Moss by any stretch of the imagination, but what I was most worried about was that Michael might be turning into my own real life Pete Doherty.

With an air of confidence I ventured out into the living room doing my best too-cool-for-school rock chick impression.

'Hey,' I said as I casually ruffled my hair in the direction of our new friend, who was resting on the floor and hanging over the coffee table that was reflecting Michael. I followed it up with 'What's the story?' But my provocative entrance was ignored.

In my attempt to make eye contact with Michael's companion I had at first missed what he was doing. Right enough, he was talking about coke, well, I could only presume it was cocaine: he had it piled high in a giant mound in the centre of the table and had already started to chalk up tube lines of the stuff for himself and . . . 'Austin,' exclaimed Michael. He pointed at the guy without looking up.

I positioned myself on the couch after kissing Michael on the back of the neck, and now 'Austin' decided to make eye contact with me. In a far from enthusiastic tone he muttered 'Olright?' I didn't exactly feel endeared to the geezer.

Like Michael he had the look of someone creative, with his army-surplus scuzz-duds. He was Robert De Niro in *Taxi Driver* meets Ewan McGregor in *Trainspotting*. And while he pretentiously kept his high-fashion aviators on, I could tell the guy wasn't

just any sham from his Breitling aviation watch. I
recognized it from an ad in *Vanity Fair*, endorsed by
John Travolta. Very money indeed.

He may have been cute, and I might not have been
so bothered if Maddie had been with me to help
defuse the situation, but how dare he come into my
little fantasy world and disrupt my fun? I had been
waiting to meet Michael all my life. I hadn't waited
twenty-nine years to spend an afternoon looking at
'Austin' snort coke up his nose.

Concentrating on the job in hand, Michael spent
a good five minutes perfecting his queue of white
powder, and then nudged me with his elbow to ask,
'Are you in, beautiful?'

Momentarily, I was stressed as to what to say back,
but since neither man could remove his gaze from the
narcotics on the table, they were unable to see the fear
spread across my face.

'A bit early for me, hon, you crack on,' I said,
panicked but trying desperately hard to keep it all on
the inside.

Like a child with Tourette's, Michael had started to
emit excitable squeaks as he rocked on the spot while
the wonderful Austin rolled up a £20 note. This was
a side to his personality that I hadn't witnessed before,
and while it was kinda rock 'n' roll, it was also kind
of a turn-off. My safe little bubble had been well and
truly burst.

Two days ago this had been the site of passionate
lovemaking. Today it morphed into an evil den

of iniquity. Tempers were already frayed with my parents. Thank God they couldn't see me now . . .

'Cheers, man,' said Michael as he grabbed Austin's note and got his head down over a perfectly chiselled line. Trying not to wince with disgust, I lay coiled on the sofa as my new fiancé did his best Dyson impression and hoovered up, not one, not two but *three* sizeable lines of Colombia's finest brain rot. Wow. He was a total pro.

Leaping in the air, Michael let out a primal lion's roar, stretching his hands to the ceiling, shaking his shoulders out and throwing the rolled-up note at Austin, who happily grabbed it as if it was a baseball.

'Good shit, man,' praised my Herculean lover. Then he wandered out of the room, waving his hands around and performing a very bad rendition of the Fun Lovin' Criminals number, 'Barry White'.

Uncomfortable with the developing situation, I remained pinned to the couch, and as Michael marched about in the kitchen with his Colombian power powder racing around his system, I had a ringside seat for my second masterclass in how to shovel class As up your nose.

First, Austin checked which nostril was working better, by closing each one off individually with his thumbs. After deciding to run with his left nostril, he shoved the twenty up it and used his right index finger to cover the other side. With ease of movement he effortlessly devoured what was left on the table in two sweeping snorts.

Unfortunately for him he had to satisfy himself with *just* the two lines, instead of my fella's suicidal greedy three.

Not wanting any of the precious sprinkle to go to waste, he wet his finger on his tongue, like they do in the movies, fingered up the remaining dust and rubbed it on his gums. Then to finish off his house-keeping he fiddled with the end of his nose to make sure there was no coke hanging off it.

Just like Michael, he made it look like an everyday occurrence. Obviously, it was. It was only coming up to three o'clock on a Thursday afternoon, but I suppose when you have a job like Michael's that has you working odd hours, a weekday afternoon is just the same as another person's Saturday night. Or so I reasoned.

As if he had just snorted a personality, Austin's pout started to relax from a harsh scowl to a more pleasant half-smile.

'So, you're the latest?' he asked, making me cough with a nervous laugh. 'Y-yess, I suppose you could say I'm the latest.' I was far from impressed.

Seizing my opportunity to gather a little background knowledge of Michael, I asked, 'So how do you guys know each other?' Unfortunately, his mobile rudely interrupted my interrogation with an irritating beeping and he headed off to the hall with a brief 'Sorry.'

I remained stuck to the couch. There were now *two* relative strangers pacing the additional rooms, and I strained to think what Maddie would do. This sort of thing wouldn't faze her in the slightest, I thought. I just needed to act cool. It's not as if it was the first time I'd seen someone do coke in my presence. I'd seen plenty of people partake of illegal substances back in Dublin, but without Maddie, Parker, Lisa or even Anna by my side, I was feeling a smidgen vulnerable.

Snapping into vixen mode and adopting the relaxed pose of a veteran groupie, I hung my bare legs on display and started to twiddle a loose curl around my finger.

Michael returned to the living room, with an open bottle of JD, a bottle of Coca-Cola and three tumblers.

'Close your eyes,' he demanded, his piercing brown eyes looking serious. Worried by his unpredictability I said, 'What?' But he just smiled. 'Close your eyes for me, heart-breaker.'

I did as he said. I could hear him place the glasses and bottles on the table, and then immediately a powerful scent wafted up my nose, giving me a fright. I jolted my eyes open, only to see Michael waving a sprig of rosemary in front of me.

'I picked it for you from the garden. There were no flowers to be seen, but this does smell beautiful . . . Just like youuu,' he cooed.

It wasn't quite Interflora calling, but I did see the romance in his gesture. He was still sweet, even though he was ridiculously high as a kite.

And just as we were starting to enjoy a moment

locking lips, Robert De Niro came stomping back in, proclaiming, 'Daz and Charlie are on their way.' Not knowing if they were terms for more drugs or actual people, I sat back and sipped quietly on the Jack and Coke which Michael handed me.

'WHOO-HAA!' he whooped, like Al Pacino in *Scent of a Woman*. 'I feel a big one going down!'

Staring out the window, I noticed that it had started to sheet rain – tears from heaven, indeed. How the hell was I going to get myself out of this mess?

'I'M IN SUM BAR, OR CLUB TYPE PLACE IN CHEL-SEE,' I shouted down the phone to Maddie. *'AN I'M WASTED!'* After about ten hours' drinking, I suddenly felt the need to call home again.

And while I couldn't really make out what she was saying, apart from, '. . . coming home? . . . OK? I'll kill 'im!' it was a comfort in itself to know she was at the other end of the phone – even if I couldn't hear her over the pounding bass of the dance music.

Slumped on a toilet, I sat and stared at myself in the full-length mirror on the back of the door. God, I was a state. I could easily be that bird from the Prodigy's 'Smack My Bitch Up' video.

Looking at my screen to see if I was still connected, I shouted down the phone, 'I MISS YOU . . . I'M FF-FINE . . . TALK TO YA TOMORROW, HON!' And then threw the phone back in my Prada bag. Thinking, duty done, I'd have put her mind at ease . . .

As I thought about rising to my feet, I wondered had I fallen asleep in the toilet? I was convinced I had lost time somewhere. I had a track record of taking power naps.

After gathering the energy to stand up I misplaced my footing and fell forwards against the door with a bang.

Very ladylike I thought, bursting into fits of laughter.

Pulling up my cerise Kylie pants, I safely positioned my bag on my shoulder and, taking a deep breath, I unlocked the door and tried not to fall down. Greeted with a disapproving frown by the toilet attendant who sat surrounded by the contents of a pharmacy, and several women availing themselves of her perfumes, deodorants and lollypops, I pulled the face of a six-year-old girl and stuck my tongue out at her the second she turned her back.

I was sorry I hadn't applied some make-up in the cubicle, for the main area around the sinks was dimly lit and the smoked-glass mirrors only made me feel even drunker. It was a couple of moments before I realized the toilet woman was glaring at me again, so I smeared lip gloss everywhere from my top lip to my chin and all places in between, and made my way out, only to have to stumble through several other heavy doors.

It was then that I became aware I hadn't a clue where I had left Michael sitting.

Scanning the busy room, I could only see bodies

and flashing lights and waitresses and people walking past me on mobile phones.

Trying to get my bearings I propped myself up against a cigarette machine. Bringing my right index finger up to extend from the end of my nose, I pointed to the left of the room, at each table, and worked my way across to the bar to see if I could jog my memory. It didn't work.

It was too dark, there were too many people, too much dry ice . . .

Turning to a nearby group I asked if I could sit at the end of their couch for a minute. But I didn't wait for a reply, and plonked myself down beside them regardless.

After about five minutes I felt like a complete fool as the women around the table had started making comments to their partners about me.

Just as I started to probe my bag for my phone, dropping an eyeliner and some English money that Parker had given me on the floor, Daz appeared out of nowhere, put his hand on my shoulder and asked, 'What cha doin' over 'ere kid?' His Liverpudlian accent sounded warm and compassionate.

'Oh, thank God.' I jumped up immediately and threw my arms around him.

We had bonded throughout the day, as he filled me in on his Irish roots. His mother Kathleen was from Dolphin's Barn in Dublin. And his real name was Darren.

'You're OK, gal, wer just ova 'ere.' He smiled as he spoke, and led me masterfully by the hand through the swarms of people, back to safety.

'Look who I found,' declared Daz, holding my arm in the air like a trophy.

'We were about to send out a search party for ya,' explained Michael as he gave me a solid hug. 'Don't do that again. You gave me a fright. You've been gone nearly an hour.'

Settling back into the group, I clung to Michael as if we were magnetically charged. Sod him, I thought, I had given myself a scare and didn't fancy the idea of getting lost again either.

Despite the fact that he picked up his entertainment of the group from where he had obviously left off, I gripped his hand and refused to let go. Thankfully, he didn't protest.

'I need to talk to these people. If you want me, just squeeze my hand, OK?' he said, before embellishing some anecdote about a model who refused to take her clothes off after being booked to do a poster campaign for a power shower.

'It's not my fault you forgot to shave your *bush*, you dumb fuck, I said to her.' His New York accent resonated thicker than before. 'I said fuck it. A big bush is retro, so we stripped the bitch and shot her . . .' His audience howled with laughter.

After about twenty minutes I had started to sober up, and asked Michael to get me another drink.

'Do you wanna do a line instead to wake you

up?' he asked. 'No thanks,' I said, my face wincing as I spoke, 'it's not really my thing.'

'Well, how about some jungle juice?' He pointed to a glass of Coke with a small plate resting on the top of it.

'Huh?'

'Some gone with the wind? A little unfaithful? Some amyl nitrate? Oh, poppers. That's what they call it in Ireland. You must have heard of poppers?' His eyes lit up with excitement.

'Umm, OK. I've heard of poppers, but what does it do?' I started to feel open to the power of his persuasion.

'It makes you wanna dance — and it's legal.' He winked, urging me to try it.

'Promise you'll mind me?' I pleaded, glancing nervously at the innocent-looking glass.

'I promise,' he said, rubbing my back and giving me a peck on the cheek. 'You'll get a kick out of it.'

Feeling safe in his arms, I grabbed the glass and asked him what to do.

'Hold the plate over it until you're ready to take a big breath.' His instructions came as if he were telling a child how to tie her shoelaces. 'When you are, take it off, take a deep breath then hold it for a few seconds and cover the glass up. It's potent stuff. It's not good to stink the place out.'

'That's it? I just breathe in and hold it?'

'That's it, heart-breaker. But be ready, it'll probably blow your head off.' He laughed at my innocence.

Feeling like a rebel wild child I stuck my face in the glass of Coke and took a deep breath of something with the distinct odour of smelly socks. Gross, I thought, as I struggled to hold my breath.

And as I replaced the glass on the table I released my inhalation and instantly felt a rush of blood erupt through my body and explode across my face. My cheeks were on fire, my heart started to pound, and it felt like it was going to surge out of my chest.

As Michael looked on like a proud boyfriend, a wave of emotion flooded over me and I took it upon myself to straddle him and push him to the back of the couch, which was carpeted with people's jackets and coats.

'Do you feel good?' he asked as I pinned his arms back by the wrists. 'Yes, baby,' I replied, coming over all light-headed, 'I feel very, very, very good!'

I kept kissing him like I was a Hollywood starlet until several members of the group started shouting, 'Get a room!' Reluctantly, I sat back down to face the group. In milliseconds I was bored and demanded, 'I want more!'

Happy to oblige me, Michael handed me the glass again. Fearlessly I took a second, deeper breath of the poppers.

This time I held it in for longer. And just like before I felt the rush of blood rippling over me. My heart pounded again, my head went dizzy. I had never experienced anything like it before. I felt hot. I felt like I wanted to dance.

And dance I did. Stepping up on the table, I thrust my hands in the air and tossed my hair to the beat of, 'Where's Your Head At?'

I didn't know.

I didn't care.

I was living in the moment, and it felt great.

I was being a bold Eva. And I loved it.

The diva was back . . .

4

9.55 Saturday morning, I was stepping out of a black cab and ducking into Liverpool Street Station. The sky was grey. And so was my mood. Sorry – change that to thunderous.

With three days to go till Valentine's Day, I didn't want to be booked on a cheapo no frills flight back to Dublin. I wanted to be boarding a BA to Vegas. But it wasn't to be. Michael had been called back to the Big Apple on an urgent job, and the party was well and truly over.

'The industry needs me,' he teased. And that was as much of an explanation as I got.

Luckily for him his flight wasn't till later, so I left him in bed, our bed, looking as edible as ever. His tired eyes and wayward hair just added to his appeal. 'I'll call ya later – ya big ride,' were the last words he shouted as I shut the door, in his newly acquainted Dublin accent.

I cursed the cold as I stared back up to the bedroom

window, where we had spent so much quality time nuzzling and analysing the world's problems. I had hoped he would have waved down or blown me a kiss. But I was probably being petty.

We had grown close in our time together. We'd laughed, been intimate; Michael had even feckin' proposed to me, but had yesterday confessed that it had just been a wicked ploy to make him stand out.

Stand out indeed. I felt as if I'd been catapulted up in the air and then dropped from a height like on a ride at Alton Towers. Despite my best tough girl act, I still found it hard to control my emotions. Maybe I'd watched too many rom-coms, because I still believed – hoped for – fairy tales.

Stupidly I had thought Michael serious when he asked me to marry him. How naïve! My heart then sank, well, it kept sinking, especially when he told me my booking number for the flight and said, 'It's just the way it's gotta be, heart-breaker!'

I felt totally despondent. I wasn't the heart-breaker. He was.

Like a stroppy teenager, I dragged my well-smacked ass and my few belongings to the nearest taxi rank and prayed for news of a bomb scare at the airport. For once, I had no such luck.

Much to my annoyance, the train was crammed with people with oversized jackets and fake-fur-rimmed hoods. But my diminishing luck somehow allowed me to find a seat; a small sanctuary where I could obsess about my phone with two hands.

Unable to concentrate, I clasped it tight and continually flicked through the few precious photos of us with stupid cheesy grins, which we had taken while lying in bed.

By the time I had reached the airport, I had texted his 'cell' several times, but had got no reply. He must have fallen back asleep.

It had been seven days and seven nights of utter debauchery.

My bones ached. My skin was blemished, and my nails looked like they had tried to scrape their way out of a cave.

I felt and looked a wreck.

But it had been wild.

It had been an adventure of the rock 'n' roll variety, and one to tell the grandkids. Well, a watered-down version anyway.

But my week away from home had nearly killed me. And as I approached the Ryanair check-in desk, queuing alongside the businessmen with their cheapo laptop cases, the hassled mothers with their irritable children and the young professionals with their iPods, I realized I had become an outlaw to society, a vagrant, a person without purpose or use. OK, so I'm sounding a little dramatic. But that's how I felt.

Numbed by the alcohol in my system, I mulled over all the problems I would face when I arrived home. I had been putting it to the back of my mind, but money matters had become critical. Rent was due. My MBNA credit card was maxed at about €12,000.

And bills from Bupa, Eircom, the TV licence crowd and Vodafone had been shoved in a pile at the back of the microwave. It was better than putting them straight in the recycling, I thought.

But how could I forget Annette? Crap. I had been admiring how glossy a woman's blonde hair was in the adjacent line when I remembered the text from Barron's wife, threatening me. Get a solicitor, eh? This should be interesting. I own nothing apart from a few designer labels and some jewellery. If she can squeeze blood out of this stone I'll kiss her myself!

Another wave of depression hit me. Although I was a girl who was attracted to wealth, I had amassed none of my own, and had frittered away all my previous earnings on frivolous things like entertainment, taxis and holidays to Marbella. My mother was forever nagging me about saving for a house, or the possibility of putting some money aside for a rainy day. Unfortunately this week the outlook was for a monsoon, and the kitty had not only been spent, the bottom of the barrel had been licked clean.

Knowing my luck, there will be nothing more than a tin of chick peas and Weight Watchers' rice pudding in the cupboard, and I'll be left thinking, why did I buy this stuff? I don't even eat it.

Things would have to change. But then I glanced back down at my phone, its battery power was running dangerously low now, and proudly smiled at the happy screensaver of Michael and myself.

Would I have swapped the last week of terrific sex

with such a hunk for a sensible millennium of work and early nights in Dublin? No chance!

With just enough cash to grab a Tropical Twist smoothie and a bag of popcorn, I sat at Gate 82 waiting to board. Feeling a renewed sense of excitement I couldn't wait to get home and fill Maddie in on all the nitty-gritty details of my true romance.

She'd be waiting for me in Dublin Airport arrivals at 1.30 to take me home. Shame I only had a token menu from the Ivy to say thank you . . .

The lift home with Maddie was strained. She looked worse than me, but every time I asked her if she was OK, she'd just bark back at me, *'I'm fine!'*

She hadn't seemed remotely interested in the fact that I had met Paul O'Grady at 6a.m. in some restaurant place that still served us champagne.

'I didn't know both his parents are Irish,' I rambled. 'Now, I think his mother is from Gardiner Street, or did he say his dad was from Gardiner Street? Either way one of them is from Dublin and the other is from Mayo. He was great craic, you know. Really friendly when he heard the Irish accent.'

But I might as well have been reading her the shipping forecast, for the interest she showed.

The real alarm bells started ringing when I said that I had bumped into Chris Evans at Zilli Fish and that he'd bummed money off us for a bottle of wine.

Many moons ago, Maddie had met him at Renards

with me, when he had just signed that massive £75 million deal with Virgin. That was before he had fallen in love and married Billie Piper, and they had only shared a quick snog, but she always thought that if she had played easier to get, she might have been the one with the red Porsche birthday presents and the Vegas wedding.

'OK, stop the car,' I ordered. 'Something's up, so just spit it out!'

'If you don't shut up you can get out and walk.'

Maddie's tone was so serious I believed her.

We spent the next fifteen minutes in silence.

When we pulled up outside my little house in Stoneybatter, we sat for another moment in deafening silence. I hated to see Maddie upset. But I was afraid to say anything that might to make her worse.

Eventually, Maddie spoke. But she kept her eyes focused directly above her as if keeping watch for passing birds that might shit on her car.

'So how are you fixed for money these days?' Her question sounded loaded.

'I'm screwed,' I told her honestly.

'Hmmm. Me too,' she whispered, almost as if she wasn't speaking to me, but to herself.

Worried she'd fly off the handle if I asked her if she was all right again, I patted her hand, which was all tensed up and almost decapitating the gearstick, and asked her, 'Do you want to come in for a cup of tea, hon?'

Realizing her bad mood, Maddie strained a fake

smile and declined my offer. 'I'll catch you later, babes. I've a job at 3.30.'

'Call me later when you get a chance?' I pushed, but with a quick 'Yeah' she had pushed me on to the path and screeched off down the road in her super-sexy silver 3 Series BMW.

I then spent the next ten minutes scrapping through dirty underwear and old razors in the side panels of my Samsonite to find my house keys.

Suffering with a bad case of ringxiety, I felt emotionally dependent on my phone.

It was Monday morning and there was still no word from Michael.

So far I had growled at Parker, my sister Ruth and some young PR twit who was wondering did I have a contact number for the model Glenda Gilson and had made the fatal error of ringing me.

I hadn't held, smelt, kissed or spoken to my boy in forty-eight hours. The frustration was positively killing me. Why hadn't he phoned? Was he OK? Maybe his plane crashed? No, I would have heard on the news. But maybe he was in a car crash and he's in hospital injured with amnesia? That wouldn't have made the news.

I know, I'm being stupid. He's probably just been busy, or playing hard to get. That must be it. Blokes always have their own rule-book for how many days they should leave it before they call a girl.

Hmmm, I wasn't happy.

Then again, maybe he left his phone by mistake in Frankie's place and that's why it keeps ringing out. My mind kept racing, thinking of the endless reasons why he hadn't got in touch.

Damn him anyway . . .

Tuesday night, Valentine's night – *and* supposedly my wedding night – the Bitches of Eastwick found themselves slouched on Parker's couch, stuffing their faces with aromatic duck, ribs, sweet 'n' sour chicken and far too many prawn crackers, while struggling to stay focused on Woody Allen's *Match Point*.

'This is shit,' groaned Parker, with his usual attention span of an ant.

Maybe it was just because I was in such a foul mood, but I had to agree with him. I hated everything about this movie – the cinematography, the weak acting, Jonathan Rhys Meyers's irritating English accent. Even the way the very gorgeous Scarlett Johansson pouted annoyed me.

'I hate to admit it, but you're right,' I sighed. 'This is possibly the worst movie I've *ever* seen!'

'It's drivel. It's not just shit, it's about as exciting as our sex lives right now,' declared Maddie as she sucked on a spare rib bone suggestively.

'What you mean is it's lacking in spunk?' teased Parker.

'Ha, very droll, Mr Pink,' snarled Maddie, 'but not everyone gets as excited about body fluids as you, my dear.'

Feeling the need to interrupt Parker before he embarked on a rant, I offered, 'Anyone for more chicken balls?' But of course that just set Parker off on another tangent. 'Chicken balls . . . Tennis balls . . . I need hunky male balls, Goddamn it. What are we doing here apart from dribbling Hoi Sin sauce all over my suede couch? Thank you very much, Eva. But come on, this is depressing. Let's go out and play.' Parker's eyes bulged passionately.

Like a man on a mission, he gave his best hurtful truth justification for why we should entertain his impulse demand.

'Look, face it, Eva, he's just not that into you. That's how the saying goes. If he was, Michael would have called you by now. So put it down to a cute holiday romance and let's hope you didn't catch any STDs off him.'

I managed to force out 'Ah, thanks darlin',' before my eyes welled up with tears and my heart felt like it was pounding from my throat.

As Maddie pushed her plate aside to comfort me, Parker swung his attention to her and unleashed his tongue in a similar attack.

'And as for you, Missy, you've been more ho lately than all the hookers on Leeson Street put together. It's about time you left some straight men for us gay boys and pointed your friend here in the direction of your STD guy, Dr Freedman.'

Totally gobsmacked, Maddie and I sat holding hands on the edge of our seat in total silence. We both knew he had valid points, but we couldn't believe he could be so hurtful.

'Jaysus, Parker, you're some bitch. I'm kinda getting the hint that Michael – the bastard – isn't going to ring me, but do you really need to be such a bully about it?' My voice quivered as I spoke.

'Sorry,' conceded Parker, 'but you've been moping about him since you've got back. He's obviously moved on.'

'Oh, *all* of three days, jeez, I'm so sorry for being such a thorn in your side.' My response shifted quickly from self-pity to anger.

Temporarily Parker was left speechless, he knew he'd gone too far, and he could sense that neither of us was in the mood to entertain his cynical monologues.

After an awkward silence while both Maddie and I just snarled at him menacingly, he took a deep intake of breath, rearranged his shirt over the large G of his Gucci belt and then huffed his way towards the hall and disappeared into the bathroom. Maddie and I took one look at each other and at the same time whispered, 'Let's get outta here.'

Practised Houdini artists, we had slipped out of Parker's apartment in seconds, closing the door gently behind us, before screaming like escaped mental patients as we ran down the back stairs.

By the time we skulked out the front door we were totally out of breath, but energized by the exertion.

'What now?' I asked, ready to take on any possibility.

Reaching for inspiration, Maddie's face curled up in one of her cute frowns. A wave of devilment flashed in her eyes.

'Let's go to a dirty pub and get drunk,' she said, but in a tone that indicated: this is what we're doing so don't argue with me.

Happy to oblige I offered up a few potential boozers, but Maddie had decided exactly where she wanted to go. With a strut that was more gangster than catwalk, she began dragging me in the direction of Pearse Street in predatory fashion. If she'd been an animal she would have been frothing at the mouth. Instead she was a model, so she just flared her nostrils and flicked her mane of hair in a spirited manner.

After several pint bottles of Bulmers, which Maddie bought since I'd nothing but shrapnel in my pocket, our problems inevitably got worse.

For some reason Maddie hadn't pandered to my frustration with Michael, and in fact had been nothing but a bitch to me for no apparent reason. Finding ourselves in a grotty pub, just as she had wished, had done nothing to improve her mood. Then again, she hardly got the welcome she'd been hoping for.

Her efforts to flirt with the middle-aged barman who looked like Brendan Gleeson in *The General* were rebuffed.

Then she tried to make friends with the locals with a playful toast that consisted of her winking like a pirate and putting on the worst Dub accent to ask, 'All right bud?'

But her greetings were as welcome as a bloody 12-ounce Angus steak at a dinner party for vegans and eventually she gave up trying to be popular and turned her heightened anxiety towards me.

Despite several sloppy texts to Michael, I received no reply. And just as my tolerance level of Maddie had reached its limit, a gorgeous guy walked in the door.

He was tall and blond. Best of all, he had a mate.

Two days later I'm sitting staring at a text from my landlord to say that he was sorry to have missed me yesterday, and that he'd be over at 6.30p.m. to collect his rent, when my mate from *So Now* magazine, Elizabeth, rang.

'Hey stranger,' she asked, all bright and breezy. 'How's unemployment treating you?'

'Comedian is it now?' I snapped back, unnecessarily cold.

'Sorry, hon, not funny I know. Anyhoo, what's the diddly dory on Robert?'

'Who's he? The man with my winning Lottery ticket?'

'Eh, Robert. The sex-tremely shy guy who rang the office just two minutes ago, asking for your number. He said he met you in some pub on Valentine's night and that he wanted to ring you to find out if you were OK? And to see if he could take you out for a drink?'

'You're kidding me.'

'Nope, he sounds cute. What happened?'

'I'm not sure exactly. My mate Maddie and myself, you know the model chick?'

'Oh yes, she's one of your bitches?'

'Ha. Yeah her, well we were out for a few drinks and we ended up in some kip of a pub. We were both in foul moods, and then we met these nice blokes and it all got a bit bizarre.'

'What ya mean?'

'Ah, Maddie just went a bit mental. She got pissed off that I was hitting it off with this guy Robert. I'd totally forgotten his name. Anyway, she didn't like his mate and in a desperate bid to steal some attention from my fella, she started doing a lap dance with a fecking hoover she found shoved in the corner.'

'Dirty dancing eat your heart out.'

'Ha! She can be totally mad. It's funny now that I think about it, but when your man completely blanked her and continued talking to me, she flipped and dragged me out the door, before I even got a chance to swap phone numbers.'

'Well, I'll business card his number to you now, and you can rectify that.'

'I'm mortified. I couldn't ring him.'

'Why, have you had any better offers recently?'

'Not exactly.'

'Well then, call him, and then don't forget to call me with the details. See ya.'

'Here, before you go, don't suppose you've heard of any work going around? I'm fairly stony broke.'

'I'm afraid not. But I'll keep my ear to the ground for you.'

'OK, thanks.'

'Here, you never know, this fella could just be your winning Lotto ticket.'

That evening, arriving late so I wouldn't have to buy myself a drink, I found that nice guy Robert looked cuter than I remembered him in the not-so-grotty pub in town where we'd arranged to meet.

As he stood at the bar to order me a glass of white wine I observed his physique from the comfort of a cosy snug.

Checking him out from head to toe with a head tilt that probably made me look like a used-car salesman checking out an ole banger, I was reasonably pleased with what I could see.

Although he was wearing a fairly dodgy navy and red striped rain jacket that looked like something my dad would wear, I did notice what a nice ass he had through his jeans and thought how much happier I was sitting here than in the hallway of my rented house, trying to explain to my landlord that I had no money to pay his rent.

That's a problem for tomorrow, I thought. I'll turn off my phone just in case he tries to ruin my date with silly demands for cash.

It's not like I'd miss any important calls. After all, it

seemed my fictitious fiancé had forgotten my existence completely.

'Pity Maddie couldn't make it for a drink,' he said with a deadpan stony face as he returned with my wine.

'Really?' I asked, slightly worried.

'No,' he smiled, 'I think I've enough excitement right here in front of me, thanks very much.'

Over the course of our very pleasant evening, I had learnt that Robert was an architect in a small but progressive firm, and that he was very close to his mother Rose and his brother Stuart.

Daddy apparently died several years previously, and since then apple of his Mammy's eye Robert drove Stuart and herself to the grave every week for a family reunion and to leave fresh flowers and a packet of ginger nut biscuits.

No joke!

'He always loved a ginger nut,' he told me.

Unsure if he was kidding, I remained composed to wait for the punch-line. It never came.

He even had the innocence to say, 'And you know, every week they're gone!'

The sarcastic witch in me wanted to ask, 'Did you ever think it might be rats eating the biscuits?' But I thought better of it. Instead I nodded and gave encouraging smiles.

Some men can be so easy to keep happy I thought.

I also learned everything there was to know about

rock climbing. He was fanatical. As were his mates Nigel (whom Maddie had rebuffed), Oscar and Barry. They all seemed very close, like they were cast from the same mould.

I pondered the idea of how I could fit into their clique. As a group we didn't look good on paper.

They were athletic and religious.

I clearly was neither!

The mother was in fact a devout Opus Dei disciple, which scared the bejaysus out of me as I was more familiar with the work of Doris Day and barely knew the words of Our Father . . .

Following in her moral footsteps, I was witness to Robert taking a few phone calls from a priest to set up an event that involved helping inner city street kids. The first call made me notice Robert for what a decent skin he was. But by the second, and then the third – like Diana, I was beginning to feel there were three of us on this date.

As I became increasingly uncomfortable with the phone calls, I began to get freaked out by his laughing and joking with 'Father Benedict' in Irish. He casually switched between English and Irish during each conversation, but kept all the jokey stuff in our native tongue.

I wasn't sure if he did it to show off, or just to be mysterious and mask what he was saying. Either way it bugged me, as of course I couldn't understand a word he was saying.

I might have been proud to be Irish. That didn't

mean I actually spoke the language!

It was all very incompatible. Alien, in fact. Robert was so earthy and wholesome in his comfortable mountaineering boots and windcheater. I almost felt like the she-devil in disguise around him.

As I tried to gaze intently into his eyes and appear interested in his charitable banter about refuge centres and soup runs or whatever, I'd find myself just trying to work out whether his eyes were in fact hazel or a muggy freckled green.

I struggled to sound virginal. Obviously *that* was a far stretch, but I enjoyed his genuine sincerity, even though I knew he was far too healthy for me.

He was, after all, just muesli on legs.

Maybe I'd been hanging around with Parker too long, I must have turned into the female version of him . . . I'd have to find a yellow brick road, and hopefully some bird called Dorothy who would take me to meet a wizard and find me a heart!

Heck, another week . . . another challenge. It was time for a new Eva. I would have to be proactive in creating some good karma for myself.

If the truth be known, my heart still ached for my wild man from New York. I'd sacrifice everything for another wonderful moment in time with him. Every song on the radio seemed to be written with us in mind, especially any songs by Damien Rice. His voice made me cry as I sang along to the words of 'Cannonball'.

As I battled to stay focused on the hunk in front of

me, I remembered I couldn't afford to buy a round of drinks, so I called it an early night, not entirely sure if I'd ever see Robert again.

He was far from a Mr Maybe, but he'd definitely do as a Mr OK For Now.

The next morning I woke up feeling somewhat melancholy and lethargic. The house felt cold, and in no way invited me out of my bed.

By lunchtime hunger had dragged me up, but I wasn't to be satisfied with a carton of carrot and coriander soup. I now hungered for company.

On a Friday afternoon my choices were limited so I worked my way through my mobile phone for inspiration. After a few 'Sorry, no' texts, good-time Anna agreed to call over. As she worked in some advertising firm that her brother ran, she was always a safe bet to skive off work early.

I told her I wanted to talk about creating a new me, and she said she'd be more than happy to discuss all my problems.

Although she was hard work at the best of times, and only palatable in small doses, I needed someone to moan to.

To her credit she was incredibly witty, but a total mouthpiece. While it was great to listen to her tell you about other people's fiascos, you always had to be on your guard not to expose your own personal dramas. Though today that's all I wanted to talk about.

An expert interrogator, she'd strain blood from a

stone, and no matter how determined you were to remain tight-lipped, Anna would always manage to steal a nugget of intimate information.

More than happy to race over to mine at a minute's notice, she arrived clutching a bottle of Pinot Grigio and a packet of Maltesers. It was her standard gift. Though she'd never eat or drink either. I think it was her ploy to loosen me for gossip, while watching me get fat in the process.

What a devious bitch!

Anyway, twenty minutes into our 'wait-till-I-tell-ya' I heard a key in the front door. And before I even had a chance to put my wineglass down, my landlord was filling the living room doorway.

'Miss Valentine,' he bellowed, 'you've been avoiding me.'

As my heart sank as low as Australia all I could do was drop my head and shelter my eyes in embarrassment. This was the situation that I had been trying to avoid. I just couldn't believe my landlord had cornered me so soon – *and* with feckin' Anna in the room.

Fuck!

Knowing the game was up, I conceded defeat by raising my hands in the air, and apologetically saying, 'Pat, I'm so sorry.'

Not missing a beat, Anna jumped up off the couch as if she'd been poked in the backside with a cow prod, and stuck her arm out in his direction.

'Hi, I'm Anna,' she chirped, with the squeakiness of a cheerleader.

Somewhat disarmed by her front (that being her snappy introduction, and the pert twins that were wrestling to burst out of her tight Juicy Couture T), his facial expression softened as he explained, 'I'm Pat. Eva's disgruntled landlord.'

Reaching for words, my jaw just hung heavy as if I was waiting for someone to pop a pill in my mouth. Seeing this window of opportunity, Anna took her chance to pounce.

'So would you have many houses out for rent, Pat? Is there good money in it, Pat? Has Eva not been coughing up the readies, Pat? Are you going to throw her out on the street, Pat?'

Stunned by the barrage of questions my rent-starved landlord stood silent for a time, before telling Anna, 'You're adorable' and gesturing me to the kitchen for 'a quiet word'.

The conversation that followed was short and to the point.

It involved a lot of me saying, 'No, sorry', to all of his questions connected with money, before I finally said, 'OK, I can do that', which was to his final demand for me to be out of the house by Sunday night. There had been no point in lying to him. I had no savings left. I had been surviving off loose change collected in old jars and what I found by rummaging through old jackets and handbags. All such hiding places had now been raided.

There was no way I could make this month's rent, and since I had initially sweet-talked Pat into letting me stay without a deposit, I had no choice but to vacate immediately.

Feeling like I had been hit by a ton of bricks I wandered back into the living room – my soon-to-be former living room – and poured my woes out to Anna. Before I realized what I'd said, I had divulged just how bad my cash flow was, and how I couldn't go home to my parents with my tail between my legs, because they wouldn't have anything to do with me.

After obviously soaking up enough juice, Anna used the excuse of a phone call from her brother to leave me with my problems. She promised to call later, but I knew that was just her way of letting me know she'd want an update.

There was no way she could stay with me now armed with all this hot gossip. She'd need to get out and report it.

Not only had Eva Valentine been dumped after being used for sex, she'd just been evicted from her home.

Surely things couldn't get any worse?

Or could they?

Actually things could get worse.

I had always suffered badly with period cramps. If there was a special occasion like a birthday or Christmas, though especially if I was away on a bikini holiday, my period would arrive. My time of the month seemed to regulate itself around parties, as if my body was trying its hardest to sabotage my ability to have fun.

But I was never going to enjoy today. It was a cold damp Sunday morning and I was sitting in the window of my living room, staring down the road waiting for Maddie to collect me. Me and my two suitcases, my three black bags full of jackets and handbags, and the one brown box I had obtained from the corner shop and into which I had dumped the assorted freebies I had collected in my several years of journalism.

Those lost, forgotten years.

The fact that I had the worst cramps imaginable just added to the glamour of the whole exercise.

I truly never remember being this miserable.

Of course there had been many other times when I had been hysterical with the trauma of a relationship breaking up, but this was just plain ole misery. Now that my bags were packed I just wanted out of the house.

I had said goodbye to each of the rooms and thanked them for looking after me, but now I just wanted to be gone.

Originally Maddie had said she'd pick me up at 10.30, but she was being her trademark late self and her tardiness was doing nothing for my mood.

It was 11.45 before she came screeching up the street, knocking my neighbour's wheelie bin and all of its rubbish across the road in the process.

Unapologetic, she just barked at me to start filling the boot of her car while she used my loo.

Charming I thought; so much for a shoulder to cry on.

Typically, Maddie returned by the time all the hard labour had been completed.

'Are you done?' she snapped, as she jumped in the front seat of her car. 'Come on, let's get out of here.'

Stunned by her lack of sympathy, I counted to ten, then a hundred, in my head trying desperately hard to keep my cool.

'So enough about me,' I said in my best sarcastic tone. 'What's eating you, Miss Narky Knickers?'

Biting her top lip, Maddie let out a big sigh before glancing in my direction and telling me, 'It's not all about *you*, love.'

Totally hard-done-by, my temper snapped as I unleashed a tirade of abuse.

'Eh, no, sorry, actually *today* is all about me, I'm the one whose life has fallen apart. I'm the person who's just been evicted from their home. I'm the one who's lost their job and has no prospects. Yes, *today* is all about me!'

Obviously counting numbers in her own head, Maddie strained a fake smile. 'Are you finished yet?'

But I wasn't.

'Where do you get off being grumpy with me? I've just had the worst run of luck lately and then you come along all bitchy and clearly feeling sorry for yourself. What did ya do? Break a fuckin' fingernail?'

We had only got two minutes down the road before Maddie swerved the car into a pub car park, clipping her shiny hubcaps on the kerb and threw her real Prada handbag on to my lap.

'Open it,' she demanded.

Furious with life, never mind Maddie, I sat with my arms crossed, refusing to obey her demand.

'Open it,' she repeated and her eyes bulged as she spoke. But I was a woman in pain, and was not prepared to jump to her orders.

'Why should I?' I snapped. 'Are the answers to all my problems hiding in your precious handbag?'

Grabbing the bag back off my lap, Maddie started to shake with anger, but I wasn't about to flinch. Weakness was not something us women readily showed.

'You really are a total bitch sometimes,' she snarled.

Not wanting her to have the last word, I barked back, 'Yes, well, that would probably have something to do with the company I keep.'

As the two of us sat fuming, looking out of our respective windows, I decided that maybe I should try and make up, especially since she had all my worldly possessions in the back of her car. Unfortunately it took about five minutes before I buckled, and by then the atmosphere had become extremely tense. So much so that I could see an actual vein on the side of Maddie's neck bulge and pulsate under the pressure.

I wanted to ask if she was auditioning for a part as Dracula's girlfriend, but thought best not to mention it.

Instead, I decided to act as if nothing had happened.

That approach sometimes worked, and at least then I wouldn't have to apologize.

'Parker was such a pet to let me move in with him but he said he'd have to leave the apartment by 12.30. If I don't get there beforehand, I won't be able to get a key off him until tonight.'

Almost snorting, Maddie cracked a smile of frustration. 'Sorry, is our little argument delaying you from getting on with the rest of your day?'

Knowing that she'd appreciate my boldness, I smirked back, 'Very much so. Now can we get a move on?'

Rolling her head and rubbing her shoulders to relieve the stress built up in them, she whispered, 'In a minute.'

I could see she was building up to something. I just couldn't work out what.

'I need you to forget about your madness for one minute, hon, and just listen. I really need you to listen.'

I hated us bickering, so I pulled my cheekiest cheesy grin and waited for a lecture.

My cheeks had begun to ache before she started to speak.

Shaking out her hands, she placed them back on the wheel before looking me square in the eyes. 'I'm in trouble Eva, and I don't know what I'm going to do about it,' she said.

'Trouble? You're in trouble? Are you trying to steal my thunder?'

'I swear to God, this is bad. Right now I'd take your life over mine.' She started to laugh.

'Have you taken any funny pills today? You're acting a little strange if you don't mind me tellin' ya.'

'Sorry, I'm just a bit giddy with my nerves, but I am serious. I'd swap you your big arse an' all, to take away my problem.'

'Go on then, spit it out. It can't be that bad.'

'Open up my handbag.'

'Jaysus, not this again, I'm afraid to stick my hand in it now in case something hops out and bites me. What's in the bloody bag? Tell me.'

'Remember I used your loo back at the house?'

'Yeah.'

'Well, I was gone longer than I normally would be.'

'Yes, I did notice. I got to shift all the heavy stuff on my own, thanks.'

'Well, I had to wait.'

'For God's sake Maddie, for what? What did you have to wait for?'

'The test. I had to wait for the test to work.'

'OK, maybe I'm just a little thick today, so I'm going to need you to help me out here. What test? What did you have to wait for?'

No sooner had the words come out of my mouth, than a light bulb went off in my head.

'Maddie, tell me this is not what I think it is?' Taking her bag back off her, I opened it up and found a pregnancy test sitting inside.

Gobsmacked I lifted it out delicately with my thumb and forefinger, knowing that she had of course peed all over it.

'So this is the mystery test then, yeah? Now I'm not too up on my pregnancy tests, hon, but I'd wager that blue cross is suggesting that you're pregnant. Is that true?'

'Mmmm.'

'WHAT? What's Mmmm? You're pregnant? Since when? And more importantly, by whom?'

'Mmmm means yes. Secondly about three weeks, and thirdly by a guy I'll never see again.'

'Maddie, have you lost your mind? Where were you three weeks ago? Do I know him?'

'I got pregnant – jeez, I can't believe I just said that. Anyway, it happened the night we were all in London. After you went off into the distance with your New Yorker, I met this guy and we hit it off.'

'Literally! Did you get his number?'

'No.'

'So, what are you going to do? Are you going to try and find him? Are you going to keep it? Jesus Christ, Maddie, that's wild. You're fuckin' mad. I can't believe you let yourself get caught.'

'Thanks. Thanks for the words of encouragement.'

'Sorry. It's just a bit of a shock, that's all.'

'Ya reckon?'

'You've obviously been hanging around me too long. My bad karma must have rubbed off on you.'

'Well, do you think you could take your smelly karma back? I don't want it. And I don't want this baby either.'

146

5

'I'm back,' screamed Lisa. 'And I've been having the best sex ever!'

It had been nearly a month since I had last seen or heard from the Princess, and as always there was a big story to be told.

So she took me for lunch at Le Café to fill me in.

'OK. I've been in rehab, and I had the most wonderful time. I think everyone should go. I truly feel like a new woman.'

'Rehab? For what? Addiction to spending money? I thought that was a natural female trait?'

'Exhaustion.'

'Excuse me?'

'Well that would be on my official file. I thought it was very LA to be checked in under exhaustion. Everyone from Lindsay Lohan to Robbie Williams has used it. I flirted with the idea of sex addict, but since Daddy was the only one who would take me in,

I thought it best not to. Of course Mother just laughed at me when I asked to go.'

'Hang on a second, all this time you've been un-contactable, you've been locked up in a loony bin? Let me guess, you were hanging out with a load of stars in the Priory?'

'No, the Priory is so nineties. I have no interest in sharing caring-time with Z-list celebrities such as Kerry Katona, thank you very much. How very common. No, I discovered a very sexy retreat in Wicklow. It costs the earth. All the big names have been.'

'Like who?'

'Oh, it would be far too indiscreet to say. I made a promise in group therapy not to divulge, but I can tell you about Francis.'

'Oh, yeah, tell me all about your new crazy friend then.'

'I will, but not before you fill me in on some of your own craziness.'

Two hours and several hot chocolates later, we had swapped our war stories. It turned out that although Lisa's problems were merely attention seeking, she had found herself a Bob Geldof who had placed a large Band-Aid over her neediness. Although equally as scruffy, and apparently 'Just as creative', Francis was a 53-year-old alcoholic artist with commitment issues, who had introduced Lisa to outdoor tantric sex, smoking hash and Oscar Wilde. Having finally found her G-spot or 'F-spot', honouring Francis with the credit, Lisa had indeed emerged a new philosophical woman.

No longer obsessed with her image, or 'superficial shell', as she called it, Lisa had come over all Mother Teresa and wanted to help people. With me being her first pet project.

Quoting the Gospel according to Wilde, Lisa explained, 'Those who have much are often greedy. I want to change that. I want to do good by people.'

Stunned by her change in personality I sat in silence as I watched my friend's evolution.

It was overwhelming.

'Experience is the name everyone gives to their mistakes,' she preached, 'and I have made more than most. But Francis has made me see the light, and I've learned from them.'

It was when she said 'To love oneself is the beginning of a lifelong romance' that I stood up and screamed, 'Enough already!'

Her Wildean wisdom was brilliant, but bordering on spooky.

But who was I to judge? She was happy. The happiest I'd ever seen her, in fact. And I was afraid to tell her that no amount of Botox could irradiate the creases forming around the broad smile she was now wearing. Let's face it, it could have been worse. Lisa could have discovered Scientology in rehab. At least she was keeping it retro.

By five o'clock Parker had joined us. He was only meant to be picking me up, but since he hadn't seen

Lisa in ages either, he decided our frozen pizzas and cheese nachos could wait.

In no time at all we had become quite the old married couple. No sex, just plenty of arguing! He had even started giving me pocket money for helping him with his work, set-designing some new period drama based in Kilkenny, for which I had to research furniture and fabrics on the internet. But his charity could only be temporary. I would need to get my fat ass in gear and find something more permanent quick.

Not content to let me fill him in on Lisa's gossip, he demanded to hear an abbreviated version from the horse's mouth immediately.

Unable to contain himself he screamed, 'You shagged an old man in the bushes? In rehab?'

Understandably, this grabbed the attention of the entire room, which had now filled up with Trinity student types. The manager even smiled over and gave Lisa a congratulatory round of applause. The old Lisa would have been mortified at such attention, but the new improved Miss Tiswell just smiled and took it in her stride.

'Francis and I are on separate paths now. But he has steered me on course for a better journey. I will always love that man.'

Needless to say, later that evening over our convenience dinner Parker and myself could talk of nothing more than Lisa's metamorphosis.

'I thought Madonna's reinvention couldn't be

topped, but Lisa is priceless. Who knew riding some dirty aul fella could change you for the better? That musta been strong weed he was peddlin!'

Obviously with her ears burning 'The Princess' flashed up on my phone.

'OK,' she said matter-of-factly, 'I hope you've found all the lamps and curtains Parker needs, because I've got you a proper job.'

'Whatya mean?'

'What do you mean, whatya mean? I've got you an in-house PR job with my dad's company. He said he'd be delighted for you to be part of the team. So that's that sorted.'

'But I'm a journalist, Lisa.'

'No, you *were* a journalist, now you're a PR executive who gets to write loads of glowing propaganda about my dad's property in Portugal. It's perfect for you and you're doing it.'

'Oh, so do I not get a say in this matter?'

'Are you telling me you have an argument with €50,000 a year?'

'Ha! You're kidding me. Nope. I can write thousands of words on how fabulous Quinta do Lago or wherever it is, is to holiday. When do I start?'

'Good girl. You start tomorrow.'

Starting a fresh job the day before St Patrick's weekend was probably not the best idea.

Nobody in the office was vaguely interested in showing me the ropes. I was basically pointed in the direction of a large empty desk, told 'Dial 9 for an outside line', and that if I didn't like the coffee I was more than welcome to walk to nearby Baggot Street to buy some.

My first impressions made me want to run out the door. Despite the warm, friendly smile of the model on the 10-foot poster in the hall promoting Tiswell Properties Ltd no one else was as hospitable.

Trying to use my initiative, I familiarized myself with all their existing paraphernalia, but any questions I had would have to wait.

'How green will you go?' seemed to be the topic of the day – and they weren't talking recycling. And 'How pissed will you get?' was the other.

Mind you, if I had told my new work colleagues that I was dressing as the Jolly Green Giant and was going to drink myself into a coma on Mojitos I still wouldn't have impressed them.

Women can be such bitches, and I was sharing an office with three of them and one young gay lad, so unofficially four hormonal women.

And since I wasn't naturally a big fan of female company (Maddie and Lisa didn't count because they were tomboys like me), this looked like it could cause a problem. But for €50,000 I was prepared to slog it out.

After making a conscious decision that I'd have to make an effort to get on with these waggons, I put down the old newspapers which I had read several times over and ignored the fact that the others were blanking me. Imagining how Anna would behave, I worked the room systematically and learned that Emma, the young blonde, had been engaged a fortnight and was getting married to Frank, a professional golfer, in Mercia next summer.

Louise, the other blonde (but with bad roots) from Blackrock had a black cat called Naomi and was currently 'Between relationships', and was happy concentrating on her career. Yeah, right!

There was Marcus, who seemed friendly enough, but then he was fairly new to the job and was just thrilled to be living down in Dublin because 'There's not much of a gay scene in Muff, County Donegal, as you can imagine!'

Lastly there was Maureen. She was the hardest of them all, really. She offered up zero conversation. I told her she reminded me of Catherine Zeta-Jones but my attempts at wooing her failed miserably. She was a brick wall, the Berlin Wall. I assured myself she'd crack. But by 5.30 she hadn't come close to a smile and if anything, my enthusiasm seemed to be annoying her more and more.

Despite my compliments on her 'Fabulous Cartier watch' and her 'Warm telephone manner', she couldn't be frostier to me. As everyone gathered up their coats to head home, I thought what a witch she was.

It couldn't possibly have been Catherine Zeta-Jones that she reminded me of. It must have been her mother. With that, and just two steps from the safety of the front door, Maureen swung around to me.

153

Swooping real close she whispered, 'Have you not worked out who I am yet?'

Taken by surprise I stumbled backwards and asked, 'Sorry?'

'I said, have you not worked out who I am yet?'

Completely baffled I thought for a moment before mumbling, 'Emmm, the boss of me?'

'God, you're even more stupid than Annette said.'

'Excuse me?'

'You heard me. Does the name Annette Barron mean anything to you?'

Instantly my heart sank. Ground, open up and swallow me whole. Maureen was the ferocious-looking woman from the Four Seasons who had been with Annette the day she slapped me. How could I have forgotten?

Drawing a total blank on anything intelligent to say, I uttered 'Oh' before she lunged at me again.

'You had no thoughts for Annette the night you tried to steal her husband, so I can't imagine you have any consideration for her today. But let me tell you this. You failed. David must have been blind drunk to even consider a slapper like you.'

Not knowing what to do, I ran. I didn't notice who had witnessed our altercation. I didn't care.

Running in the direction of Grafton Street, I cursed Maureen, Annette and David all the way.

I then cursed myself for not standing my ground.

Why hadn't I told her he seduced me?

Why was it this snog was coming back to haunt me? Had I not paid for my sins already?

After spending half the night running up Parker's phone bill complaining to Anna about my new job, I felt better.

Parker had been working late with some location managers making decisions on rural castles and churches, and I couldn't moan to Maddie because she was in a tearful place, and was only in text communication.

I had tried to get her to go for a walk and talk through her options, but she said she wasn't up to it.

Like me, when Maddie had something weighing heavy on her mind she shut down. All she wanted to do was blank out the outside world. She wanted nothing to do with anyone, not even me, and I just had to accept her wishes and hope that she would snap out of her mini-depression soon.

With a simple text, 'I'm here for you', I abandoned annoying Maddie, and focused on annoying Anna. She would have to do. After my confrontation with Maureen I needed someone to talk to and I didn't care who; this was bound to leak sooner or later, with or without Anna's help.

My first call had been to Lisa, when I had wrongly shouted at her, asking, 'Why didn't you warn me?' But she had had no idea Maureen was a close friend of Annette's. After all, Lisa had just left for her Bramble Hill Retreat adventure the day of the Four Seasons

Fiasco. Wounded and apologetic, she did her best to soften the situation, which made me feel terrible.

She suggested she could ask Daddy to move Maureen somewhere else, but I pointed out that if anyone was to move it should be me.

Somehow I kept failing to learn from my mistakes.

I needed to start being nicer to people.

Unlike Lisa, my journey to enlightenment was stalled. I was never getting to heaven.

But was there somewhere worse than hell?

Parker later suggested my wardrobe . . .

By Sunday I was really ready to rock 'n' roll. Snubbing the chance to see Robert and his pals take part in their annual skinny-dipping swim at Dun Laoghaire's Forty Foot rocks, myself, Parker and some gorgeous young French boy called David – who sounded just like the chef Jean-Christophe Novelli if you closed your eyes – were making our way to Lisa's family home in Dalkey, which had the most amazing view of Dublin Bay, and Bono's house. Well, the roof of Bono's house.

Every year her folks threw legendary parties, with the cream of Dublin's social scene in attendance. Rich builders were always seen as sexy in Ireland. And the Tiswells were no exception. They had been quite the building dynasty, well, at least until Patrick and Patricia failed to produce any sons and neither Lisa nor the Joy-less daughter had any interest in taking over the company.

Since Parker had only got acquainted with his new

friend a few nights earlier after meeting on the internet site Gaydar, we didn't really know what to expect. But he had a really fit body, which was exaggerated by his tight fitted black shirt and tight jeans, and he seemed game for a laugh, even though his English didn't stretch much further than, 'Pleased to meet', and, 'Repeat please?'

He was really just a stopgap though.

The handsome Jeff, or Hairy Hands as Parker called him, had enjoyed several mischievous evenings with Parker after he flew us to London, but had ended the relationship abruptly because Parker wanted to be more public about their romance than Jeff was comfortable with.

Needless to say, he was a tad hurt by the rejection. But with David, he wasn't looking for anything serious, just a good time.

But none of us could fail to be in a mood to party with our regular taxi guy Johnnie Barret around, who sang to us the whole way up.

We had met him one night several years ago outside Sophie's Choice and we fell in love with him. Fanatical about Dean Martin, his life was to worship him and spread the Dino love.

Anyone who had the good fortune – or misfortune, depending on your tolerance – to fall into his taxi would receive the full repertoire of songs. He was his own sycophant. And since I was 'in the journalism game', I was privileged to be given one of his CDs, 'totally free', of his classic covers.

Poor ole Dino must have been turning in his grave as we murdered renditions of 'Baby It's Cold Outside' and 'Memories Are Made of This'.

Giddy from the anticipation of having a play day Parker was in flying form and without consideration for anyone else's eardrums wailed his way into 'That's Amore', before demanding, 'What the fuck is a tarantella supposed to be?'

As Johnnie navigated his way up the narrow bumpy roads of Dalkey, I tried desperately not to stab myself in the eye with an eyeliner pencil as I finished doing my make-up. While the very likeable David won himself major brownie points for being extremely cute on mime percussion.

What was even cuter was his face when he saw all the security guys in their black suits, wielding walkie-talkies as they requested to see our formal invites. He looked like he had died and gone to stud muffin heaven.

Of course we had forgotten ours, as we did most years, but Lisa texted us the secret code, which was to tell the main guy, Vladimir, 'Kiss me quick I'm Irish' – Mrs Tiswell's idea of a hilarious joke.

Not a bad idea really, considering he was six foot four and ex-Russian army. He was built like a bull and could have been my McDreamy any day.

Unfortunately Vladimir didn't take us up on our offer, and just ushered us through with a wink and a cheeky smile.

Beefy bodyguards aside, even as a seasoned visitor

I couldn't help but be impressed by the pomp and glamour of the occasion. I had counted over thirty security men on the road, all in monkey suits, and we hadn't even got close to the massive marquee yet.

Thousands of large white lanterns lined the road of the manicured garden, which would look stunning later, and even though the weather forecast had promised hailstones and perhaps snow, the party people were out in force as they queued in their Mercedes to get the ladies and their heels as close to the front door as possible.

Once we were inside, leggy models in short green cocktail dresses and pretty boys in green dickie bows offered us a variety of novelty drinks on trays, which included everything from Green Frogs to Green Diamonds.

Although Parker thought it was very uncool to drink such nastiness he managed to grab a Green Fantasy off some poor innocent young Matt Damon look-alike; I think he scared the poor boy by whispering, 'You can share my fantasy any time!'

Appropriately, I grabbed a glass titled Green with Envy, and our little French boy went all patriotic and picked himself up a Green Guinness. We made our way through to the main marquee where a fella who looked like the fat bloke from the Commitments was belting out a version of 'A Nation Once Again'.

Positioning ourselves at a corner which was near the bar, loo and had a clear view of the stage, we settled in for an afternoon of *craic agus ceol*, aka fun and music.

After doing her welcoming rounds Lisa joined us, as did some of her cousins, whom I had met several times before, but even though they told me their names again they left my head the second they entered. Either way, they were a good bunch and were just as able to entertain as the next.

As the afternoon progressed into the evening, we had worked our way through the Green Monsters and Green Demons and had moved on to Absolut Hunks and Mad Cows. Neither were on the menu, but the very accommodating barman Jordan, who didn't seem to mind us telling him that he looked so much better since he got the boob reduction, was keen to match a 'Bitchin' cocktail' to our personalities.

Of course Parker was thrilled, but then he had told Jordan that he worked in the film business and that they were currently looking for fresh faces.

It was a cheesy line, but it worked more times than not.

There was a powerful smell of stew wafting from the other side of the marquee, but Parker told us all that 'Eatin' is cheatin'!' and that a game of Truth or Dare would take our minds off the hunger.

The craic really kicked off when one of the girls who was clearing our table of glasses got caught up in our high jinks.

In the middle of Lisa's story of how she was a girl who liked to swallow rather than spit out bodily fluids, Parker piped up, 'Eh, sorry, as a matter of interest, do you spit or swallow?'

Although I was half cut I was mortified, but she didn't seem fazed.

Not flinching for a second, she revealed in a deep Aussie accent, 'Oh mate, I gargle!' Everyone at the table fell about the place laughing.

By this stage the live rebel music had been replaced by a DJ and it was time to express ourselves.

Dancing around the table we swung our arms in the air and gyrated like strippers in a rap video. People began to stare, but their disapproving faces made us want to dance bigger and bolder as if we were auditioning for Louis Walsh.

Thankfully the Tiswell family had seen this all before, and even though Lisa's mum came over to say hi just as I had knocked over somebody's pint, she just gave one of her own half-sozzled waves and told us, 'I'm dee-lighted you're all having fun.'

We were having the perfect day, and everyone was in high spirits; that is, until Parker's ex, Jeff, walked into the marquee.

I spotted him walking in our direction and had to warn Parker, who was now sitting on the bar singing to our new pal Jordan.

What a tragedy, to interrupt such a pitch-perfect rendition of 'Can't Get You Out of My Head!'. Parker literally fell off the bar as I pointed Jeff out as he chatted to Lisa's dad just a few feet away. Instantly he turned to David and said, 'Take your top off.'

A little confused, he said, 'Pardon?'

But Parker wasn't taking no for an answer. 'I said

take your top off,' he demanded. 'You're not bringing much else to the table, so the least you can do is take your top off and show us those muscles of yours.'

And then like something out of a Diet Coke break ad, he did, clearly chuffed to be back at the centre of Parker's attention.

By now several women who had been looking on in disgust were drooling with lust. Just as I was thinking what cocktail they should order, Jeff approached the group and with a sheepish smile asked, 'How have you been?'

Pretending not to notice, Parker fondled David's pecs while telling him to 'Flex them again', to hoots of laughter.

Doing my best sober impression I told Jeff that things were great but if he was planning any more trips to London to count me out because the men there were shits. Paris or New York I could handle, but he'd have to dump Florence for a bigger bus.

As soon as the word 'dump' left my mouth, I could see Parker's back physically tense up.

It was obvious to all that Parker was deliberately ignoring his presence, but Jeff put his hand on his shoulder and pinched him. He refused to turn around.

After making the decision to recognize Parker, he wasn't going to give up easily, so he stood his ground and asked, 'Are you going to ignore me all night?'

While the rest of us made loud gasping noises, Parker glanced down at Jeff's hairy hand, which was still on his shoulder, before darting a bored look at me. I'd seen that pissed-off face before and it normally signalled trouble.

After a cold silence he hissed, 'Do we know her?' It was totally mortifying. He was acting like a spoilt child, and he continued his tantrum by pushing Jeff's hand away.

Trying to stifle my nervous giggles I brushed past Parker and invited our naked chef to the bar, but Parker was having none of it.

'He's not going anywhere, Eva. If anyone is leaving it's Jeff here, he's very good at walking away. Aren't you, Jeff?'

After several requests for a word in private, a wounded Parker finally conceded, and the forlorn duo walked off in the direction of the gardens.

They were gone about twenty minutes when we got the nod that the fireworks were about to start. As everyone was handed a hot whiskey and guided out on to the patio, the Tiswells' legendary firework display blasted off into the sky. They always splashed out a 'minimum of €200,000', on fireworks, according to Lisa, just because they could. And that was loose change compared to the cost of the bar tab.

The most my folks would fork out for a special occasion would be a couple of bottles of Lidl cheapo wine to wash down some vulgar beef curry. They were never big on entertaining, bless, as Mother dearest was forever worried about stains.

Maybe it was her lack of social skills that made me

go extrovert? Who knows? I'm not sure I have the energy to care any more. She says tomato – and I say where's my next drink coming from?

As a spray of green, white and orange lit up the cold dark sky, I could see in the distance that sexual sparks had started to fly yet again between Parker and Jeff. Although they weren't kissing, there was a lot of laughter and tactile hand-holding. They looked really good together. It was just a pity that such a sweet guy as David had to be the pawn in Parker's gambit to win back Hairy Hands.

Four slices of white toast smothered in butter and marmalade, two cups of Barry's tea and a large bottle of Ballygowan water later, and I felt somewhat ready to ring my mother.

'Hi, Mum.' I did my best to sound cheery.

Her lacklustre attempt at 'Eva' didn't!

'I was just ringing to wish you happy St Patrick's Day. How are things with you?'

'I can't talk now. I'm just out of the bath. Your sister is having us over for lunch.'

'Oh. That's nice . . .'

'Anything else?'

'Eh, no. I suppose not. Just called to say . . .'

The phone line had already gone dead.

It might have been a bank holiday, but Parker still had to work, much to my irritation.

Both Maddie and Lisa were spending the bank

holiday with their families. Maddie said she was curled up on her couch, depressed and watching *Pirates of the Caribbean* with her nieces and nephews, which was 'doing her head in', as her folks spent the afternoon in the kitchen arguing again about her dad's drinking; the Princess was skiing with her folks in Chamonix.

So I invited Robert over to the apartment to keep me company.

I had been avoiding his texts over the weekend, but I was bored and he was happy to oblige.

Wanting to erase what a disappointment I was to my next of kin I planned to raid Parker's champagne stash. He normally didn't mind, once I admitted to taking it.

'Laurent Perrier rosé is not for wasting on fools,' Parker would say. 'Dom Perignon is for footballers and Cristal is for gangster rappers. Laurent Perrier is for the more educated and cultured among us. Though if the fool is cute and you get a ride out of it, go for it!'

While the journalist in me had managed to extract plenty of details about Robert's life, I had told him very little about myself.

Totally out of character, I was a typical woman when it came to dating, and usually blabbed inappropriately about ex-boyfriends and my personal downfalls. Even though I know I shouldn't reveal the particulars of previous relationships to new men, I'd forever find myself saying, 'I once went out with this musician', or 'The doctor I used to go out with always told me to drink a glass of water within sixty seconds of waking up to kick-start your metabolism.'

But with Robert I hadn't bothered to try and impress him with the importance of my former lovers. I thought my world too vulgar to embarrass him with. To him I was a blank canvas. Someone who obviously had the luxury to take a career break – yeah, right! And now I was this chick who lived in a three-bedroomed penthouse apartment.

On the outside it all looked very rosy.

Despite my casual approach in getting to know Robert, when I heard his voice over the intercom I felt a flutter of excitement.

As much to make myself feel good as in preparation for our date I had shaved all relevant areas, as there hadn't been any cash for waxing of recent times. Applying my natural, I-look-like-this-all-the-time make-up, I spent twenty minutes with my trusty GHD styler getting a perfect sheen look and donned my favourite Rock & Republic jeans which give me the best bum, and my sexy gold chiffon top that hung low on one shoulder. Checking myself out in the hall mirror as I waited for Robert to come up in the lift, I thought I looked hot. Maybe it was the muted artificial lighting, but that mirror was always kind.

I'm going to have sex today, I thought. And as soon as I saw him step out into the hallway, my mind was made up. I definitely fancied a mouthful of muesli.

★   ★   ★

'I never knew holy boys could get kinky like that!'

'It's good to learn something new every day, I think,' smirked Robert.

'Well thank you,' I replied, quite stunned by what I had just experienced, 'that was indeed quite a lesson.'

Dumbstruck at this quiet boy's sexual practices, I topped up my glass of champagne with the bottle I had brought into the bedroom, and took a large mouthful to cleanse the palate and settle my nerves.

It had proved a very successful lubricant to slip us both into a state of undress. And in Robert's case, had drastically helped to alter his personality; although I hadn't remained shy about my carnal intentions, with direct comments such as, 'We should shag soon so we can bypass the awkward getting-to-know-one-another stage.'

To be honest, I actually surprised myself by being so forward, but after recent events I wasn't prepared to let any more opportunities get away from me.

He had been utterly respectful and gentlemanly during our first date, not pushing past a romantic snog or placing his vice-gripped hands on the base of my back, and just about slipping the tips of his fingers inside the top of my jeans. Today though, he had let go of any inhibitions and truly let his animal instincts take over. No honestly, he seriously let himself go!

The games all began when we had been sprawled on Parker's couch watching *Will & Grace* and I had lost a handful of dry roasted peanuts down my top. I had lost interest in the episode as I'd seen it a hundred times before, when I started play-acting with the old pub trick of throwing a nut in the air and catching it in my mouth.

Suggestively I opened my mouth, but playing the hapless girl I let several nuts disappear down my cleavage.

After I'd sent out all the right signals, my date saw this as his moment to make a move and took on the role of bounty hunter.

With a fresh confidence he winked. 'Finders keepers,' he said as his powerful fingers lowered my chiffon top to reveal my white lace bra and my breasts, which shimmered fantastically from a light dusting of Melon powder from MAC.

Remaining still, I calmly looked down to his hand on my chest, and then raised my eyes to meet his. With the most subtle smile, I gave him permission to continue, and waited for him to make the next move.

'You're so very sexy, baby girl,' he told me before lifting several peanuts away from my skin with his devilishly long tongue. And before I had a second to reply his hand delved into my bra, scooped out my left breast, and he wrapped his warm mouth around my nipple.

Gently humming he curled and swirled his firm tongue, flicking and licking and sucking and biting. Darting me a playful look as he popped my second breast over the bra, he then nuzzled his face between my chest as he mumbled, 'Hmmmm. Home.'

Not sure what to say to that I just quietly moaned, as sex talk had never really been my thing.

Without wasting time, his rough hands worked downwards and unzipped my jeans and inched them off past my ankles as he kissed my thighs, knees and several bruises I had acquired on Saturday along the way.

Light-headed from the champagne, I decided to let go of my hang-ups about my body. I had put on at least half a stone since London and I was conscious of the extra bulge. But it didn't seem to bother Robert. He was definitely in the zone.

In a moment of clarity, I thought it best not to romp on Parker's suede couch, so I took hold of Robert's wandering hands and a bottle of LPR, and led him in the direction of my bedroom.

As I knelt on the edge of the bed, the underwire in my bra dug into my chest, so I unhooked it at the back and dropped it to the floor like I was performing in a burlesque show.

Crawling on to the bed beside me, Robert brushed up to my ear and whispered, 'Have you any stockings?'

Confused I asked, 'Do you want me to get dressed up to undress for you again?'

'No,' he said, a little embarrassed, 'I want you to tie one around my cock.'

Not wanting to appear unworldly, I stepped over to my dresser and started rooting around in one of the drawers for a spare stocking. Trying desperately not to spill any Bridget Jones knickers or woolly tights on the floor, I finally found an unopened pair boxed up at the bottom.

Hesitant to open the packet as they cost €30, I turned to him and asked, 'Do you really want one?'

Leaving no doubt in my mind, Robert jumped off the bed and grabbed the packet out of my hands, ripping the stockings out of the plastic in seconds. Throwing the lot on the bed he stripped himself, leaving a small pool of clothes on the floor and then shuffled up beside me.

His cock, as he called it, was long and narrow. It wasn't the prettiest I had ever seen. Michael's had been perfect and not even Michelangelo could have designed it better.

But Michael wasn't here and Robert was. So long and thin would have to do.

'I'm going to tie this here,' he explained as he placed my expensive barely black stocking around the base of his dick, 'and when I reach orgasm I want you to pull it tighter – it helps to intensify the orgasm.'

Nodding in bemusement I wondered what exactly was in it for me. 'So what's a girl get in return for her stocking, then?' I asked.

'Patience,' he whispered, as he pulled me down the bed on to the flat of my back, before removing my matching white lace thong, which he threw to the floor to join the rest of the clothes.

I wriggled my hips with nervous excitement as

Robert, his dick neatly tied in a bow, crouched down over me and began to munch his way across my belly and down to my neatly shaved vagina.

'Tell me what you like,' he said as he began to stimulate my clitoris by softly nudging it with his nose.

'What you're doing there is nice,' I said, praying that he didn't want to start a dialogue. But I was out of luck. He was in the mood to talk.

'Do you like it when I tease you there?' he asked in between his sloppy vaginal kisses.

'Oh, yeah, that's good,' I offered, trying not to sound too awkward.

'And how about this?' he asked again as he started to insert what felt like two fingers inside me.

'Yeah, yeah, that's really good,' I said again, hoping that he would shut up.

But he wouldn't. The questions kept on coming.

'Do you want me to lick you harder? Do you want me to do it faster? Does it feel better when I rub you with my nose? Can I stick a finger up your ass?'

I felt like telling him to shut the fuck up, but I was horny now and I just wanted him to get on with it rather than give me a spot quiz.

Then without thinking and almost as a knee-jerk reaction to his interrogation I blurted out, 'Just worship me!'

Chuffed with himself, as if I had shared a fantasy with him or something, he submissively ducked his head and said, 'Oh, yes please. I will be your slave.'

171

Biting my lip so as not to call him an eejit, I snapped back, 'Get back to work then.'

In hindsight, it was a pretty comical moment, but it shut him up temporarily as he used all his digits to make me climax.

He didn't succeed.

I faked it.

Somewhat unsettled by his rattle-tattle I wasn't able to fully concentrate on the job, but it was still pleasant enough once he was gagged.

But just as I pushed him off I saw his dickie bow waving at me.

He looked ridiculous. Letting out a loud laugh, I had to shrug it off as an orgasm aftershock.

I was just lucky I hadn't made the mistake to point. Not that I think he would really have noticed. He was extremely focused on setting up the second act of our sexual play.

With no wardrobe change he switched location to the full-length mirror on the wall and positioned me in front of it on my knees. 'I want to be able to see everything,' he said lustfully as he took up his position beside me.

Let's make this quick, I thought. If Parker comes home and hears grunts and groans coming from my bedroom he'll barge in on top of us.

And if he finds Robert wearing women's clothes he'll have a field day. I'd never live it down.

Either that or he'll try to freak me out by asking to watch.

With my right hand I took hold of the shaft of Robert's dick and gently started to stroke it. With my left I held his balls and massaged with my fingers. And just as I had started to lick the head of his dick, the chatter started again.

'Oh yeah,' he groaned, 'go on, you dirty bitch.'

Not sure I'd heard him right I continued what I was doing and built up more momentum.

But I wasn't mistaken.

'You're – nothing – but – a – dirty – whore,' he blurted out, jerking as he spoke.

Assuming that it wasn't said to mean offence, I kept with it. Massaging and licking and rubbing and pulling. In between each lunging motion I looked at him in the mirror. He was snarling and grinding, it was very primal, though a tad gay looking as he posed with one hand on the wall to steady himself, and the other on his hip.

Then just as my mind had started to wonder what Parker might think of this, he screeched, 'Stick a finger in my ass!'

Snapping back to reality I passively inched my middle finger towards his anus, separating his legs further apart on the way. Wishing I had a pointy stiletto to throw up there – then again, he'd probably love that – I darted my finger as hard and as far as I could.

'Jesus Christ, woman!' he screamed, as he fell against the mirror. 'Did you not think to grease her up a little?'

173

'Sorry,' I mumbled, then tried again. But he wasn't taking any chances. 'Just suck my balls,' he demanded as he took control of his cock and began to pull himself off.

'Just a dirty bitch,' he whispered under his breath, 'Just – a dirty – fuckin' – whore!'

And just as I thought I had taken enough verbal abuse, he screamed again, 'Pull on it!'

Not completely sure what he meant, I tugged down on his balls with my mouth. But he wasn't impressed.

'The fucking stocking!' he screamed.

Now praying for this to be over, I did what he said, and as he ejaculated partly over me – now literally making me a dirty bitch! – and partly across the mirror, I pulled on the stocking and winced in case I decapitated his manhood.

Despite his running commentary during the build-up, when he actually orgasmed Robert was mute apart from a few groans.

Pushing me away he stumbled to the bed and collapsed in throes of laughter.

'Are you all right?' I asked.

'Ha. Yes, sexy. You did good.'

At ten o'clock Parker arrived home mentally drained after spending the day ordering people about. He loved his job, but always came home shattered after twelve hours of arguing with art directors over which shade of grey makes a wall look mythical.

Tossing his black Gucci man-bag of drawings across

the floor, he kicked off his pointy black Gucci shoes and fell on to the couch beside me.

'So how is the dark prince of Gucci this evening?' I asked, trying to appear sober.

'Fucked. Think pretty Thai boy working the strip in Bangkok. That's how fucked I am.'

'Fair enough. Glad I asked.'

'Sorry pet, how was your day? Are you all right? You look very flushed.'

Although all evidence of my perverse afternoon had been banished, Parker had a sharp eye and was able to sniff out sex at ten paces.

Trying to be evasive, I asked him did he fancy anything to eat, but he wasn't to be distracted.

'You're all red in the cheeks. What have you been up to?'

'Nothing,' I said, looking extremely guilty.

'Listen, I'm not in the mood for twenty minutes of guessing games. Just tell me now because you have the look of boldness about you.'

'Hon, you wouldn't believe me if I told you.'

'Oh-mi-God. That good? Tell me, tell me, tell me.'

Bribing him to make me one of his fabulously sinful hot chocolates, I explained the whole sordid scenario as I watched him make froth on the fancy gizmo on his €3,000 coffee machine.

Studiously he remained quiet through my whole story, and as he popped three large pink marsh-mallows into my giant mug and handed it to me, he darted me one of his serious looks and told me to sit down.

'Now don't get angry with me, but I've a theory.'

'About what?' I asked, but I didn't really want to hear his answer.

'I'm being deadly serious. And I don't want you to shoot the messenger.'

'Just tell me.'

'OK, but you're not going to like it.'

'Parker . . .'

'He's gay.'

'No he's not.'

'He's gay. Well, bi. But he definitely likes boys' bums.'

'Grow up.'

'He's gay and I'll prove it to you. Trust me, I'm a fag!'

'God, you're full of it sometimes. Listen, I know he's only a temporary fixture. As far as I'm concerned Robert is my Mr Good Enough For Now guy. Ha! That is if I can afford to keep him in expensive stock–ings.'

'Hi, Maddie, can you talk?'

'Not really. I've just told my mother I'm pregnant. She didn't exactly take it well.'

'What did she say?'

'That I was a no good embarrassment like my father.'

'They're still arguing, yeah?'

'When are they not? You know, she almost started frothing at the mouth she got herself so worked up. All this, "you're nothing but a dirty whore" and that I got what I deserved.'

'Wow. We're like two peas in a pod . . .'

'What ya mean?'

'Sorry, hon. I was just thinking out loud. Listen, I just rang to say that I think you're being really brave.'

'Thanks.'

'No I'm serious. I don't know how I would have handled the situation. I know you hate it when I get mushy, but I just wanted to tell you you're deadly and that I'm here for you if you need me.'

There was silence at the end of the phone.

'Maddie, are you there?'

'Yeah, I'm just . . .' sniff, 'I just . . .' sniff, 'I have to go . . .'

'Maddie?'

'What?'

'Keep the chin up, hon, it'll all work itself out. I promise ya.'

6

'He's going to have them lasered for me!' screamed an excited Parker down the phone.

'I just left you five minutes ago. What are you talking about?' My nerves were frayed. It was my second day at work and I felt like I was about to step into a war zone.

I kept telling myself to think of the money, but it was useless. The fear of seeing Maureen again was turning my stomach. That, or the Tropicana orange juice I had necked for breakfast was gone off as Parker said.

'Jeff. He's just rung me to say he'll get that furlining zapped off for me. It must be love.'

'Hang on, are you talking about his hairy hands again? You can't be serious? You're not actually going to push the poor bloke to get the hair on the back of his hands removed – are you?'

'Yes, it's gross. I feel like I'm being groped by a giant

silverback ape when he touches me. And anyway, he offered.'

'Mmmm, just out of the blue he offered. You're such a diva. Listen, I'm very happy for you and your gorilla, but I'm about to walk into my own version of hell. I gotta go.'

The hairy hands saga would have to wait till later. I was standing on the bottom step of an impressive Georgian building which was now my place of work. It had a fabulously huge fire engine red door, with tall white pillars surrounded by delicate stained-glass windows. The kind you see on postcards.

In nature the colour red signals danger. If I were looking at a traffic light it would be telling me to stop. But despite the warning signs I still had to pass the threshold and face the ramifications.

But I had nothing to stress about. When I arrived into the office, Louise told me that Maureen was on annual leave and that I had nothing to do but drag a sack of invites to the post office and answer any calls that came through on Maureen's phone.

Happy days.

With little to do other than physically be in the office, which was fairly cold and bare with its stark white walls that reached up high to old ornate cornice work and coving, I busied myself with sending e-mails to friends I hadn't seen in ages.

Catching up on old correspondence was only ever done when I was really bored. And my mates from around the world knew this. But they were guilty of the same crime.

Approximately once or twice a year I'd hear from old pals who had defected to foreign spots as far afield as Australia or Hong Kong. All of whom had gone on to lead much more successful and fruitful lifestyles abroad.

There was Christian, who moved to Johannesburg, who was far from a religious man. He found his happiness down the bottom of a diamond mine instead of helping the missionaries.

He now lives with five Dobermanns, two cleaners, one gardener and ten security cameras, that he sits and watches each evening as he has his dinner alone.

There was also my old friend Anna Maria, who flew down to Sydney while taking a year out from studying Business & Law at UCD, but she fell in love with one of the few straight men on Bondi beach and never returned.

She now has six kids under five, three girls, three boys, with her youngest, Sam and Jake, being six-month-old twins.

Her last e-mail was to say her mother-in-law René was moving in to help out with the kids, and that her husband Thomas had been diagnosed with skin cancer. I had terrible nightmares for ages after, imagining myself in her shoes.

I had visions of myself climbing a mountain of dirty nappies but never quite making it to the top. All the while some shrivelled-up old bat was standing over me telling me I was doing everything wrong.

Argh! It was my idea of hell.

But she felt blessed by all of her healthy children and her ability to produce them.

'Not everyone is lucky enough to be able to have kids,' she boasted. I agreed with her, but told her it wasn't her duty to repopulate on behalf of eggless women across the world.

The last of my globetrotting friends was Jean. She was my best friend from primary school, and to this day we share very little in common, except the aptitude to keep in touch. Despite her mother's best efforts to split us up, because she didn't think I was a suitable friend for her studious princess, we always stayed in touch via notes, letters and now e-mails.

According to her mother, I was a bad influence on Jean because her free time would be better spent at home practising her piano scales and reading Enid Blyton. Although I only wanted to drag her to the nearby park and climb trees or look at the local flasher expose his bits, I wasn't deemed suitable company, and to this day I still can't work out why.

My own mother wasn't as concerned with my extra-curricular habits. She always preferred me to be outdoors, not because of the fresh air, but so I wouldn't be in dirtying her house.

I was never allowed to bring friends over to hang out, God forbid ever asking for a sleepover. No, my mother just didn't like children that much. I think she expected us to pop out of the womb fully functional adults, with impeccable manners and the ability to understand the saying, 'Only speak when you are spoken to.'

I was halfway through writing a generic e-mail to the gang explaining the ups and downs of life as a single girl in Dublin, when Maureen's phone rang.

Snapping into work mode I diligently picked up the receiver and in my best phone voice said, 'Good morning, Tiswell Properties Limited, Eva speaking, can I help you?'

A confused female voice at the end of the phone line asked, 'Is this not Maureen's number?' 'Yes, it is,' I explained, 'But she's on holiday this week, can I take a message for her?'

'Oh right, eh, no. It's a personal call. I'll ring her mobile.'

'OK so. Bye now.' I did my best to sound professional and cheery.

I was just returning to my e-mail, explaining how I'd been the star of an erotic porn movie with a guy called Robert, when Maureen's phone rang again.

'Hello, Tiswell Properties Limited, Eva speaking, can I help you?'

'Is that Eva Valentine?'

'Yes it is, hiya, who's this?'

There was silence.

'Hello. Is there anyone there?' I said.

'It's Annette Barron.'

My heart sank as panic set in.

'Listen, Annette . . . I don't want to argue with you, so I'm just going to hang up.'

'Don't!' she pleaded, with a quiver in her voice. 'I'm sorry I slapped you before. And I'm sorry I threatened you. I was extremely upset, as you can imagine. But I need to talk.'

'I've nothing more to say, Annette. I've already said I'm sorry and I meant it. I've no interest in your husband. You're just going to have to take my word on that.'

'I really need to talk to you though, in person.'

'I don't think that's a good idea.'

'Please. What time do you take lunch?'

'Annette . . .'

'Please,' her voice sounded emotional again. 'It won't take long.'

'Emmm, one o'clock, I suppose.'

'Thank you. I'll be waiting outside.'

As I hung up the phone a wave of claustrophobia flooded over me. Annette was coming to see me and would be waiting for me at the front door.

Could there be a back exit?

Should I just leg it now?

As I plotted a possible escape route, I could feel my temperature rising as if I'd been plunged into an oven. I felt trapped. And the black woollen poloneck jumper I was wearing wasn't helping matters.

I was terrified of seeing this woman. What if she wanted to hit me again?

Tugging at my polo to allow air at my neck I began

to feel nauseous and dizzy. This was the nightmare that just kept giving. Was I ever going to be free of this bad Barron karma? As total panic gripped my body, I started to hyperventilate.

Feeling like a ton of bricks had been dropped on my chest I gasped for fresh air but couldn't catch my breath. All I could think of was to run outside. As I got up from my chair in slow motion to head to the door, everything blurred and then blacked out . . .

The next thing I recall was Marcus standing over me asking, 'Are ye all right luv?'

'Wha . . . What happened?' I felt strangely calm as I lay on the floor.

'Ya crashed, darlin. Ye've been out cold a few wee minutes.'

Trying to piece it all together I remained still on the floor as my senses of smell, touch, sight and sound returned.

'Drink this,' ordered Emma and handed me a plastic cup of water, almost spilling most of it on top of me.

'Yeah . . . thanks,' I muttered, trying to elevate myself to a sitting position.

'That was one spectacular fall, Eva. One minute you were running across the room and then the next you just dropped to the floor. You're lucky you didn't crack your head on one of the desks.'

As if someone had flicked a switch, I promptly felt pain, a heavy throbbing pulse at the front side of my head. Lifting my hand to my forehead I could feel a sizeable bump forming.

'I've hit something.' I looked around at my assembled audience for suggestions.

'It was the floor ya hit, luv,' chuckled Marcus, trying to stifle a giggle.

'Sorry for laughin' but ya looked so funny. You looked like a fat Sonia O'Sullivan collapsing across the finish line.'

'Thanks for that.' As if my day wasn't bad enough, I'd just been called fat.

'Ach no. I meant just fat compared to her. That one's got more of a man's body than I do.'

'What time is it?' Suddenly I remembered why I had got so upset.

'It's a quarter to one,' offered Emma. 'Are you hungry? Is that why you collapsed? You should just go for lunch now.'

'I'll go to the loo first,' I said, thinking out loud, and shuffled in the direction of the hall. As I let the door swing closed behind me I could hear the office erupt into fits of laughter.

'Did ya see her go?' cackled Marcus hysterically. 'Poor wee lass looked a state!'

'A fiver says she's pregnant,' laughed one of the girls.

'Ha! A tenner she's a dipso,' laughed the other.

Normally I would have run back inside and let them know exactly what I thought of them. But I hadn't the energy. I was going to have to face Annette in a couple of minutes. I had to pull myself together.

After a mini pep talk in the toilet mirror, I brushed myself off and strutted back into the office to collect my handbag and jacket.

Big girls don't cry, I told myself as I stuck my right arm into my beige belted mac. I was just going to have to face Annette and be done with it.

Unfortunately by the time I had tunnelled my left arm through the other sleeve the tears had started to flow. So I slumped at my desk and began blubbing like a baby. Not caring who saw me I sobbed and yelped, until I heard Marcus in the background whispering loudly, 'Check out crazy.'

Just like she said, Annette was waiting for me outside. She was pacing the pavement talking on her mobile, but the second she saw me she hung up with an abrupt, 'She's here.'

Dressed in a full-length cream wool coat, with large gold buttons, which matched her silky smooth hair, she looked the picture perfect wife. It was such a tragedy she wasn't a contented happy one.

'My car is just down the road. We can talk there.' Her words were precise and calculated. As if she'd rehearsed them over in her head.

Trying to hide the fact that I was an emotional wreck, one who had just suffered something close to a mental breakdown just minutes before, I followed Annette's lead and remained silent. Best not speak until spoken to in such a predicament, I thought.

Once seated inside her gorgeous silver CLK Merc,

Annette didn't waste any time in setting the record straight.

'Understandably, I'm not your biggest fan, and even if this were a different situation I still don't think we would be friends. But woman to woman I need you to be honest with me.'

Stunned by her candour, I released some stress in a long sigh and smiled. 'Sure.'

'Did you come on to David, or was it the other way round?'

'Listen, Annette—'

'Just answer the question, please. I feel my husband has been lying to me about any number of things, so tell me. Was it you, or was it him that did the leading on?'

'Him.'

'Are you sure?'

'Very . . .' I held my breath, waiting for her reaction.

As my confirmation began to sink in, her eyes welled up with tears.

'I know you're telling the truth . . . I've only been fooling myself.'

Not sure what to say to the woman, I just sat frozen in my seat. What was appropriate behaviour when you tell a woman her husband is a lying, cheating scumbag? Should I hug her? Or just get out of the car and walk off?

Choosing the latter I pulled at the door handle and with a forced smiled said, 'I'll go now.' But she wasn't letting me go yet.

'He's done this before. David. You aren't the only woman my husband has chased behind my back.'

'Men are bastards,' I told her, trying to nip her story in the bud.

'Do you know where he is today?'

'I don't think I want to—'

'Paris. The bastard is in Paris.'

'Oh.'

'And do you know who he's with in Paris?'

'Annette, I don't really—'

'My fucking best friend, can you believe it? Maureen is in the most romantic city in the world with the love of my life. Bitch!'

'Are you sure?' I stupidly asked. My stomach was rumbling with hunger, and now I had shown interest in hearing her story, which I truly didn't really want to hear, and all of a sudden food was far away.

'People warned me about her, you know. They said she was only ever out for herself. But I loved her. She's my best friend. *Was!* I did everything for her. I would have given her my last euro. My jewellery, anything, but not my husband, I can't believe the bitch took my David.'

With that, Annette hung her head in her hands and wept. All the while I sat uncomfortably in silence.

'I knew he played the field,' she continued. 'But I let him get away with it because he always came home to me. He was a lovable rogue – but with Maureen? That's just unforgivable.'

As she delicately soaked up her tears with a spare

tissue she pulled from her glovebox, making sure not to smudge her mascara, she settled her emotions and apologized for crying.

'You must think I'm some eejit? Huh?'

'God, no . . .'

'And you'd be right. I've been so stupid, but not any more . . . I'm going to make fools out of them.'

'Jesus, I don't think . . .'

'What? That I should leak it to the papers? Bloody right I will. I found his credit card bill, all the hotels, all of the meals. I found everything. And I'm going to tell whoever will listen.'

'If you do that there's no going back. Are you sure you want everyone knowing your business?'

'I reckon all of Dublin probably already knows my business. That's probably why I feel like such an eejit. I was the last to know.'

'Listen, it's his loss,' I told her, as if auditioning for the role of her new best friend.

'No. I'm the bloody sucker here. But I'm going to screw the both of them. They'll wish they never ever met me.'

Five minutes later I was standing in the queue at Spar waiting to pay for my chicken and stuffing sandwich and Diet Coke when it dawned on me. If Annette goes to the papers about David's cheating, I'll probably get dragged into it again.

Maybe she was just venting and won't do anything about it?

She's stood by and let him cheat before, so why

would she jeopardize her cosy lifestyle in her Ranelagh mansion now?

Concentrate on getting to the till, paying for this stuff and consuming it before you collapse again, I told myself.

As soon as I'd walked back to the office and stuffed my face with my plastic lunch, a weight lifted. With food in my belly the world seemed a better place. Annette would come to her senses and deal with this privately. Otherwise, she would be the fool she thought she was.

'The Wife, the Mistress, the Publisher and the Hack. That's some headline to be part of, Eva.' Parker took great pleasure in sifting through the Sunday papers.

'The stunning one-night-stand Eva Valentine has been pushed aside . . .' he gasped. 'It is said that she was no match for the worldly-wise temptress Maureen O'Brien. Ouch. That gotta hurt? But on the bright side, you're famous again. You'll be the envy of all the wannabe slappers about town.'

'Brilliant. Just as my mother was starting to thaw out with me.'

'Oops, I forgot about Poker-Up-Her-Ass Valentine. Ah, there's no point in stressing about it.'

'Yeah well, I hate being the fuck-up. Ruth is always the perfect one. I'm sick of this never-ending story.'

'OK, word of advice for you. Either stop getting caught out, or stop being a bold Eva.'

'Very profound words, Parker, so who told you that – the Dalai Lama?'

'Eva, seeing that giant cold sore on your top lip has gone some way to cheering me up.'

'Well I'm glad it's brought someone else joy. I'm never leaving this apartment again.'

Maddie and I were curled up on Parker's couch wearing our matching sloppy velour tracksuits watching *Murder, She Wrote*. We were equally fed up with life and the current day we were living through.

It was the nasty episode where Jessica visits Ireland, full of dodgy American actors with dodgy Oirish accents.

I should have been in work, but Lisa rang to say her dad had been on and thought it best I took a couple of days off to let things cool down.

'Would it not have been cheaper to just hire a few local boyos for this? The accents are nearly as bad as Colin Farrell's in *Alexander*.'

'Ha! You'll never get over the night he snubbed you at the Haven, will you?'

'He didn't snub me, Eva. He was sober and in a grump.'

'Mmmm, he just preferred the company of his boys that night.'

'Yeah, that Castleknock clan hang out of his arse whenever he's home.'

'You know, the person who did it always appears in the first scene, or something like that.'

'What are you talking about?'

'Sorry. The murderer is always supposed to appear in the start of the show. *Murder, She Wrote.*'

'Oh, fascinating stuff.'

'I thought so. So how've you been feeling?'

'Eva, I don't want to talk about it.'

'Ever?'

'Not today anyway.'

'You really need to clear your head, hon. Start talking things through. Like your plans.'

'I don't have any yet.'

'Ah, Maddie, you're going to have to make a decision soon. If you don't want to keep this baby you have to take action sharpish. And before you jump down my throat, I'm not saying I think you should have an abortion. I'm just saying, if that is your choosing, please do it sooner rather than later.'

'I know . . . I'm just very confused at the moment. I mean, havin' a baby is huge. It's almost too massive a deal to think about.'

At the mere mention of an abortion, you could see Maddie curling up into a tighter knot in a defensive reaction, but she was still putting on a plucky face. And while I didn't want to cause her any more upset, she needed to be pushed into facing the harsh reality.

'Yeah well, it's a bit late for that,' I stressed, 'your back is up against the wall on this one.'

'Ha! Kinda like the night the little fella was made.'

'There she is. I thought you'd lost your sense of

humour completely. And what do you mean little fella? You couldn't possibly know yet.'

'Little fella was just a figure of speech. Get over it.'

'I'm allowed to be stroppy, have you not noticed the growth on my face?'

'Mmmm, yes. As I said, Eva, that cold sore of yours has cheered me up immensely.'

The next morning I got a call from a more confident Maddie. Her voice sounded stronger than of late.

'My mum says I'll go to hell if I have an abortion. And she's probably right,' she said defiantly.

'Maddie, your mum doesn't have to live your life – you do.'

'I know, so meet me at Le Café in about an hour. I want to tell you my decision in person.'

'Why, what is your decision?'

'See you in an hour.' And with that she hung up.

Was she going to go through with an abortion? Was she going to get the boat to England like thousands of young Irish women before her? She sounded happy whatever her decision. I just hoped she'd made the right choice, whatever that might be.

By a quarter to twelve the two of us arrived at the front door of Le Café looking like twins. In co-ordinating Gap sweatshirts, black leggings and tan Ugg boots, we looked like the grungy students we never were, especially me with my ugly cold sore still invading my face.

I gave Maddie an air kiss and waited to gauge her mood. I didn't have to wait long.

'For the record, I'm fine. So you can relax. I'm genuinely grand. I'll tell you all when we get in.'

With my plastered fake smile I held the door for her and said a prayer that I'd approve of her decision. Please, please, please don't want an abortion, I thought. Neither of us were overly maternal creatures but I was sure that she'd regret such an action later in life.

But I was soon distracted from my obsessing by the cute manager's smile, and turned my nervous energy into trying to hide my cold sore with my hair.

'Ladies, it's so lovely to see you both on such a grey day. You are like two beaming rays of sunshine,' he teased.

Chuckling back, an extremely upbeat Maddie retorted, 'Jaysus, you'd say anything. Any chance of a table for two?'

'Why of course there is every chance,' he smiled. 'Follow me.'

So far, so good, I thought. Let's hope this lunch continues on such a positive track.

Once we were seated the conversation remained light and breezy following some silly joke our host had made about 'minding the gap'!

Over bread rolls and soup we had avoided the abortion issue superbly. But as Maddie strayed into inane chat about how she thought she was wearing the wrong foundation for her skin tone, I knew she was just avoiding the giant elephant in the room.

'OK, enough with the Michael Flatley tap dance. What's going on, missus? You've gotta tell me, because I feel like I'm going to burst.'

'All right,' she conceded, fixing herself on her seat. 'Just give me a second.' And with a deep breath she threw me a calming smile and started to speak once again.

'I know my mother is going to hate me whichever decision I make, so I've given this a lot of thought and come up with the best solution for me.'

Practically on the edge of my seat, I could feel my eyebrows almost lift off my face with the anticipation. 'And?' I questioned nervously.

'Well, when you think about it, having an abortion is not really my style. Basically I've been caught and I suppose I'll have to live with the consequences.'

'So is your mind made up?'

'Yep. I'm gonna keep him or her.'

'Are you sure?'

'Yes, Eva, I'm sure I'm sure.'

'Yeaee, we're having a baby!'

Hearing my cheers the manager came promptly over to the table asking, 'Everything OK?'

As I swept my hair across my face again I wanted to gloss over the details and tried to play down the situation, claiming, 'Oh, we just got some good news, just a mini victory for mankind.'

'That is a cause for celebration, very good. How would you like two glasses of my finest Pinot Grigio on the house?' he asked.

Without a second of hesitation Maddie screamed, 'Oh God, not for me.'

Automatically picking up on her snappy reaction, he gave me an inquisitive look before turning back to Maddie. 'That's not like you, are you sure you wouldn't like a glass?' he asked.

'No honestly thanks, I'm off the booze.'

'Really, why? Are you pregnant?' He laughed.

In shock we darted each other a look, before Maddie stuttered, 'No, eh, God no, just taking extra care of myself, that's all. Me pregnant? Are you joking? As if!'

Looking extremely confused, he cleared the table and took our order for two teas.

'Wow that was close,' Maddie sighed, running her hands through her hair to relieve her stress.

'Damn right,' I sighed. 'He nearly saw my fecking cold sore,' I teased. 'Anyway, where were we? Oh yes, we're having a baby, yeaee!'

'Emm, what's this *we* shit? Are you offering to carry this foetus for the next four and a half months? Share the morning sickness? Which I've been told should be renamed morning, noon and night sickness . . .'

'Ah come on, I'll be holding your hand *and* fat ankles the whole way through it. Ha! This is so exciting, a mini baby Maddie. I hope this London geezer was good-looking? I don't think I could love an ugly baby.'

'Fuck off . . . Of course he was good-looking. At least I think he was . . .'

'I know it's hard to think straight, but are you happy now that you've decided to keep the baby? And how do you feel about devoting the next twenty-one years of your life to it?'

'Don't call my baby an "it". I always thought I'd have boys, so until I hear otherwise, I'm carrying a little man. Troy.'

'Troy? Who or what is Troy?'

'I've always liked the name. He's my baby and I can call him what I like. And if you have any opinions on it, you can keep them to yourself.'

'Wow, fair enough. Is this the start of your raging hormones?'

'Listen, girlfriend. You ain't seen nothing yet!'

As a waiter returned with our teas, so did the manager, carrying a little pink cupcake. Placing it in front of Maddie, he gave her one of his cheeky winks and said, 'I thought a baby bun might be apt for this mini celebration of yours. Enjoy – your secret is safe with me.'

As he walked away from the table the two of us raised our hands to our mouths and just stared at each other in silence.

It's amazing how easily people figure things out. From now on Maddie would have to be so much more careful. Small mercies that Anna wasn't anywhere in the vicinity, otherwise it would have been game over for Maddie's secret.

*   *   *

Three days later, the Princess flashed up on my phone.

'Hey, Lisa, are you well?'

'I'm good, Eva, thanks.'

'What's the story?'

'I've got bad news, I'm afraid.'

'Are the family OK?'

'They're all fine, thanks but there's bad news for you I'm afraid.'

Knowing damn well it was something to do with the job, I sheepishly asked, 'What do you mean?'

'Dad was on . . .'

'Ah . . .'

'I'm sorry darling, but Maureen has threatened to quit if he doesn't remove you from the office. She's been with him fourteen years, and . . .'

'It's fine. I understand.'

'It's just that he's nowhere else he could put you.'

'Listen, it's grand, genuinely.'

'He's really sorry.'

'Forget about it. It's like water off a duck's back to me at this stage . . . I wonder what Wilde would have said in this situation now?'

'Well, I was just thinking that myself and . . .'

'Lisa, I was joking.'

'No, but I've a few quotes here and—'

'Hello . . . Hello . . . Sorry, you're breaking up . . . If you can hear me . . . Hello . . . Hello . . . Ah! You're gone . . .' Not able to swallow Wildean reason I cut her short and hung up.

I was in a fragile mental state and this news was just another blow to my already broken heart.

I had been hoping that the Tiswells' charity life raft would have lasted longer.

Too bad my old ghost ship went and sank it.

'Tell me what I have to celebrate again?'

'Well, the herpes has finally gone from your top lip and there's the fact that you will no longer scare young children and old people in public with your hideous appearance.'

'Parker . . .'

'Sorry, it's your thirtieth birthday, Eva. You are now officially old.'

Parker as always was never one for subtlety and took great pleasure in winding me up. But it wasn't as if he was lying. It was my thirtieth birthday, and depending on which way you looked at it, I suppose I *was* now officially old.

'On the bright side, I should really command more respect now that I've left my twenties behind.'

'Ha! Who fed you with that bullshit?'

'It's true. A woman with lines on her face is taken more seriously.'

'A woman who has lines on her face just looks like a woman closer to the grave. So are you saying you'd never have Botox?'

'Don't be stupid, of course I would. But I'm hanging by a thread here and I'm trying to stay positive.'

'You're right. Be old, jobless, homeless and proud.'

*   *   *

When I arrived at Henry's Bar 7 everyone I knew was there and greeted me with a big, 'Surprise!'

Unfortunately the biggest surprise was when I approached the reserved tables and tripped over someone's handbag and gave everyone a bird's eye view of my left nipple as it broke free from the several layers of titty tape I had concealed it with.

My backless, bottomless and frontless micro mini black dress did little to hide such a Janet Jackson wardrobe malfunction!

Tangoed to within one inch of my life and painted with heavy black eyeliner not too dissimilar to Amy Winehouse, I was in diva overload, and felt fantastic. I was the centre of attention for all the right reasons tonight, and I was going to milk it.

As everyone told me how well I looked, which I graciously accepted, even though I wasn't normally great at taking compliments, I sat myself among the throng and got stuck into the glass of pink Anna handed me.

Anna was never my favourite person in the world, but she always got a party going, and tonight I wanted to party.

'Now anyone who's not here is going to catch up with us later at the Haven,' continued Anna. 'Farrelly and his crew are still barred from here after their rows with the doormen, so they send their apologies, and Smith and his gang are going to some gig at Vicar Street first, but will be down after.'

As always, she knew everyone's plans. She was so exact about things that I almost felt like she knew what colour underwear you were wearing. But she was as funny as she was dangerous, and after years of battling with her mean streak, had become quite generous with old age. What age that was, no one was quite sure. 'We're only talkin' Hollywood age,' she'd say. And that had been stuck at twenty-seven for as long as I had known her.

Since there was no sign of Robert yet, whom I had invited purely because I didn't want to be snogless on my birthday, I was free to flirt with whomever I chose. Not that there were any suitable candidates in view so far. But the night was young.

As I scanned the bar for fresh talent, I spied three familiar faces waving at me. They were the typical middle-aged, pot-bellied wannabes who were constantly on the make, and always in their little group hanging around bars and clubs. Lusting after whatever had a pulse.

'What are those Daddy Sleazes doing here?' I asked Anna. Knowing she'd be the one with the info.

'Shut up, I asked them in. They'll keep buying us champagne all night. All you have to do is go over to them and chat for a little bit. Just make them laugh, make them feel included and then blank them for the rest of the night.'

'I can't stand those eejits.'

'Who cares? You're drinking their champagne as we speak. They've bought everything on the table so far.' Guilted into submission, I thought it best to get the thank-yous out of the way, so I adjusted my tit-tape, glossed up my lips and made my way across to the boyos at the bar.

Surprisingly my charm offensive went well, and after several minutes of hair flicking and some bad golf puns from me, I was able to make my escape by introducing the lads to Cathy.

A sweet girl, she wasn't exactly my idea of sparkling conversation, but she was a petite pretty blonde and could stomach hours of mind-numbing banter from blokes like these three because all she was interested in was money.

All I had to say was, 'They're inheritance boys and big golfers', and she was all over them like a rash!

With my duty done, I returned to the group only to find Robert being smothered by Parker. Like a pro-tective father he had put his arm around him, and was in the middle of a big talk.

'I'm just telling Robbie here . . .'

'It's Robert.'

'OK, whatever. But I was just letting him know that if he hurts you, I'll hurt him.'

As neither Robert nor myself quite knew if he was serious, I thanked him then informed him that Manuel his favourite barman had just appeared, be-fore hopping on Robert's lap and snogging the face off him. 'Hey is that a mobile phone in your pocket? Or are you just pleased to see me?' I asked, searching for more compliments.

'Let's just say that whatever's in my pocket right now is rock hard, and is available to you for good vibrations.'

Quite clearly turned on by my appearance, his choirboy persona had definitely been left at home; now his alter ego kinky stud was out to play for the first time in public.

Although I had been left a bit freaked by his willy-wear on our last encounter, I was determined to have fun at my own party.

And since the chances of me having sex with anyone this night were next to none considering the amount of alcohol I was planning to consume, I was safe from his advances. Well, Parker had been put under strict instructions that unless Harry Connick Jnr landed in Dublin and demanded to have his wicked way with me, Parker was the only man allowed to take me home.

So for now, kissing and dirty-talk was as much intimacy as I was striving for. And with Robert, the kissing was tongue-tinglingly good. Even if he was more than a little off the wall.

As the night continued, more and more of my social drinking buddies turned up, with the one obvious exception of my best pal Maddie.

I told everyone she'd had a big job in Belfast modelling for some hotel group, and that she had to stay over because the MD of the advertising company had fallen in love with her.

It was a believable lie, yet it didn't stop Reuters

trying to do a bit of detective work on the finer details.

Just as some of the group started to dance on the couch, the owner of the bar, Neil Jacobs, walked over to us wielding two bottles of peach schnapps.

'Call this a party?' he laughed, dumping the bottles down on the table in front of me. 'What you need here is the master party boy to get things started.'

'Sorry, are we not rowdy enough for you?' I was half insulted that he didn't think people would be having fun at my birthday.

'Gather round, everyone,' he ordered, ushering boys to their seats while helping girls to step off his couch. 'We've a drinking game to play.'

A legendary character on the Dublin scene, Neil was all about the show. Whether it was at the races, in a restaurant or in his own bar, Neil would always be holding court with naughty party games or by telling fantastically absurd stories.

'So what's the game, Neil?' I asked, already seated, eager to consume even more free booze.

'It's the cigarette packet game,' he explained, ripping the plastic off a packet of John Player Blues he'd taken out of his jacket.

'Very catchy title,' said Parker, in his best sarcastic drawl.

'Excuse me. You better behave, Mr Pink Panther, or you won't be allowed to play,' Neil retorted, well able for any of Parker's jibes.

Not wanting to be excluded from any fun, Parker saluted and smiled. 'Yes sir – no sir!'

We were like primary school children listening to a teacher read a story as Neil explained that we had to pass this flimsy piece of plastic around the group using only our lips. And every time someone dropped the plastic he'd make us neck a mouthful of peach schnapps straight from the bottle and would also tear the plastic into a smaller strip.

All of a sudden we realized the pitfall of who we had sat down beside.

Thankfully I had Robert to the left of me but there was some unknown girl to the right. She had introduced herself as 'a friend of Anna's', and was a stunning brunette. Although there were several guys that I would have preferred to park myself beside and touch lips with, I felt relieved that I hadn't got someone unpleasant, even if she was female.

Before the clear plastic baton had reached me, it had been dropped several times and had been torn down to a minuscule size, with all blameable persons being semi-drowned in Neil's sickly sweet poison.

Everyone huddled around the two tables was getting extremely horny. We had all become excessively loud with the excitement, and Neil felt obliged to tell us to calm things down every few minutes.

'This is a respectable establishment, lads,' he'd say. 'Keep it down,' before creasing up with laughter.

As the plastic made its way towards me, I could

feel myself getting caught up in the naughtiness of the game. So far there had been boys locking lips with other boys as they sucked the piece of plastic off their neighbour – all of them announcing how 'secure' they were in their sexuality.

Then came my turn to be passed the cellophane. As my new acquaintance turned to me with her glossy long chestnut brown wavy hair and twinkling doe eyes, she arched one eyebrow and gave me a devilishly cheeky wink before leaning forwards and pressing her full lips against mine.

Closing my eyes as if we were sharing a proper kiss, I pushed my lips against hers, and was temporarily lost in the smell of her sweet perfume.

I had never been this close to a woman before, yet it didn't feel strange or weird. In fact it felt perfectly normal, and wonderfully enjoyable. Actually it was better than that. It was fantastically erotic. Why the hell hadn't I kissed girls before? And why did all these people have to be here? I could be lost in this kiss – this plastic-cover-coated kiss – all night! Of course with everyone chanting, 'Go Eva – go the diva!' I doubled up with a fit of the giggles and dropped the plastic down my top.

As Neil automatically reached for his bottle my new girlfriend wasted no time. Saying 'Let me fish that out for you', she softly slid her dainty fingers under the fold of my dress and retrieved the nearly invisible piece of plastic from my right boob. 'Here it is,' she said, then bit her bottom lip suggestively.

Was this gorgeous girl coming on to me, I wondered? But I had no time to react. Neil had almost viciously grabbed my chin and had started to drown me in peach schnapps.

'Extra helpings for the birthday girl,' he screamed. To which everyone cheered.

Neil ordered me to start the game again with a fresh piece of plastic, since the last piece was too small. I turned to Robert, who I had almost forgotten was still with me.

He had a strange look on his face, as if he was jealous. Then as if he felt he had to reclaim his woman, he quickly licked a few stray splashes of peach schnapps off my arm before puckering up.

He lingered as we swapped the plastic, but all I could think about was this chick beside me flirting.

As we mirrored tongues through the plastic, Parker and Anna chanted 'Get a room', so I sheepishly pulled back and let him move on to Lisa, which he did very quickly, before snapping his head back to me with possessive eyes and squeezing my thigh.

Instantly a look of disappointment shot across her face, which was pretty amazing as her regular Botox injections rarely allowed such emotions to be shown.

Looking like one of those latex sex dolls with her mouth gaping open as she tried to suck in the piece of plastic, she threw me an evil eye as if to say who the fuck does your boyfriend think he's snubbing? Turning to an old boyfriend of hers, Adrian, she gave him a dramatic snog worthy of an operatic performance penned by Andrew Lloyd Webber.

As the group whooped and cheered, Robert pulled me close and in a serious voice said, 'You looked like you enjoyed that.'

'You're a phe–nom–enal kisser.' I rolled my tongue as I spoke, trying to distract him from my lesbian tryst.

'No. I'm talking about your *other* kiss.' He pointed to my gal pal like she was the scene of a crime.

I pulled a serious face and told him, 'Yes I did!' He wasn't my boss, and he certainly wasn't going to give me grief on my birthday.

As I reached for my glass, my lesbian fantasy next to me noticed I was running low on champagne.

'Let me fill you up,' she smiled before grabbing a bottle of Laurent Perrier rosé from one of the two ice buckets between the tables and topping up my glass to the brim.

'Cheers.' I raised my glass in a toast.

'My name is Lucy, by the way. Lucy Ormond,' she replied. 'In case you'd like to know.'

Just then a very boisterous Neil tapped me on the shoulder and stuck a bottle of peach schnapps in my mouth. 'Another splash for not paying attention,' he said.

Thankfully only a tiny drop fell from the bottle, as it was as much as I could stomach. I returned to flirting with Lucy. The coast was clear as Robert had since taken leave for the Men's in a huff.

'I'm Eva Valentine. It's my birthday.' I gave her a coy look as I spoke.

'I know, I was a big fan of your column,' she gushed. 'And you know what else? Our initials spell LOVE. It's an anagram, Lucy Ormond and Eva Valentine. Cool, huh?'

Gobsmacked, I just raised my glass again and clinked it against hers. 'Pretty cool all right . . .'

When it was Lucy's turn to pass the plastic to me again Robert was still lost in frustration somewhere else so I took full advantage of the freedom. Instead of sticking to the rules of the game – not that there were any formal rules – Lucy peeled the plastic off her Angelina Jolie lips, grasped the back of my head and pulled me in close for a deep kiss.

I didn't restrain myself.

I felt like I was in a movie.

So there we sat in the middle of this large group of mutual friends kissing passionately.

I felt like a porn star.

As long as she was kissing me, I'd kiss her back, I thought. But then the group went quiet. And I couldn't help but wonder why.

Pulling back our lips made a strange popping noise that made us both laugh and eased the awkwardness of the moment. As I looked up I realized all eyes were on us. But the fun had left the group. No one was laughing or joking any more.

Looking at Parker, who was sitting opposite me, I tried to work out his expression.

'What?' I asked indignantly.

But he gave me no reply. His eyes widened and with an outstretched finger he pointed for me to turn around.

Thinking they must have organized a surprise for me like a strippergram I spun round on my chair with a big smile on my face.

But oh, how wrong could I be.

Instead of some greasy bodybuilder in a dirty fireman outfit I found an angry David Barron standing in front of me with overtly aggressive body language.

Shocked, I did what any three-year-old trapped in a thirty-year-old's body would have done and spun back round on my chair.

If I couldn't see him he wasn't there.

Or maybe he'd take the hint that I wasn't up for a chat and walk off?

No such luck.

'Have you any shame?' bellowed the voice behind me. I didn't reply. I just sat rigid on the stool.

'We can have this out right here or we can do it outside. Which would you prefer?' I could hear the anger in his voice as it quivered when he spoke.

'Listen, there's no place for that kind of talk,' said Neil, sizing him up. 'I think you should leave.'

'Well I think I should stay, as I've a few things I want to say to this bitch here who broke up my marriage.'

'Steady on there, pal.'

'I'm not your pal. Now get the fuck out of my way.'

'Right, that's it, you're outta here.' Neil signalled to

his doormen to remove Barron, who had now started to grab at me and had managed to pull my hair.

'I'm not going anywhere. Now get out of my face. I'm not leaving till I speak to that bitch.'

By now several of Neil's security guys had pushed their way through the busy Saturday night throng and had grabbed hold of David's shoulders.

'We can do this the easy way, or the hard way,' explained one of the extremely wide men.

'Sorry, lads, there's just been a misunderstanding. There's no problem.' David switched his tone immediately. The shock of seeing the bouncers reminded him of his manners.

'Get him out of here,' demanded Neil.

'Who gives you the right?' squealed David. 'Somebody get me a manager?'

Neil didn't bother explaining his title. His hired help had removed David from our reserved area and they were now halfway across the bar with him, heading in the direction of the door.

Extremely shaken, I was huddled in Parker's arms, each of us as frazzled as the other.

'It's OK, he's gone now,' Parker tried to calm me with his powers of observation.

But I was unimpressed by his lack of support.

'Minister for the obvious!' I screamed back.

'I'm sorry pet . . . I'm not very—'

'What? Good in a crisis?' I wasn't taking any prisoners. I needed someone to vent my anger at.

'I'm sorry . . .'

'So you said.' I shook Parker's arm off my shoulder. 'I was about to be attacked and you just remained glued to your seat. Thanks a million.'

With that I picked up my bag and stormed off to the loo, with Lisa and Anna trailing behind me.

'You sure pissed him off,' quipped a clearly delighted Anna. 'Ha! I wonder did anyone get his rant on a videophone. We could send it in to TV3 news. I can see the story now: Publisher gone mad.'

I hadn't the energy to scold her for trivializing David's attack. He had really scared me. When Neil started to push him back I was almost sure he was trying to hit me.

I wanted to cry, but I couldn't allow myself. Not with Anna still in the Ladies with us. She'd be sure to out me as a cry-baby. Not that she hung around long enough to see any tears. When she realized I wasn't going to flip out and start bitching about him, she got bored and said she'd see us back at the table.

'It's your party and so you're allowed to cry.' Lisa could see the emotion in my eyes as she wrapped her arms around me and cuddled me in close.

'Thank you,' I snivelled, before weeping uncontrollably for the next ten minutes.

As I climbed to the top of the stairs on the way back from the loo, I saw what looked like Parker snogging . . . Wait, it couldn't be . . . Was that Parker kissing *Robert*?

Furious, I stormed over and pulled the two of them apart.

'What the hell is going on here?' It felt like my head was about to explode.

Strangely cocky, Robert explained, 'Well if it's OK for you to kiss other girls, why isn't it OK for me to kiss other guys?'

'Yuck! You never told me you were gay.'

'I'm not gay.'

'I think you are,' interrupted Parker, as he pointed to his pouted lips in his camp Austin Powers way.

'No I'm not. I suppose you could say I'm bi-curious,' Robert rationalized as a smug grin rippled across his face.

'Ha! I wonder how bi-curious your mother would be to find out your biblical habits? And as for you – ' I turned my hostility back to Parker. 'What do you think you're playing at?'

'I was proving my point.'

'What point?' I demanded.

'I told you I'd out Robert. I needed to prove it to you. Here's the proof, *voilà*!'

'Well thank you very much, Parker, aren't you just a doll.'

'Don't get stroppy with me. You knew I was gay at the start of the night. I'm not the one lying to you, now am I?'

'I'm not lying to you, Eva. I was merely getting into the spirit of things.'

I rolled my eyes at the absurdity of the situation.

'Well I think this abuse is pretty rich coming from the girl who just had a full-on kiss with another bird,' said Parker.

'I had two, actually.'

'What do you mean?'

'I've just had two full-on kisses with that "bird" and her name is Lucy.'

'Lucy the lipstick lesbian, eh? She's cute stuff. You don't see many of them down the George.' Parker did his best to ease the tension.

Realizing he couldn't compete with another woman, let alone challenge her to a fight outside for my affections, Robert threw in the towel and left in a huff.

'You're both mental,' I could hear him mutter to himself as he barged through a group of people who had been listening to the argument. By the looks on their faces, they were disappointed it was over.

'My gaydar is never wrong,' boasted Parker, chuffed at a job well done.

'Ah Parker, how could you? I've never seen you kiss a bloke in public. Why did you have to do it with him, and on my birthday?'

'I've done you a big favour, pet. I knew he was on my bus.' He put his arm around me and started to walk me back in the direction of the others. 'Now he's out of the way, you can have loads more fun with your new VBF.'

Lost for words, I silently strode back to my friends. All of whom seemed to have visibly moved on from the drama and were back dancing on the couches.

Had I really been kissing a girl in public?

Did this mean I was gay?

I sat back down on my stool. There was no sign of Lucy or Neil.

Relief, I thought, taking a large mouthful of champagne. I was just reaching in my handbag for my mobile to text Maddie the scandal when a small hand slid around my waist.

'I see your boyfriend has just left.' I tilted my head to see Lucy smiling at me. 'It looks like I have you all to myself,' she whispered.

'Listen, I'm not sure . . .'

'Shhhh.' Lucy placed her soft hand over my face to stop me from talking. 'Relax,' she purred. Her pride and confidence were overflowing.

Not sure how to react, I followed my gut instinct. 'You're dangerous,' I told her.

'Yes I am.' She raised her glass of champers to toast the revelation. 'And it's gonna take you till tomorrow morning to find out just how dangerous I can be . . .'

7

'You better behave yourself, or else I'm leaving the two of you at Malaga airport to be sold into white slavery,' Parker barked at me and Maddie.

It had been a miserable Irish summer and he'd been desperate to get away to the sun. It was June and I was still out of work, which meant I was now completely broke apart from whatever odd jobs Parker threw my way.

The summer months were always considered silly season in print media circles because whenever you sent off e-mails to people looking for work, they'd bounce right back at you with the blunt message that they'd be out of the office for the next three weeks.

Thankfully my pauper status didn't stop fun being had, as Parker kindly forked out the €800 for my ticket. And although Maddie was one of the most successful models in the country, raking in a fortune with editorials and press work, he went and paid for her plane fare too, mumbling something like, 'God forbid I show any favouritism.'

Of course that didn't mean we were going to treat him any differently. Somehow we had been conditioned to expect such luxuries in life. I used to joke that every day was Valentine's Day for me and that meant I deserved gifts all year round, but I can never recall when this spoilt behaviour began, since my mother was always such a controlling force.

But today Maddie and I were giddy with excitement, and had combined our efforts to tease Parker. As a double act we could be dangerous, but it was taking very little to wind up Parker today. He was currently having a mini diva strop because Maddie had told him his belt didn't match his shoes and then I'd pointed out that his salmon shirt complemented the broken veins in his cheeks.

He was never comfortable out of his black uniform, bless, but every summer he made the effort to 'Marbella-rize' his wardrobe.

'I don't think there's much of a slave trade in the south of Spain, dear,' pressed Maddie. But seeing that Parker was about to throw another wobbler, I calmed the situation by saying, 'Yes, but there's hundreds of dangerous pimps' and signalled to her to shut up.

As we boarded the 3.30p.m. Aer Lingus flight to Malaga, there were plenty of familiar faces also going out for some sun, sand, sea and sex.

To me, Marbella and Puerto Banus always felt like an extra suburb of Dublin, as there were so many Irish with property there. Sadly, many of them couldn't give away the apartments and villas that they had invested in in the nineties – even if they threw in lifetime golf club membership or an around the clock live-in hooker, but, either way, it was still considered flash.

There were so many recognizable faces there that it was impossible to book a spray tan or a hair appointment without bumping into half the regulars of the Haven.

Normally I would have been there already to hang out and flirt with the rich Type2 boys from Dublin, who tell their girlfriends and wives that they're just away on golfing trips. But since I had been out of work for ever, this June bank holiday weekend was my first chance at summer lovin'.

By now, Maddie was four months pregnant, but being such a skinny bitch she was defying nature and still had no signs of a baby bump. She also hadn't suffered any nausea. I was the one who had started to feel sick – at the fact that she was still slimmer than me.

But today we were looking for devilment as we took our seats on the plane and scanned for possible playmates. Things were looking miserable as the seats filled up with couples, but then four Hulk-like fellas bounced their way through the aisle, knocking against passengers with their large carry-on rucksacks, and banging into lockers with their bulky shoulders and cauliflower ears.

'Check out the rugby players,' squealed Maddie, totally forgetful of her mumsie state and how unacceptable it is to consider sex with a bloke while pregnant with another man's baby.

'They're farmers,' moaned Parker. 'Redneck, culchie hick farmers.'

Now, usually Parker would have been horny looking at such a posse, but since he was 'in love' with Jeff, he was very much the devoted boyfriend.

Although 'Hairy hole', as Maddie had renamed him, wasn't coming with us to Parker's family villa, he would be joining us in seven days, which gave us one week to listen to Parker complaining.

Whilst the fact that Parker had become a one-man man and was utterly faithful to Jeff was wonderful, there was nothing fabulous about his mood when his boy was out of town. Think Glenn Close in *Fatal Attraction* and you'd be able to imagine what sort of nightmare Parker had become when he couldn't be with his lover. Obsessing about Jeff had become a constant hobby.

'Jeff would never eat avocado – they're far too fattening.' Or, 'Jeff prefers Liquid Silk to KY Jelly because it's not as sticky' or, 'Jeff hates Victoria Beckham because she reminds him of an old trannie he used to secretly date!'

His prattling was as endless as it was pointless. But we were his friends and he was allowed to be annoying occasionally. And the fact that he was bankrolling my social life was another good reason to humour him. Yes, just as Lisa had cleared up her bout of verbal Wildean diarrhoea, Parker started spewing the Jeff Alexander guide to a perfect life.

On reflection, I supposed I had bored everyone long enough about my phantom photographer boyfriend, so it was my turn to be patient. But just because Parker wasn't in the mood to be mischievous didn't mean that Maddie and I had to play vestal virgins.

She was single – although secretly knocked-up – while my love life was complex, to say the least. Although Robert and I had made up after our little tête-à-tête at my birthday, things had never been the same. Occasionally we'd ring each other for a bootie call, but although it would act as the perfect stress relief as required, our partnership was never to progress further than the purely functional.

As for Luscious Lucy, as she was now named in my phone, well, I still didn't understand where we stood.

I had apparently snogged her several times in as many months, but had only vague recollections of each encounter. Copious amounts of alcohol was always part of our mating ritual.

It turned out the doe-eyed beauty had a young prince of her own, and although he'd once said that he thought it was arousing that she liked to kiss other girls, in reality it just made him jealous, which was very understandable.

Through a drunken haze I remember the last time she placed her lips on mine, as it resulted in a rapturous round of applause . . .

*   *   *

It was on the dance floor of Sophie's Choice and Lucy had been dancing with her equally cute boyfriend when Parker and I cosied up next to them as bold as brass.

A complete minx herself, her naughty switch flicked on the second she saw us, as she promptly started shaking her ass with some sexy Shakira moves to tease me.

I can still picture her leaning over her boyfriend's shoulder and whispering, 'You look hot', while giving me a wink.

Brazen was the only way you could describe this chick. And it was hard not to adore her, which I did tremendously.

As far as I could recall, her fella took the hump with her not-too-subtle flirting, and marched off the dance floor leaving the three of us happy to compete in an erotic dance-off.

Thrilled with ourselves we strutted and gyrated like we were Rihanna dancing under her 'Um-ber-ella!' But after some over-amorous twists from Lucy and myself Parker declared, 'Gooseberry ain't my colour' and went off to find devilment with Jeff.

As soon as we were left to play on our own, we became sandwiched together like magnets. Spinning in circles and performing like contestants on *Dancing with the Stars*, we owned the room and no one else existed. Despite being petite Lucy's grasps were firm, and with her arms snugly around my waist I felt bulletproof.

Laughing and flirting, grooving and swirling, we ripped up the dance floor and refused anyone else space in our drink-induced fantasy. Unable to control ourselves we started to kiss right in the middle of the dance floor . . . passionately.

We shared a magical moment, as her sweet tongue rolled around in my mouth and her hands gave my hips a tight squeeze.

All I was aware of was her strawberry lip-balm and the hint of coconut that left her long flowing hair as I fingered it.

When the song changed to a more hardcore dance track, we pulled back from our kiss and stared straight into each other's eyes, smiling like Cheshire cats. I was just about to tell her how much I'd like to get naked with her when a large cheer came from the direction of the bar. Automatically we turned, to see a gang of six lads cheering and clapping at us.

'Great show,' one of them shouted. 'Don't stop now,' cheered another.

If we'd been sober we probably would have been mortified, but we weren't, so we fell about laughing and cheekily took a bow.

The next thing I remember was Lucy's boyfriend taking her by the hand and manhandling her down the stairs of the club with her jacket and handbag over his shoulder. That was a couple of weeks ago, and I haven't seen her since.

Although she still very much occupies my thoughts I've thought it best to leave well alone. I wanted and needed a boyfriend and a protector. As much fun as Lucy was, no man would ever consider taking me on if I spent my Saturday nights kissing girls. Well, except a pervy one, and I didn't want to end up with a swinger. The city was full of them, but that was not the type of life I had dreamt about as a young or grown-up girl.

After waking up with the fear of what I'd done, I'd stayed away from clubs in case I was recognized for my lesbian exhibition.

Today, I was sitting on a plane, which officially meant I was on holiday. It was a break away from guilt and the harsh reality of my failure in life. And now that I had locked four eligible hunks in my radar and had smuggled several snipes of Moët in my hand luggage for myself, it was time to let the party games begin.

Clearly up for a bit of boldness we received several loud, 'How-si-goin?' before the hunks finished shoving their bags into the overhead lockers.

Maddie was just about to go down and introduce herself to the lads when a very matron-like hostess told everyone to take their seats. So instead she did what she always did on planes: took out some paper and started to write a note.

'Hello tasty boys – especially you in the Irish jersey,' it began. 'Are you looking for fun on this trip? XXX.'

Wasting no time, she nabbed a less fierce air hostess and asked her to pass the note to the boys, who were making general fools of themselves. Within seconds there was a big cheer, with one of the lads screaming, 'Absa-fuckin'lutely!' in a thick Corkonian accent, followed by the other three moaning, 'Shut the fuck up, Bugsie.'

After much rummaging in jackets, the boys located a pen and our note was returned with, 'The fella with the Irish jersey has a small mickie. But the rest of us are hung like donkeys. Are ya up for makin' the high mile?'

At this stage I had necked back the first mini bottle of bubbles, and had moved on to my second, so feeling a little finicky I sent a note back: 'Sorry lads, but did you mean the Mile High Club?'

Although the plane hadn't even left the runway yet, several groups looked as if they were about to complain about the sound pollution. Noticing this, the air hostess refused to accept the note from the boys to give to us and told them to keep it down.

Ten long, laborious minutes later our Airbus was finally in the skies, and Maddie was hot out of the traps and over to get acquainted with the guys. Of course I was too embarrassed to go with her, so I giggled and waved from my seat while Parker tutted with mature disgust.

'You're behaving like fishwives,' he barked, pulling a snooty face.

'What's a fishwife anyway?' Knowing well that he wouldn't have an answer.

'I don't know.' His tone was almost a growl. 'But

you two are acting like common little tarts, I'm embarrassed for you. I'm putting on my iPod now, and if anyone asks, I'll disown you.'

'Well you can act like a grumpy old bear for the rest of the flight if you like, but I'm going to enjoy myself. You've approximately two hours and twenty-five minutes to lose yourself in the Scissor Sisters, so I hope you have enough battery power. Good luck!'

With that I jumped out of my seat and sauntered up the aisle like it was a catwalk. Not that any of the guys noticed; their eyes were transfixed by Maddie and her tight white T.

She always had great pert boobs, but since she'd got pregnant, they had almost doubled in size, even though the rest of her hadn't.

I had just snuggled up beside Maddie and pretended to be interested in some story she was telling about Sinatra's Bar in Puerto Banus, when the angry hostess got on the intercom again and told everyone to take their seats as we would be experiencing some turbulence.

Maddie didn't look as if she was prepared to give up on her games, as she told the boys, 'Hold all those thoughts, as I'll be bringing sexy back!' She gave me a poke in the ribs and pushed me towards our seats before I even got a chance to open my mouth.

'Eh, thanks for that,' I snapped, as I fixed my belt buckle in a hasty fashion.

'They're dickheads,' she whispered, still waving in their direction.

'Excuse me?'

'And we'll have to make a sharpish exit off the plane as well. Because I jokingly said that we were here for your hen night and you were looking for a final fling before the big day.'

'So what's wrong with that? The blondie fella looked kinda cute. I've done worse – *you've* done worse!'

'Agreed, but I think they're bad eggs.'

'Since when have you been so picky? I'm going to give the blond one my number.'

'No, you're not.'

'Why not?'

'Because . . .'

'Fuck sake, Maddie, just tell me why not.'

'Just leave it.'

'*Why?*'

'Cause they've got Class As on them and I don't want to be exposed in the papers as the model who's been smuggling a baby, and now drugs!'

'Fuck off . . . How do you know?'

'The loud one in the jersey said he had coke on him and did I fancy a line?'

'Get outta town. Jaysus, they're mad bastards. So, why were you still flirting with them? Telling them you'd bring sexy back. I presumed you were talking about me.'

'Get you. Actually I was, kinda, but I was just trying to get away from them subtly.'

'Subtly? You're one of those bitches who give

women a bad name: "I said Yes, Your Honour, but really I meant No".'

As the plane started to swoop and dip in the wind pockets Parker opened his eyes and pulled off his earphones. The colour had drained from his face and he gripped the armrests of his seat in panic mode.

'I'm fucking hating this turbulence,' he moaned, terrified. 'I'm hating it more than Jodie Marsh's wardrobe, I'm hating it more than that smelly Pete Doherty . . . actually, I hate it just as much as Colin Farrell's dirty fingernails. *Fuck!* I'm hating it—'

'OK, calm down. Don't get your G-string in a twist, it'll pass soon.' I tried to sound composed, but Parker was normally the sensible one in these situations while I was always uneasy with the rocking.

'Listen, I've a good story for ya, to take your mind off falling out of the sky.'

'Thanks, pet,' he said in a sarcastic whisper.

'Maddie, tell Parker about your DR-uggie mates.' The captain surfed the wind as I spoke.

'Sh-ushh,' Maddie glared, looking around her as if she was being followed. 'Keep it quiet.'

Intrigued, Parker leaned over my lap towards Maddie on the outside seat and demanded she filled him in on her news.

'They asked me – if I wanted – a line of coke,' she mumbled through her hand.

'No way?'

'Yes way . . .'

'And then what?' Parker's attention span already seemed exhausted.

'That's it. Turbulence hit, we were told to come back to our seats, and now here we are.'

'Ri-VET-ing.' Parker resumed his white-knuckle pose, while the lads up front whooped and cheered as the plane swooped three times downwards.

We spent the following two hours avoiding Pablo Escobar and his mates thanks to continued bad weather and the trolley-dolly service of tea and coffee, ham sandwiches, giant Toblerones and Burberry perfume. By the time we landed, our stress levels were at an all-time high, what with Parker's new fear of flying and Maddie's anxiety of being linked with reckless coke-heads.

Thankfully everyone scrambled for their bags before the seat-belt sign had been switched off, so the guys couldn't make their way back to our seats. Instead Maddie waved them on and told them she'd see them at the luggage reclaim, before turning to me and saying, 'They'll have to catch me first.'

As we waited in our seats for the queue to ease, Parker busied himself with his phone, and his mood instantly lifted. 'Look I'm a Moviestar,' he said proudly, showing us the network coverage on his mobile before a message from Jeff beeped through.

'Ah look, he says, "Missing you already . . . I luuve U xox." Ah, isn't he the best?'

'The best *ever*,' Maddie and I gushed in unison, knowing Parker was far easier to manage when happy.

With that all our tensions eased and we were three happy campers on tour again.

With Maddie's wild men out of sight, we made our way to Passport Control thrilled by the sight of the warm Spanish sun.

'I'm going to be sitting beside the pool with a strawberry daiquiri in my hand in about ninety minutes,' beamed Parker, stretching his arms out as if he was catching some rays.

'And I'll be lying right beside ya trying to hold my belly in,' smiled Maddie, with a deep intake of breath. 'You never know, I could catch the eye of my first future husband!'

'I hope he likes children,' I teased.

'Well Heidi Klum bagged Seal with someone else's baby,' she answered back with an air of optimism. 'And then she had more with him.' With that she skipped off to wave her passport, content in the knowledge that happily-ever-afters can happen.

'What do you mean there's a problem?' I was surrounded by several Spanish Policia who were trying to escort me to a nearby door marked PRIVADO.

'No, give me my passport back – I've done nothing wrong. Parker – Maddie!' I was pushed inside a small concrete room with a desk and a few chairs and told, 'Wait here' by an angry policeman wearing a bulletproof vest.

As the door closed behind me, I dropped on one of the chairs in shock, my heart pounding with fear.

What did they think I had done? Was this a case of mistaken identity? Was it some elaborate practical joke?

Moments later the heavy door swung open and Maddie and Parker were pushed through it. Thank God, I thought. At least I wasn't alone in my abduction.

'I demand an explanation,' Parker insisted in his best butch voice. Maddie hung on to him for dear life. 'You can't do this to us,' she added weakly. 'We've done nothing wrong.'

But once they were inside, the door was slammed shut again, leaving us dazed and confused.

Maybe it was her hormones, but Maddie burst into tears, and although we were trying to remain strong, Parker and I weren't far behind her.

In a panic Maddie screamed, 'What the fuck? What if they want to do one of those anal examinations? I don't want some bitch sticking her rubber gloves up my ass.'

'Sounds all right to me,' chirped Parker.

'Not funny,' I said, trying to fight the tears. 'We're in some serious shit here. What the fuck do they think we've done?'

'They've taken our phones,' said Parker, as if talking through a plan in his head.

'I've still got mine,' I said and rooted in my hand-bag. 'But who will we ring?'

'Jeff,' urged Parker. 'Hurry up and turn that bloody thing on before they come back. He'll know what to do.'

But as if the police had been listening to our conversation, the door crashed open again as I was staring at my Nokia doing its lengthy connection light-up ritual.

'You won't be needing that just yet,' said one of the two plainclothes men who walked into the room. He had an Irish accent. 'I'll mind that for now.' He signalled to me to hand over the phone, which I did and then instantly regretted.

'What did you do that for?' Maddie was turning from emotional to hysterical.

'OK, listen up, people, calm down and we can get through this a lot easier.' The man, who was wearing a blue short-sleeved Ralph Lauren shirt and navy jeans, had a recognizable south Dublin accent, and even though it didn't seem to sedate Maddie, it went a small way towards calming my nerves. After all, at least these guys were from the same town as us. Surely they'd be less likely to throw us in a foreign jail and throw away the key? My mind began racing, just like my heartbeat.

'I demand you tell us why you're holding us here. We've just arrived for our holidays. We're not smuggling people or drugs.'

'If you take a seat I'll explain.' The same man spoke, while the other observed.

Realizing we had no option but to co-operate, after checking out each other's eyes we hesitantly sat down and faced our kidnappers.

As Maddie continued to weep, the second man – in

a white short-sleeved Ralph Lauren shirt and navy jeans – handed her a tissue from his pocket while the main man readied himself to speak.

'You're wondering why we've pulled you in here. Well, let me introduce myself and my colleague. My name is Detective Hugh Ormond and this is Detective Mark Fitzsimons and we're—'

'Are you charging us with an offence?' interrupted Parker.

'If you would let me finish, sir, I'd like to explain.'

'Yes, well I've a pregnant woman here who doesn't need this sort of upset,' explained Parker as he put his arm around Maddie to comfort her. It only seemed to make her worse.

'What . . . do . . . you want with us?' blubbed Maddie, then erupted into another tearful episode.

'If you'd let me explain,' said the man in the blue again. 'As I said, my name is Detective Ormond and this is Detective Fitzsimons and we're part of the Garda National Drug Unit.'

'What?' Parker was aghast.

'We've pulled you in because we'd like to find out your exact relationship with John Mathews, Cormac Bulger, Jack Gannon and Ray Gannon.'

'Who?' the three of us asked together.

'Oh come on. Do you expect me to believe you don't know who I'm talking about? We've just stepped off the same flight, and we were witness to your contact with these four men.'

'We don't know them,' snapped Parker defensively.

'This eejit started flirting with them, but then changed her mind.' He pointed to Maddie as he spoke, which evoked even more cries.

'Oh, th-is is all my fault now, I suppose,' whimpered Maddie. 'How was I to know?'

'Know what, Miss Lord?' Detective Ormond asked while scanning her passport.

'Nothing . . . I know nothing . . . Can we just go?' Maddie was an extremely bad liar. And our trained Gardaí could smell a stinking rat.

'We can do this the easy way or the hard way, Miss Lord. All we need is a little co-operation from you and then you can leave.'

'I'm no snitch,' blurted Maddie, stupidly signing her death warrant.

'Jesus Christ, Maddie,' moaned Parker, fully aware she was digging a deep hole for herself. 'Just tell them what the men said to you.' He glared at Maddie and then at me. I remained quiet and frozen on my chair. The less attention I brought to myself the better.

'OK, Miss Lord, we're all ears.' Detective Ormond smirked as he spoke.

'Shouldn't I have a lawyer present or something? Am I under arrest or what?'

'So far this is an informal inquiry, Miss Lord, but if you want to make life difficult for yourself we can arrest you all under the Misuse of Drugs Act, search your bags and we can make it all very formal.'

'No,' I screamed, without thinking. 'Sorry, no, we'll talk, well, Maddie here will explain. Won't you,

Maddie?' I squeezed her hand and raised my eyebrows for extra effect.

'Yes, Maddie,' agreed Parker, 'showing loyalty to four men we've never met before is hardly worth being banged up in a Spanish jail for, now is it?'

'Why me?'

'*Maddie!*' Parker's fuse had almost burnt out.

'OK, OK,' she muttered, trying to prepare herself for her big revelation. 'They offered me a line of coke on the plane – that's it. Are you happy now?'

'I don't think this is the time for attitude, Miss Lord. I'd like to point out that we can hold you here over the weekend, and we are more than happy to keep you company until you decide to tell us the truth.'

'But that is the truth,' pleaded Maddie, perking up. 'I've never – we've never – met them before the flight today, and I had no idea who they were. Honest, I was just having a laugh with them, and as soon as they asked if I wanted a line of coke, I backed off. You've got to believe me.'

'Do you really expect us to believe you've no relationship with these men?'

'Yes – I've never seen them before.'

'But we saw you with them. What was it that you were passing to them on the plane?'

'Just a note.'

'Saying what?'

'Stuff.'

'Miss Lord, must I remind you that we can hold you and your friends here for the weekend.'

'Fuck sake . . .'

'Excuse me?'

'Sorry, just stuff,' she sighed, with agony in her voice. 'I was just messing, having a laugh.'

'And?'

'And I was flirting with them. It was just innocent stuff. Have you never had fun with strangers before?' The two detectives just looked at each other and then turned their gaze back to Maddie.

'Your friend here informs us you're pregnant.' The detective gestured at Parker. 'Does the father of your baby approve of you "flirting" with other men?'

'I'm not with him,' she mumbled under her breath.

'Sorry?' asked the detective again.

'I'm not with him,' she repeated, her voice louder. 'I'm an unmarried mother-to-be. So there, are you happy now?'

'Not really, Miss Lord. I don't believe a word out of your mouth. I don't believe you're pregnant, and I don't believe you've never met the four men we have under surveillance. I think you'd better make yourself comfortable. Because we've a lot more questions to ask.'

The two men stood up from their chairs and left the room, leaving us to stare at each other in bewilderment.

'I've told you everything I know.' I was in a different room on my own being interviewed by the same detective, Hugh Ormond.

'Have you been drinking, Miss Valentine?'

'Yes, and I'm not trying to be sarcastic, but what has that got to do with anything? I wasn't planning on driving anywhere. I had kinda hoped I'd be sitting at my pool drinking more by now, actually.'

'If it's all right with you, Miss Valentine, I'll be the one asking the questions.'

'Sorry.'

'It's OK, we just have to be clear on everything. These are very dangerous men you've come into contact with.'

'Yes, well it'd be a lot easier to avoid international drug dealers if they wore T-shirts to state who they were.'

'Believe me, it would help our job considerably too.'

Thankfully, after much aggravated discussion, it looked like the two detectives were coming around to our explanation of events.

The four men Maddie had been flirting with turned out to be small-time drug lords who were travelling to Puerto Banus to meet up with Russian gangs to open new avenues for smuggling Class A drugs. We had foolishly introduced ourselves to these flash Harrys who were under investigation by Europol and being followed by the Drug Squad.

After I'd given him all our contact details, of where we were staying and how long we were planning to stay for, Detective Ormond handed me back my passport and stood up to walk me back to Parker and

Maddie, who had each been interviewed separately before me.

'You're free to go now. Is there anything you'd like to ask me before we release you?'

'I thought we weren't under arrest?'

'You weren't, but you could have been.'

'Emmm, by any chance are you related to a good-looking brunette named Lucy?'

'She's my younger sister.'

'You're kidding.'

'How do you know my skin and blister?'

'She's . . . just a friend of mine. She's a good girl.'

'Oh I better look after you, so. Otherwise I'll never hear the end of it.'

Fifteen minutes later Parker, Maddie and myself were sitting in the back of a scruffy white minivan being driven to Marbella.

It wasn't exactly Parker's style, but the detectives insisted they get us to our villa, and since thankfully we had too much luggage to fit in the back of one of their Policia cars, we were ushered into a rattling unmarked tin can instead.

The driver didn't seem to have a word of English, so the three of us sat in silence during the fifty-minute journey to Parker's villa. All that could be heard over the noisy Moroccan music in the front was the beeping of texts from our mobiles.

Parker of course was bombarding Jeff with his tale of injustice, while Maddie filled Lisa in on her ordeal of being accused of being a liar, slapper and criminal.

I plucked up the courage to send Luscious Lucy a message to say, 'Today I'm very glad I met you. For once you delivered me out of trouble instead of leaving me in it xxx.' Understandably she was probably a little confused by my text. 'Are U drunk?' she replied. Far too exhausted to give her a full explanation, I texted back 'YES'.

'It's definitely a first for me, ha, being arrested,' chuckled Parker as he sipped his second glass of white Faustino.

We had finally made our way to our favourite restaurant, Fernando's, and were awaiting our usual order of *lobster au gratin*, crispy pork belly and sweet BBQ ribs. It was the same order every visit and the same randy waiter Amancio who served us, which meant the same harassment every time I visited the Señoritas. Of course we called him Armani the lean mean pestering machine, as he was the image of the ultra-stylish flamenco dancer Joaquín Cortés – long hair, attitude and all.

Although I pretended to tire of his advances, which came in the form of drawings on napkins, red roses and decorated desserts, Amancio – who every year would tell me that his name meant love or loving – always made me feel the sexiest woman alive.

'You are so beautiful – be my woman – can I make loff to you?' He was your typical intense Spanish gigolo. I just had to forget that he fed the same passionate bullshit to at least six or seven other women a night.

'We weren't arrested,' I retorted as I watched Amancio's tight ass glide across the room. 'Stop saying that. That's how we get ourselves into trouble.' I also warned him to stop going on about the fact that we'd been held by the Gardaí.

'Just like the time we discovered those remote control mini vibrating eggs,' chuckled Parker.

Maddie and I looked at each other, 'Ohmigod,' squealed Maddie, 'do you remember?'

Raising my glass of wine, I toasted the air and answered, 'How could we ever forget?'

Several years back we'd been enjoying a posh meal at Shannon's restaurant in Dublin when a friend of Maddie's called in with presents for her. He owned a sex shop on South William Street called Miss Naughty, and he had a bag full of goodies for her as a thank-you for a modelling job she'd done wearing some of his kinky lingerie.

In the bag there were jingle balls, gloves with vibrating fingers, bizarre clips for places that didn't need clipping, DVDs, lube gels, lipsticks, a five-gear Rampant Rabbit, nipple tassels, edible undies and two remote control mini vibrating eggs.

It was adult game heaven. And of course we weren't going to wait till we got home to enjoy the goodies.

After receiving filthy looks from the neighbouring table for swinging the blue rabbit in the air and revving the speed control like we were at the starting grid at Mondello, we decided we needed to be more discreet with our fun. So Maddie and I nipped to the loo to try out our hard-boiled eggs, leaving Parker at the table doing rotten impersonations of Wacko Jacko with his buzzing glove.

The two toilet cubicles were free so we raced in and cracked open our presents, with the excitability of one of those MTV Sweet Sixteeners when they run to find out what expensive car their daddy has bought them.

Thinking we had the place to ourselves we continued a dialogue through the walls, along the lines of, 'Which way up do you slip it in?' And 'What if it gets lost in there? Will you fish it out for me?'

Feeling secure that we had adjusted our sex toys adequately, we threw open our doors to find two hor- rified middle-aged women standing waiting for us to vacate.

Respectfully we made apologies for being so loud, then ran out of the Ladies in hysterics.

Resisting the lure to try out our new gizmos till we returned to the formality of the table, we exercised our pelvic floors on the way back up the stairs, which, for me anyway, was extremely satisfying in itself. Giggling, we sat down to the sound of the gloved one as MJ singing to the next table about how bad he was.

Although they were trying their best to ignore him, he persisted. When he managed to get the daughter at the table to smile, he felt he'd achieved a small victory and abandoned his harassment.

'So what have you two brassers been doing?'

'We're practising to become chickens,' explained Maddie.

'Yeah, don't make us laugh, we might just lay an egg,' I chirped.

'Don't tell me you stuck those stupid things inside you?'

'Yep,' we replied in unison.

'What's it feel like?' Parker asked with usual perverse interest.

'Like I've been impaled on a plastic egg,' said Maddie. Parker was unimpressed. 'Not exactly erotic stuff,' he grumbled. 'I thought it was meant to vibrate like this glove?'

'We haven't switched them on yet,' I told him. 'Would you like to turn me on?'

'Ha, there'd be a first,' cackled Maddie.

'I wasn't always a poof, you know,' said Parker, pushing his hair across his forehead in a very gay fashion. 'I have had sex with two women, you know.'

'Ewww, doing depraved things with your Barbie dolls doesn't count as having straight sex,' tutted Maddie.

'I'll have you know I fought the good fight against finding the female form repulsive till well into my late teens. And during that time I went to great lengths to satisfy two lovers.'

Both Maddie and myself sat silently in shock.

'Honestly. I lost my virginity to a 47-year-old friend of my mother's, Doreen. We had a sexual relationship for two years. And then my second liaison into uncharted territory was with a butch young thing by the name of Christina. She's since shaved off all her hair, shortened her name to Chris and was last heard of living with another skinhead, by the name of Bernie, in Christchurch.'

'So are you tellin' me you'd know how to tickle my fancy, Mr Pink?' I waved the small remote under his nose.

'Clearly I'd have no interest in doing that manually, but technologically speaking, I'd love to.' Without delay he'd grabbed the device and turned the button to HIGH.

'*Jes-us!*' My yelp from the power surge between my legs could be heard around the dining room. 'Easy does it, Parker. You don't want to electrocute me.'

'Death by two-second orgasm,' he chuckled.

'Is it that good?' questioned a now eager Maddie, experiencing her own tingling sensation.

'Just switch it on.'

'I can't, I'm scared,' said Maddie.

'Then give it here,' ordered Parker like the play master. 'I'll give you manners.'

'May the force be with you,' smiled Maddie as she handed over her remote.

Removing his glove, he took the two remotes and placed one in each of his jacket pockets, then struck a pose like John Wayne.

'Now I finally have the power to control you two witches. Whenever you're disobedient, I must punish you. You have been warned.'

'I've been a very naughty girl,' cooed Maddie. And like a coiled-up elastic band he snapped back 'Take that,' all the while keeping his hands hidden in his pockets.

'Ahhhh – switch it off,' squealed Maddie, 'stop it, stop it now!'

'OK, OK, but I can't forget *you*, my pretty.'

And with that Parker switched off Maddie's vibrator and asserted his power over mine.

Just as Maddie ceased screaming I took over, and he persisted in playing this tag tennis screaming game until the *maître-d* came over to the table and asked us to keep the noise down.

Recalling our wild days always helped to cheer us up, but despite having finally unwound from the day's events, I was definite that I didn't want people to think that I had been arrested in Malaga.

I had been fired, dumped, evicted, fired again and now this. Detained under suspicion of having dodgy mates was too much to comprehend, but I didn't think I could cope if Anna caught wind of us three being hauled over by the Gardaí.

She might have been back in Dublin, but that didn't stop her soaking up gossip from the Costa.

'You have had one toxic year, Eva Valentine. You and Britney Spears should hook up and compare notes. You know, you could give her a run for her money in the car crash stakes. All you need to do is cut off that fabulous hair of yours and replace it with some cheap hair extensions and you're matched.'

Now in familiar territory Parker was back to his old self and thankfully not moaning about missing Jeff.

'Actually I was thinking of adopting some peasant children from some impoverished country, and then allowing a tabloid journalist to witness me locking them up with a couple of pitbull terriers just to outdo her.'

'Don't talk about babies like that. It freaks me out.' Maddie's little face looked bruised. Even though she knew we were messing, her hormones lately seemed to react badly to news of neglected children.

'You know Britney went to get her spray tan done the day she handed her kids over to K-Fed,' explained an animated Maddie.

'Who fucking told you that?' demanded an un-impressed Parker.

'I heard it on TV3. Lorraine Keane said it so it must be true.'

'Mmmm, I wonder will our brush with the law make it into their Daily Dish?' Parker winked at me as he spoke.

'Jesus Christ, you don't think? Really? Fuck . . . no . . . ah, God . . . fuck . . . no!' Maddie went into a near hypo.

'Calm down, hon, don't mind him, he's only winding you up. Aren't you, Parker? I said: aren't you, Parker?'

'Of course I am, little Miss Up-the-duff. But I think you have to be more careful who you talk to in the future.'

'Excuse me?'

'I'm serious. I think you need to concentrate on yourself and forget about flirting with randoms.'

'Get her,' squealed Maddie indignantly, 'that's a bit rich considering you're all loved-up. How easily you seem to forget what it's like to be lonely.'

'Trust me, pet, you won't be lonely for long. When the invisible junior here pops out, you'll never be lonely again. Stressed, exhausted and possibly frumpy – but not lonely.'

Maddie was just about to face up to Parker when Amancio arrived at our table bearing delicious-smelling food. 'Exquisite ladies and da beautiful Parker – ' he winked at me while placing our meals in front of us – 'dinner is served.'

Half starved, Maddie couldn't stay angry at Parker as she tucked into her ribs with the ferociousness of a wild animal.

'Ea-zy, tiger,' smiled Amancio in his warm Spanish accent. 'Watch the threads, I've a lady I need to impress tonight, huh?' He kissed my hair and then disappeared as quickly as he had arrived.

'I know I can't talk, but you'd never know where that fella's been. You could catch rabies or anything.' Parker for once was talking a little sense.

'I know, but he's very cute and an amazing kisser. He's one of my most steady boyfriends. Five years, sorry six years we've been coming here . . .'

'Yeah – and – every visit – you let him – molest you. It's disgusting,' Maddie somehow managed to say in between sucking the life out of her spare ribs.

'Now girls, handbags please. Just because he fancies Eva instead of you doesn't mean you have the right to totally diss him. He's a fine figure of a man. If a little riddled.'

'I'm eating.' The word 'riddled' didn't sit well when I had food in my hands.

'Sorry. OK, I think we need a toast.' Parker composed himself with his freshly filled glass.

'Here's to—'

'Escaping jail,' I interrupted.

'Yes . . . But hang on, raise your glasses, girls. Let's toast all the positives.'

'Which are?' Maddie's back was still up.

'Well, friendship. Unless some sugar daddy steps up and offers to pay for dinner I'll be forking up the lettuce tonight, so that must mean something.'

'Thank you Parker' – 'Yes, thanks Parker.' We dipped our heads in appreciation and embarrassment. Without him, this whole trip would not have been feasible.

'OK,' I took it upon myself to make a speech, and stood up.

'I'd like to make a proper toast, to dear friends, also known as partners in crime.' Both Parker and Maddie squeezed out a giggle. 'Parker, under that sarcastic venomous tongue of yours lies a good heart . . .'

'You've just got to dig deep . . .'

'Yes, thank you, Maddie. As I was saying, Parker you are my hero, without you these last few months I would have sunk, and I want to formally thank you now. So cheers to you.' Together we clinked our glasses.

'And to new friends we haven't met yet.' Parker and Maddie looked at each other with puzzled faces.

'Maddie's baby,' I whispered.

'Oh thank God,' gasped Parker, holding his hand to his chest for dramatic effect, 'I thought you wanted to go cruising for more felonious fellas. I don't think my heart could take any more excitement for one day.'

Just then Amancio caught my eye and waved at me to follow him outside.

'Oh, sorry guys, I'll be back in a minute,' I put my glass on the table and tousled my hair for a fuller look. 'I've gotta go see a man about a dog.'

'Watch out for the rabies,' laughed Parker as I stepped past him on a mission.

I didn't care about the other women, I needed some Amancio lovin'.

If you can't beat 'em, join 'em, I thought. What goes on tour, stays on tour – let's hope!

'*Por favor*, can I have *dos* well-done burgers, *uno* club sandwich, but hold the bacon – no bacon, emmm, *tres grande agua sin gas*, and *tres grande* Coke Light . . . *Gracias*.'

It was 5p.m. Parker and myself had only managed to make it down to the pool, and this was breakfast. Maddie was none too impressed. Possibly thinking she was German, she had placed our towels on the sunbeds closest to the bar and beside the shower unit at 8a.m. She said she couldn't sleep with the loud drunken snores from Parker and me.

Although we had our own extremely fabulous private pool at Parker's family villa, we always gate-crashed the neighbouring five-star hotel as we didn't have a live-in chef and the only passing tits were crested or blue ones!

Great for parties when you had a gang but quite lonely if you're hungover and in the mood for people-watching.

'So? Have fun last night?' Maddie was trying to hide her jealousy. She had felt sleepy after the meal and had had to retire early so we dropped her back to the house before hitting a few pubs and clubs.

'I couldn't tell you,' groaned Parker, as he carefully lathered Factor 25 on his face, making sure not to coat his rectangle-rimmed black Prada shades.

'Ask the disco diva here beside me. I felt like an irresponsible parent going off and leaving you on your own, but the energizer bunny here was a woman possessed, and there was no way she was going home till she'd wiggled her wobbly bits in everyone's face.'

'Well, neither of you would have noticed if I'd gone missing in Fernando's after those footballers came over to the table,' complained Maddie.

'They were new in town,' I pleaded, 'and needed some guidance. They'd only been given the names of a few dingy bars, so I decided to take them under my wing.'

'You mean your bingo wings,' chuckled Parker.

'Listen here, Mr Universe, I'd had a stressful day and needed to forget about my worries. You were hardly an unwilling participant.' One of my final memories of Parker was of him balancing on a brick wall singing Mika's 'Grace Kelly' at the top of his lungs, while I was screaming at the barman I had earlier snogged, because he wanted me to get into his tiny car and wouldn't take no for an answer.

Eventually he had driven off in a huff, and Parker had dismounted with a few screams of his own when he looked at his scuffed shoes.

'So did either of you girls get lucky?' enquired a now inquisitorial Maddie, hungry for gossip.

'Well, I got lucky with everyone from the waiter to the barman . . .' I was still technically drunk, so in my mind this revelation was hilarious.

'Yeah, and probably the toilet cleaner in between,' said Parker.

'Ha, there were no loo attendants that I can remember. There was some other fella I kissed on the stairs of the Maroon Bar, but I think he wanted to buy me for the night so we did a legger.'

'So you had a laugh anyway?' Maddie's voice mellowed as she saw the waitress return with our drinks.

'I think Eva may have got us barred from Sinatra's, but yeah, it was a pretty fun night – how you feeling today *bella mama*?'

'Bored!'

'Well, we can't have that, *ma chica*. How can Sue

249

Ellen here and myself make it up to you? Can we
take you down to that hotel on the strip beside the
cosmetic surgery hospital and look at all the Bridies in
bandages? That's always worth a giggle.'

'Nah, it's fine, I'm just a bit restless in myself. I'll
feel better after some food. I thought you guys were
never going to reappear.'

'You know, she's had her feet done now.' Only one
half of my brain seemed to be working, which resulted in a ridiculous half-assed statement.

'What?' rhymed my pals.

'Lisa,' I said, as my tired eyes locked into a stare at
the gnarled feet of a glamorous granny several sunbeds
up. 'Lisa's had collagen or something injected in the
balls of her feet. Apparently it's very much in vogue.'

'Why would you have collagen put in your feet?'
Maddie asked now, examining her own.

'Are you telling me she thinks she has too many
wrinkles on her feet? That woman is barking, I tell
ya,' said Parker.

'No.' I snapped out of my daze. 'She said models
and high-powered businesswomen get it so they can
stand in high heels all day.'

'Are you sure? It sounds made up.' Being a model
herself, Maddie always assumed she knew everything
about the fashion business and never took knowledge
from mere mortals well.

'It's bizarrely true, it numbs your feet so you can't
feel pain, I think. Pity you can't use it for broken
hearts, eh? Sore feet I can handle.'

'Mmmm, I thought she had outdone herself when she got Botox in her armpits to stop her sweating, but collagen in her feet has gotta warrant being committed to rehab again.'

'That's probably what she wants,' smiled Parker. 'Remember the last time she was in? She said that old alco was her best sex ever. If Jeff wasn't so damn perfect I'd consider going too.'

'Ha! I wonder do they do group rates?' I was only marginally serious.

'Group rates for single mother models, homosexuals and bisexuals please.'

'I'm not a bisexual, Parker, I'm a trisexual.' I paused for dramatic effect.

'More like trisexual two-or-three-times. 'Cause you've definitely tried most things more than once,' squealed Maddie.

Our giggles were interrupted by a waitress handing us plastic cartons of food. It was hardly fancy nosh, but I was so hungry I was considering turning cannibal.

'Can I get you anything else?' asked the friendly waitress with a big smile, clearly hunting for a good tip.

'Yes,' piped up Parker. 'Are you a spit or a swallow?'

'Excuse me?' asked the waitress, puzzled.

'Sorry, doesn't matter,' said Parker, doubling over in a fit of laughter.

'What's up with him?' Poor Maddie didn't get the joke.

'One of those "had to be there" moments,' I muttered, putting a handful of chips in my mouth.

'Typical. What did I miss out on now?' Maddie threw her hands in the air in despair.

Parker couldn't reply. He thought he'd been hilarious, and was now nearly choking. I was about to explain when a message beeped on my phone and saved me; after all, I couldn't eat and talk happily at the same time.

Rooting through the girlie pink plastic beach bag I'd got free with a magazine at the airport, I negotiated my way through spare towels and found my phone, already covered in sand from the old half-used bottles of sunscreen it was stuffed in with.

I had one new message.

'Michael's Cell' flashed up.

Fuuuuuuuccccccck!

I stared at the phone, frozen with fear. It couldn't possibly be . . . Michael?

I was terrified to open the text because of what it might say, so I flung the mobile on the sunbed and held my head in shock.

What could he possibly want after all this time? The bastard hadn't been in touch in four months.

'Is everything OK?' Maddie was the only one to notice my behaviour. Parker was still in a world of his own.

'No.' My voice reeked of self-pity.

She moved over to me and put her arm protectively over my shoulder. 'What is it?'

'It's Michael.'

'Michael who?'

'Michael New York Michael.'

'Oh fuck, that asshole. What does he want?'

'I don't know . . . I can't open it . . . You do it.'

'Did you say – Michael?' Parker managed to stop laughing just enough to speak.

'He's texted her,' said Maddie.

'I'd delete it,' smarted Parker. 'Don't read it. It'll only fuck with your head.'

'I can't delete it.' Or could I? Maybe Parker was right.

Maddie gave me one of her new motherly looks and asked, 'Do you want me to read it?'

'Yes . . . No . . . Emmm . . . OK.' Why did he have to text now? I had just stopped thinking about him and his fabulousness.

'Here,' I handed her the phone. 'Read it, then.'

Enthusiastically grabbing it, she sheltered out of the sun to look at the screen and then gasped.

'What does it say?' I had changed my mind. I wanted my phone back – *now*!

'You don't want to know,' Maddie cringed.

'Give me the phone,' I snapped, jumping up to grab it back.

Oh–my–God . . . The words 'I love U xox' were spread across the screen.

Was I reading it right? Did my long-lost New Yorker actually love me? This had to be a sick joke.

'Well, what did he say? Ask for forgiveness? Declare his undying love for you, what?'

'Shut up, Parker.' My mind was reeling.

What should I do? Do I reply? If so, what do I say? Do I tell him he broke my heart?

'Well?' Parker was now extremely curious.

'It says 'I love U xox' – it must have been sent to me by mistake.'

'I told you so,' Parker sang the words with delight.

'I told you so, what?'

'You should have deleted it. That's going to wreck your head now, because there's no way you *can't* text him back after that.'

He was right, as usual. I might not text him back straight away. But I would have to know. Was this text meant for me? Or is he already in love with someone else with a name similar to mine?

I couldn't make this decision sober.

I flagged down our waitress and ordered two Bloody Marys and a Virgin Bloody Mary. Even if Maddie wasn't drinking, she had to at least feel part of the group.

Several rounds later we had exhausted every possible excuse as to why I received the text.

(a) He was drunk and missing me.

(b) He had meant to send the text to someone else.

(c) Someone had taken his phone and sent the message to wind him up.

I was hoping he missed me, but I wasn't feeling that

lucky, and of course Parker had rubbished the idea completely.

So I told myself it was either a simple mistake or a terribly evil joke, but somehow I couldn't let it go. I had really fallen for this guy. He was the most exciting man/person I had met in years, although he was far from perfect. Surely it was worth finding out if he had really sent that message of love to me?

What could I lose? I had been stripped bare, metaphorically speaking, and lost everything that I had ever possessed, dignity included, over the last five months.

It was time to gamble.

Fuck it. When Parker and Maddie took to the pool for a swim to cool off I grabbed my phone and texted, 'Hey sexy . . . Long time no hear . . . How U?' And pressed SEND before I could change my mind.

OK, I'd done it now. Best forget all about it and get on with my holiday.

Adjusting my La Perla bikini, which really had seen better days, I stood up to join the others in the pool. There were some cute boys cooling their feet down the opposite end, so my plan was to busy myself with attracting their attention and see what fun I could find myself.

I had just stuck my big toe in the water to check the temperature when I heard my phone beep through a message.

No way? It couldn't be? Could that actually be from Michael?

I rushed back to my sun lounger so quick I nearly gave myself whiplash.

'1 New Message.'

'Michael's Cell.'

Open . . . 'Hey U, it's me. I'm in Dublin, where U @?'

Arggggggggggggghhhhhhhhhh!

8

'If my husband was ever with you, I'd never touch him again. 'Cause you're so contaminated.'

It was the statement of the evening, and it left everyone gobsmacked.

It was 16 October, so it was Lisa's twenty-fifth birthday celebration, again. As if constantly reliving the same party, Lisa never aged, in years or looks. And after an extremely boozy afternoon with fourteen of her nearest and dearest at the Shelbourne Hotel, the party was well and truly under way.

But despite the love that had been shown around the table at our five-course lunch, events took a nasty turn when her sister Joy took offence at a comment Maddie made about her husband Tristan.

It was an innocent off-the-cuff remark, but Maddie got her face verbally smacked when she said, 'I wish I could get my hands on a husband like yours.'

What was most ridiculous was that at a now robust

nine months pregnant, Maddie wasn't fit to do anything more than smile at a man; her stomach had amazingly swelled so far out that it was hard enough to get close to her just to give her a hug.

In her naïvety she thought she was complimenting Joy's husband, whom she thought was extremely plain and boring as hell, but instead the Joy-less one became viciously aggressive.

We had never been her biggest fans before, but stupidly drunk or not, she had dug her own grave as far as any sort of future friendship was concerned. If Lisa wasn't such a loyal chum, she'd have instantly told Joy off in some choice colourful language.

Her derogatory outburst witnessed by at least half of the group, Joy stormed off to grab her most desirable hubby and vacate the party, leaving Maddie with her jaw on the ground. Thankfully she had taken the initiative to leave herself, before Lisa became aware of the altercation.

As she strutted out the door with her pencil-thin nose in the air and what looked like a poker stuck up her backside, she clutched the witless Tristan with the grasp of a bitch in heat.

For all her money and looks, all anyone could see in her was her ugliness. Part of me was thrilled that she had exposed her nasty streak in such a spectacular fashion. But it had been at a cost: Maddie's pride.

Between the pressure on her bloated ankles, the pains in her side, back and nipples, the recent lack of sleep and the worry over stretchmarks, Maddie was already a basket case. She felt ashamed that she was about to become a statistic – an unmarried mother – and the last thing she needed was for her nose to be rubbed in it.

And of course, she took it badly.

But no one could have forecast the result of such a clash.

'I've nowhere to stay. Just call me Mary . . . Sooooo, is there any chance I can crash here for a bit?'

Maddie was standing at the door of Parker's apartment with several bags and a wheelie case in tow. It was the Sunday afternoon after Lisa's birthday bash the night before, and Parker had the expression of someone who was hallucinating.

'Can I come in at least?' Maddie pleaded, still waiting for an answer.

Parker stood silent, his jaw open and a frightened look on his face.

'Jesus Christ, I'm growing old here,' she complained, before brushing past him to make her way towards me on the couch.

'Cooome in, why don't you? wheezed Parker, sounding like he had been drinking whiskey for forty years.

'Everything all right?' I questioned, feeling just as bad as Parker sounded.

But it was obvious from her baggage that Maddie's home situation was in crisis.

Waddling past, huffing and puffing, she threw her jacket on the floor and lowered herself gently down beside me.

'No. Everything is not all right. I'm officially homeless. Do you think Parker will let me stay?'

'I'm in the room,' cried my hungover surrogate father. 'I'd rather you talk to me instead of that free-loader.'

As favours went, this was a bad morning to be asking him anything.

'I don't particularly want to know the answer, but why are you here? And what the hell are you doing with all these bags?'

'Well, I was a little upset last night and I kinda picked a fight with my mother.'

'And why does that land you at my door?' Parker was showing no signs of compassion for her story so far, and Maddie knew she'd have to pull harder at his heartstrings.

'Because the miserable bitch I formerly called my mother told me I was no longer welcome in her house, and that I would have to face up to my responsibilities, and that she was ashamed to face her neighbours because of the embarrassment I had brought on the family. Having a drunk as a husband was bad enough, but now having an unmarried daughter as well was like living through *Angela's Ashes*.'

Knowing I should keep my opinions to myself, I subtly winked at Maddie to acknowledge she had made a convincing argument for Parker. Having spent

decades of feeling persecuted for being gay, Parker
always sided with the underdog.

'She's embarrassed by you, yeah?'

'Apparently she is.'

'You're something else . . . you know that? And
you're looking for me to take you in?'

Afraid she'd say the wrong thing, Maddie simply
nodded.

Visibly disorientated, Parker stormed off to the
kitchen muttering before returning swigging on a
two-litre bottle of Ballygowan water.

After taking the longest possible gulp, a rehydrated
Parker seemed to be softening, but he wasn't ready to
roll over yet.

'Am I your first or last safe house to call on?'

'Eh, you're the only option I have . . .'

'There's no one else you can ask?'

'No . . . Listen, if you want me to look up the
Golden Pages for Women's Refuge Centres I will. I
just thought you might like to be my hero.'

'Ah Jaysus, do I have "EASY" written across my
forehead?' Parker smirked, before dropping his head
in his hands.

'Christ, woman, you're pregnant. You're about
to drop a baby. This apartment might look like the
recovery wing of Mount Carmel hospital, but I
know nothing about babies, and I don't think this
bachelorette pad is quite the place for a newborn.'

'But Parker . . .'

'But nothing. What if you break your waters on my

cream carpets? Or worse still, on one of my beds. If I had wanted water beds I would have bought some.'

'But I can't go back to my mother's. She hates me.' Maddie added tears to her performance for extra influence.

'Don't cry . . . Oh, for pity's sake, stop it. Ring the bloody Samaritans if you fancy spilling tears. Eva, can you do something with her?'

I had just put a caring arm around her when a seriously dishevelled Jeff walked out of Parker's bedroom in nothing but a pair of tight leopard-print boxer shorts, leaving little or nothing to the imagination.

'What's with the Broadway production out here? I'm surprised half the block hasn't knocked in to complain of the noise. Oh, I was in a beautiful sleep. Barbra Streisand and I were having a barbecue. And she was in the middle of telling me how wonderful a kisser Robert Redford was.'

Momentarily abandoning the unfolding drama, Parker melted when he saw his lover and gushed, 'To think he used to think he was straight. Bless . . .'

'Yes, party boy, I'm no longer a waste. Now what's the problem?'

'I haven't the energy to put up a fight any more. Our pregnant friend here is looking for a room. But not just for the night.'

'And what's the problem?' Jeff seemed puzzled.

'AND we're a full house.'

'No we're not. It's a three-bedroom apartment. Eva

might have exploded a clothes bomb over one room, and I might have filled more than one spare drawer in your boudoir, but the extra room is just used as a wardrobe-overflow. Don't be such a Scrooge. Of course you can stay, Maddie.'

Jeff playfully smacked Parker's behind and gave him one of his don't-argue-with-me looks. He always got his own way. It was amazing to watch. No one could stop Parker in his tracks quite like Jeff.

'There's not even an *en suite* I can call my own any more,' whimpered Parker.

'So what? Would you prefer to be lonely again? I vaguely remember you telling me you couldn't bear the thought of life without me last night. And you never wanted to come home to an empty apartment again.'

'I had always wanted to share my home with a partner, not half the cast of *Friends*.'

'Get over it,' hissed Jeff, 'it's a done deal. She's your friend and she needs our help. When you feel claustrophobic you can hide out at my place. There's three thousand square feet at the K Club which has been gathering dust ever since I met you.'

'It looks like I've been overruled. I suppose if you must stay, you must stay.' Parker was defeated and deflated, but he always got over these mini strops fast.

'Eh, now say it like you mean it,' scolded Jeff, determined to show off his dominance.

'Oh for God's sake, I would love for you to stay,

Maddie. In fact . . . stay as long as you like. You just took me by surprise, that's all.'

'Good boy. Now that's sorted I can go back to bed. Catch you later, girls.'

And with that Jeff turned on his heel, whipping Parker's bottle of water out of his hands and shouting, 'I'll be waiting' as he got to the door of their bedroom.

Somewhat dazed and confused, Parker muttered 'Sheets', before disappearing off with Maddie's bags into the room beside mine.

It was a monumental occasion.

Parker coerced into submission in his own home, without as much as a gun put to his head.

I expected pigs to fly through the window any minute . . .

Michael and I had been texting on and off for the four months since I had missed his visit to Dublin. I was sort of fed up with the whole idea of me and him since I had come to the conclusion he was a total shit and nothing but a player. But he said he was planning to return to Dublin again before the end of the year and he had teasingly said he wanted me to be his Christmas box!

I never expected the shock I would feel when I actually received a text reading 'THE EAGLE HAS LANDED!!!'

On first viewing I screamed.

On the second I felt nauseous.

On the third I texted back, 'You don't get to come till I say so!'

It took him all of twenty seconds to send back, 'SHOW ME THE MONEY @ THE HARTLEY HOTEL PENTHOUSE . . . when can u get here?'

I ran next door to show Maddie, but she was napping, so in a moment of madness I texted back, 'Order me some bubbly and wait and see . . .' I then jumped in the shower, almost killing myself on a loose tray mat, and scrubbed myself feverishly. Several minor razor cuts later, I was sitting in front of my full-length mirror dripping all over Parker's carpet as I tried to trowel on my night-time-look make-up.

It was a messy process as I was steaming up the joint, what with the shower and the naughty thoughts I was having.

Thankfully my liquid eyeliner went on straight the first time, which I took as a really good omen. So I buffed off my skin with half of my reserve bottle of Flamingo Fancy body glow and slid into an all-black balcony bra, thong and suspender set. Although it was a Marks & Spencer buy, I felt I looked as sexy as if I was wearing some kinky Agent Provocateur number.

Without a second to waste I speedily fastened up my opaque black stockings, but took care to make sure that their sexy 1940s red seam up the back was zigzag free.

To finish the look I stepped into vintage black Dior peep-toe heels and belted up my Carrie Bradshaw mac. I was subtly filthy and felt erotically charged. I couldn't wait to flash Michael the complete show. The Valentine in full glory . . . Let's hope he still found me hot stuff or I was about to make a complete tit out of myself.

As I charged out of the apartment I prayed no one else would be at the Hartley. Imagine having to sit sweltering in my mac as I swapped small talk with some of his mates or colleagues!

But the not knowing made this a sort of fantasy role-play – 'Tonight, Matthew, I'm going to be Madonna in *Body of Evidence*' – only instead of standing on a car bonnet and lifting my coat, I'd lie on the piano all Michelle Pfeiffer in *The Fabulous Baker Boys* and let Michael devour me like the tart that I wanted to be.

Thankfully I had seen the penthouse once before after attending a *Desperate Housewives* finale screening there years back, so I knew what to expect from the décor at least.

I just had to convince myself not to be overly disappointed if he hadn't covered his bed in rose petals, stacked several bottles of pink champagne on ice beside the Jacuzzi and bought an engagement ring the size of something Liz Taylor would wear.

I'd hate to build up my expectations.

But surely that wasn't too much to expect from our reunion date?

He screamed, 'Surprise!' as he opened the door. What he should have said was, 'Girlfriend, I'm gonna wake up the shallow bitch in you.'

When I say he had a spot the size of Wales on the

side of his right cheek, it's not a word of a lie. Its ugly presence was partially bearable when he turned slightly away from me as he led me down a long hallway, but it really belonged in a university laboratory.

What the fuck?

Not only was it the sort of pimple that only a rugby scrum could squeeze, its glow-in-the dark yellow hue was similar to the radioactive substances aid worker Adi Roche would campaign to have villages evacuated from.

While I was determined to focus on the rest of his face and body . . . such a cute ass . . . and what muscular hands . . . I couldn't help but stare at the alien pod on his face.

I tried to fight the gawking, but as people who own Barry Manilow noses and Lolo Ferrari bosoms will know, it's impossible for others not to gape.

'It's a spider bite,' he said after becoming aware of my Kryptonite.

'Did you get to bite him back?' I teased, hoping to sound breezy.

'I'm still picking him out of my boot,' laughed Michael as he stood at the end of the hall. And just as I caught up with him, he exposed bad news number two as he swung open a door and said, 'Miss Eva. Say hi to the gang.'

He might as well have told me he was holding a Ku Klux Klan meeting, for all the interest I had in getting acquainted.

As I stuck my head through the door my fake smile

wavered at the sight of about twenty people lounging around my seedy lust den.

It was a massive loft-style suite and it was saturated with grumpy arty types, smoking, eating and listening to some young hairy guy murder a guitar medley. Michael, as per usual, had more friends than I was comfortable with. Through gritted teeth I managed, 'Nice to meet you all', sounding ridiculously American, but judging by my reception they were as excited to see me as I was them.

'Most of them will be too stoned to remember your name,' explained Michael as he manoeuvred me round some badly stacked boxes, suitcases and camera equipment. 'So I'll pass on the intros. Fancy a drink?'

'Eh, please . . .'

Although I just wanted to run a mile from the lot of them – as this was *not* the anecdote I wanted to recall for Parker and Maddie – I thought I'd at least accept a drink to calm my nerves, and then do my Houdini. With lethargic bodies strewn all about the place, I suggested I wait outside on the back balcony while Michael fetched me a tasty beverage.

Thankfully it was mild for this time of year, so I settled myself on a large wooden chair beside a grand table, which I'm sure had hosted many a supermodel dinner party, and sulked.

The balcony had a great view of the city, and I watched the cars and shoppers go by. For a woman with such a privileged view I felt very grouchy; even more so when a passing seagull nearly shat on my shoe.

As I changed seats Michael reappeared with two bottles of Heineken. It was not what I had envisaged. But a quick beer was exactly what I needed to give me a lift. He pulled another heavy seat beside me, kissed me on the head like a child and asked, 'Well, did you miss me?'

I thought about lying and saying no. I thought about smacking him across the face and calling him a bastard, but thought better of it when I visualized his spot. Instead I counted to ten, held my composure, and calmly said, 'You broke my heart just a little. It turned out you were the heart-breaker.'

Amazingly he looked surprised, and said 'Ohhhh,' before filling his mouth with his bottle.

'Yes, ohhhh,' I retorted, confident that the truth was the way to go.

'You promised me the sun, moon and stars and then the second I walked out of Primrose Hill you seemed to forget all about me. Why would you do that?' I tried to make it sound like the hurt was all in the past, but a lump somehow leaped into my throat and caught me off guard.

And then just to spite myself, I showed total female vulnerability – tears.

What a total disaster. OK, so they weren't Sinead O'Connor, 'Nothing Compares To You' tears. They were just crafty make-a-bloke-feel-bad tears. But they weren't planned, and I was finding it hard to fight them.

'Gosh, I'm sorry, Eva,' Michael said. He took my

beer out of my hand and placed it with his on the ground – just like a re-enactment of the first night we met – and then cuddled me close.

He still had that strong smell of Davidoff. It was divine. If it hadn't been for the spot and my embarrassing dumped lover act I would have hopped him right there and given the tourists something to write home about.

But this fantasy wasn't going according to plan.

'I just thought it might have been easier on you if I broke contact,' he said, lifting my face so we could lock eyes. 'As you mad Irish would say, I'm a bit of a bollix, I just couldn't help myself with you. You were so damn fine. And may I say you look extremely hot this evening.'

'You may,' I sniffed, melting once again with his dreamy eyes. 'Now give me my beer back. I'm far too sober for this malarkey.'

'Ma-larkey?' he questioned.

'Yes, malarkey,' I replied, unsure how to explain the word.

'All-righty then.' He looked at me blankly for a second before breaking out in a giggle.

'What's so funny?' I snapped, worried that he was laughing at me for not being cool.

'Sorry, it's just I've been dying to ask one thing since you've arrived.'

'What's that, dare I ask?'

'Well . . . I was just wondering what you might, or might not, be wearing under that mac coat of yours.'

'Still got that dirty mind of yours?' I smirked, in the knowledge that he still found me attractive.

'Damn sure,' he said, as his eyebrows danced. 'And if I was to make a bet I'd say you've got a treat for me under there.'

I was just about to lift up my coat and give him a sneaky peek when some muso type popped his head around the corner. He wore ridiculous oversized white-rimmed shades, purple skinny jeans and two off-white layered Ts, both of which were too short to cover his hairy bellybutton.

'Hey bucket carrier – you're up,' he said, signalling to Michael to get his ass back inside.

He shouted back, 'Two minutes!' almost bursting my eardrum, and then turned back to me with puppy-dog eyes.

'It's fine, just go,' I said, sounding incredibly pissed off, which I was.

'It's just we've a big shoot on here tonight, so I better get the crew together and make this thing happen. Why don't you head off for a bit and I'll call you when we're done.'

'Can I not stay and watch you in action? Maybe I could help.'

'Sorry, pumpkin, I don't like any distractions while I work. Don't worry, we'll catch up later, I promise. Now you better go.'

And with that, he took my hand and started to lead me back through the throng of now busy bodies and then along the hall towards the lift.

As he kissed me goodbye at the door I felt myself slipping into a sulk again.

What a big baby I was.

'You can show me what's underneath that coat then,' he smirked, 'and—' We were rudely interrupted by the same guy again.

'Listen, fella,' he hollered, 'hurry the fuck up, there's shit here that won't move itself!'

For the first time I saw a different side to Michael, a flustered one. Without another word, he kissed me again and pushed me out the door, slamming it behind me.

I stood just outside the door for a couple of minutes trying to figure out what to do.

I was a single girl who was wearing nothing more than knickers and a coat, and had stale beer breath. Where could I possibly go?

Fuck it, I thought, calling the lift. This was the sexy city of Dublin. The possibilities were endless for a woman like me.

I didn't need to hang around here like a pathetic groupie. I was just going to step out into the night and see where the streets would take me.

The cute barman handed me a glass of champagne and said, 'Compliments of the two gentlemen in the corner. They said don't be lonely.'

I had only made it as far as Rounder's Bar downstairs in the Hartley. But it was as good a place as any to entertain myself.

As I thanked the barman I stretched on my stool to see where he was pointing, and found two attractive guys raising their glasses to me. Politely I toasted them back with their champagne, which somehow gave them the green light to get up out of their seats and walk towards me.

With no time to think, I could only fix my hair and look approachable.

'Thank you for my drink,' I gushed as the duo arrived over.

'You're more than welcome,' said the better-looking of the two, and then introduced himself. 'I'm Bill, and this is Mark.'

Since they had Dublin accents and didn't have the appearance of escaped mental patients, I kept smiling. After all, they were the best offer – well, only offer – of company I had had so far.

A couple beside me got up to leave. Bill looked at their vacated seats and asked, 'Would you mind if we joined you?' The word 'Sure' had barely left my mouth when my new mate Mark came out with a cheesy line that sort of annoyed me.

'Of course she'd like us to join her. She's too beautiful to be drinking alone.'

But I realized that I was a bit tetchy from my disappointment with Michael, so I laughed it off and said, 'Bet you say that to all the girls,' meaning every word of it.

An hour and two glasses of champagne later Bill and Mark had told me that they were part-time models and in the middle of recording an album. Apparently they had spent the afternoon putting down a 'really funky tune' in Brian McFadden's old studio and were certain that it would get picked up soon. 'But we don't need that fucker Louis Walsh,' explained Mark. 'That asshole doesn't know what he's talking about half the time.'

Tiring of their endless wannabe banter I kept checking my phone, but no calls or texts were beeping through. While it had been fantastic to see Michael, even after all this time, I couldn't get it out of my head the way that scrawny guy had barked at him.

It seemed like a deep lack of respect for the photographer, especially one who had been flown over from New York to do the shoot.

Was Michael really the guy he said he was?

I was quickly dragged back out of my daydream when the two lads started to hum melodies.

I was mortified for them!

Although I wasn't usually made to feel uncomfortable by people being loud, other drinkers had started to stare, and these guys had really started to make me fidgety. In between their 'hummmms' and 'ah-haaaas' and their predictions of the death of Westlife, I knew I had to plan an exit.

But it was only when I had stepped up and made the excuse that I needed to use the toilet that the guys showed their true colours.

'Sorry, before you go,' Bill giggled, 'well, we were actually hoping you'd settle a bet for us.'

Somehow I sensed something bad, so I just flattened my fringe on my face and sternly said, 'Fair enough. What'ya wanna know?'

Instantly the two boys broke into fits of laughter, almost spilling their pints, before Mark piped up, 'What are you wearing under your coat? Bill reckons you're on the game, so you'd have nothing on underneath.'

I was speechless.

Did they just call me a prostitute?

As I stood and scowled at them, the two boys high-fived each other, repeatedly telling themselves, 'You the man' – 'No, you the man!'

I walked out of the bar.

There was no point in telling them off. It was standard behaviour for Dublin blokes, but how could they think that it was acceptable?

It was occasions like this that left me totally disillusioned by men.

There just had to be decent men out there waiting to adore or at least be nice to me, didn't there?

I walked about for twenty minutes to clear my head before finally making for the cobbled streets of Temple Bar where I settled in Tanta Zoe's for some grub. Having devoured some Cajun chicken popcorn and a bottle of Wolf Blass, I finally got the call I'd been waiting for.

'How's my Oirish queen?' His New York tone made my heart skip a beat.

'Fairly drunk,' I replied, slurring.

'Do I need to send out a search party for you? Or can you get back to the Hartley?'

'Nope, I'm just five minutes away in a taxi. Are ya ready for me?'

'I think I'll need to sink a few beers to prepare myself for the Eva invasion. But get your tasty ass back up here, beautiful. I'll be waiting. Oh, and I've a surprise for you.'

Ah fuck. I was dreading another surprise. Knowing my luck, he'd probably have a spot on his willy too!

'Eva, you've met Lucy, I believe.'

A broad grin spread across his face as he introduced me to his drinking partner.

Although the suite was still stuffed with luggage and equipment, all previous bodies had left. Lucy, *my* Lucy, had replaced the throng. And taken up a place at the bar with Michael.

'I asked her to join us for a drink. I hope you don't mind?'

I was choked. Did I mind? I was preparing myself for a big romantic reunion, and all of a sudden I walk in on a cosy drinks party.

I felt such a fool. This was not how I had imagined things working out.

I reached for the appropriate words as we politely kissed each other on both cheeks. 'Of course. Good to see you. So, eh, how do you two know each other?'

Before Michael had a chance to speak, Lucy piped up, 'We met last night, actually, at the Haven.'

'Really?' Automatically I flipped into jealous girl-friend mode.

Realizing that might get my back up, Michael quickly shoved a beer in my hand and said, 'I'm sorry, we got in late. I was going to call you, but . . .'

'But what?'

'But nothing. I should have called you straight away. Listen, I'm a bollix. Now let's just enjoy tonight. Lucy here tells me you're a very talented dancer.'

'Oh yeah?'

'And a kisser,' laughed Lucy as she banged her teeth on her glass of white wine.

'Lucy . . .'

'Ah relax, Eva. He knows about us. I know about you two.'

'And now we all know about each other. Cheers!' Michael raised his beer and encouraged us to do the same with our drinks.

Feeling too fuzzy to argue with them I pulled up a stool beside Lucy and tried to let the shock of seeing her and my anger over the fact that Michael hadn't called me the second he had arrived in Dublin Airport float over my head.

So I tried to 'Chillax' as Michael suggested and made an effort to enjoy the mutual flirting.

After a time we moved from the bar to the lounge to play CDs – and that's when Lucy kissed me. Like everything with this pair it came totally out of the blue. While Michael was sitting on the floor shifting through discs beside the CD player, Lucy found her moment and planted her lips on mine.

I wasn't entirely comfortable with it, but I didn't fight it.

And then, like the time before, I enjoyed her touch. So I went for it and kissed her back with months of pent-up emotion inside me. I had almost been living like a saint since the summer, in between looking after Maddie and the freelance work I had picked up with some new contacts.

But while this was what I considered having fun, and I was going with the flow, there was something niggling at the back of my mind . . .

No amount of free internet porn could equal the pleasure of standing in a penthouse suite, being kissed by a gorgeously hot sassy babe, so I blanked out my worries. Even though I considered myself straight, for a moment I almost forgot Michael was in the room – well, almost! As my ears swelled to the sound of Amy Winehouse's voice singing 'Valerie', my wet tongue played inside Lucy's mouth while our hands explored the other's body.

This wasn't the evening I had planned, but it served Michael right that I could enjoy Lucy's company more than his.

Of course Lucy was taking no prisoners and started to rub the curve of my waist and work her hands downwards. As I kissed her I just wanted to get even closer to her, so I pawed my way across her face, touching her silky hair which smelt so good, and grasped the back of her head to pull her as close as possible.

As I raised my arms in beat with the music I could feel my coat rise up a little.

Lucy already had her hands on my ass by this stage and I could sense her giggle as she tucked them under my hem to touch my peachy bare bum. I felt myself surrender to the naughtiness of the moment . . . then Michael put his arms around the two of us.

'Girls, girls,' he interrupted, 'let's not rush things. You gotta let me cut in on some of the play.'

Separating the two of us he put his arms around us and guided us towards the coffee table which had six parallel lines of coke measured up on it. 'Let's not lose pace,' he said as he handed Lucy a rolled up fifty. And then as he pulled me in for a kiss he whispered, 'I want this to be a long and special night. I can't have you falling asleep on me.'

So there I stood kissing Michael as I heard Lucy snort up two lines of coke.

As we stopped she handed me the note and walked off towards the balcony doors, adjusting her nose.

Feeling a little pressurized I offered the note to Michael to try and get myself off the hook, but he wouldn't take it, and insisted I did the coke.

'I don't need it,' I pleaded, but Michael wasn't taking no for an answer.

'Don't let the party down,' he said, as he kissed my cheek, 'get them into you and let's continue the party outside in the Jacuzzi.'

Did he just suggest the Jacuzzi? I had obviously thought about us slipping into the tub and the fun we might have, but that was before I realized Lucy was part of the set-up.

Did he mean the three of us in the Jacuzzi? What was I supposed to do? I've never been part of a threesome before. What the fuck is the protocol between two women and one man? Do we all go at it at once or do we take turns? I felt my heart racing and I hadn't even done any drugs yet.

Noticing my panic, Michael stroked my head and kissed me. 'It's OK. Don't worry, we'll take things nice and slow,' he told me.

'Michael . . .'

'Eva, everything's gonna be fine. Just relax. You're among friends and I'm gonna look after you. And so is Lucy.'

He pushed the outstretched hand which was holding the note back towards my chest and whispered, 'Come with me, baby.'

Although there was a part of me that wanted to flee, there was a bigger part of me that wanted to stay and let myself be free. This was far from an everyday occurrence so, reckoning I'd be a long time dead, I gave in to temptation.

Taking a leap of faith I knelt down at the table face to face with the coke. And there was no denying it scared me. So many young people had died in Ireland due to cocaine in the last few years. Was I going to be the next casualty?

Michael knew I wasn't a willing player so he rubbed my back and kept gently coaxing me, 'Let's not waste it, babe.'

Erasing all thoughts from my head, I decided just to go for it. It was now or never. So I tightened the rolled note and bent over my lines. With huge enthusiasm I began to snort the first line, but ran out of steam half-way through it. By now the competitive streak in me came out, so not wanting to be beaten by two seem-ingly simple lines of coke – Lucy had devoured hers with ease – I gave it another shot and polished off my designated drugs with gusto.

Expecting a massive rush, I was slightly dis-appointed when it didn't hit, so I stood up, passed the note to Michael, who practically ripped it out of my hand, and waited for my energy surge.

Initially my nose froze up and started to run, which was not the glamorous side-effect I had wanted. I ran back over to the bar and grabbed a napkin and tried to mop up the dribbles without ruining my make-up. I was swaggering back over to Michael, who had already finished his lines, when my whole body started to feel weird. I suddenly felt more confident and had the urge for conversation, yet my head felt light and my stomach a little sick. It was like nothing I had ever experienced before.

I wasn't sure if I liked it yet, but I was determined not to let it get the better of me.

'I want to dance!' I whooped, slapping Michael on the bum.

It was clear he had other ideas.

'Well, I want you to take that coat off. You've been teasing me all night with that thing on.'

Despite snorting a whole lot of confidence, I wasn't quite up for a striptease for both Michael and Lucy, even if I was very much attracted to both of them. I had to think quick to distract them from his suggestion.

'Can we order champagne first?'

'Too late.'

'What'dya mean? Too late for what?' I was confused by his answer.

'I've already ordered it, pumpkin. And it's waiting for us beside the Jacuzzi.'

'Oh . . .'

'And it's pink,' he explained as he spun me around and walked me towards the open balcony door.

We stepped outside into the fresh night – and there was Lucy straight in front of us already in the steaming tub taking full advantage of the hospitality.

'Come on in,' she said, topping up her glass with more champagne, 'the water is fantastic, and as you can see it's just as bubbly as the Laurent Perrier.'

By now the cocaine was obviously starting to work its magic, as the Jacuzzi with Lucy in it was looking like a plan.

But how would I get in?

Judging by the mound of clothes beside the Jacuzzi Lucy was already in her birthday suit, which put pressure on me to strip down too.

The way I saw it, I had one of two options. Either I could run back inside, strip down to the buff and come back out with a bathrobe wrapped around me. Or I could fling off my coat and jump into the water with all my underwear still on and then remove the offending items from the safety of the Jacuzzi.

I could worry about retrieving them after several gorgeous glasses of champers.

I might have been feeling bulletproof, but I wasn't quite cocky enough to do a Patricia the stripper on it, so as Michael started to open the belt on his jeans, I quickly threw my coat back into the suite, away from the possibility of getting wet, and made a bolt for the Jacuzzi.

I had already dipped myself up to my suspender belt when Michael realized what I was doing, so he gave me one of his naughty looks, wagged his finger at me and said, 'You may run, Miss Valentine, but you can't hide.'

As Lucy poured me a glass of champagne, she gave me a devilish wink. She looked set for boldness.

'He's very organized, your boy,' she said with a broad smile.

'Scarily so,' I agreed.

'Bottoms up?' she smirked, raising her glass for a toast.

'I hope you mean that literally,' said Michael as he brushed past Lucy, his penis dangling with a semi, and eased himself into the water between the two of us. 'Ahhh, now isn't this cosy? I've two of the hottest girls in Dublin, wet and wild.'

'So are you planning any other devious surprises?' I prayed for the answer to be no.

'What other surprises could there possibly be?' he asked in retaliation, rubbing his right hand across my thigh.

'Ach, anything is possible with you,' I slurred. Maybe it was his touch, the Jacuzzi, the champagne – then again, how could I forget about my first dalliance with coke? – but the combination of all four had started to ignite a craziness in me.

I was now as horny as hell, and undid my bra playfully, thinking I was Dita Von Teese, and flung it across the decking. It was followed by my stockings, which I foolishly ripped for dramatic effect, my suspender belt and then my thin black thong. Both Michael and Lucy cheered as I removed each item. I felt centre stage.

'Now we can get the party started,' whooped Michael as he splashed the water to make us scream again. 'That's what I love to hear,' he responded. 'I want to make you holler – but first I want to see you girls kiss again.'

'Do you like to see me kiss girls?' asked Lucy.

'Damn sure,' said Michael with a smirk.

'Hang on,' I interrupted, 'since when is it about what Michael likes to see you do?'

'Oh shush now, don't get all paranoid on me. Tonight is all about you, Eva. Isn't it, Lucy?'

I darted a look at Lucy and she just stared back at me, in fact almost through me. There was a coldness from her that I hadn't seen before. Instantly I felt a wave of panic flood over me. I wanted out. I wanted to be as far away from here as possible.

So I pushed across the pair of them and announced, 'I'm going.'

At once Michael put his hand on my shoulder and said, 'Stop right there, you're going nowhere.'

But I was completely freaked and I needed to get out. As I struggled to break loose of Michael's grip, Lucy growled, 'Just let her go. Let her go home and play with her dollies, I'm not in the mood for amateur night.'

'What the fuck does that mean?' My anxiety quickly flipped to anger.

'Nothing,' snapped Lucy, taking a large mouthful of champagne. 'I just know you're out of your depth here, so it's probably best if you go now.'

'What's that supposed to mean?' I demanded again.

'Well, I'd made a bet with Michael here earlier that you wouldn't be brave enough to take us on in the Jacuzzi. Michael seemed to think you'd be woman enough for the job, but I wasn't convinced. So it looks like I've won the bet.'

'You've made a bet about me?' I turned to Michael for clarification but he just shrugged his shoulders and continued to drink his champagne.

What should I do? My head was spinning. I was so frustrated. I wanted to walk out and take a stand, but I also wanted to prove myself. I *was* woman enough for this. I could be part of a threesome, yeah, I was going to show them just how impressive a lover I could be.

'Well fuck you two!' I screamed, reaching for the bottle to top up my glass. 'I want champagne kisses, so who's going to give them to me?'

Boisterously I took a mouthful of champagne and put my glass back down at the side of the Jacuzzi. Then automatically I leaned in to kiss Lucy. In my hazy state I thought: well, I'll show her.

In the background I heard Michael starting to get really aroused, but this kiss was all about Lucy and me. They weren't going to push me out of the fun. I was all about the fun!

As we pressed lips I could feel the bite of the bubbles from the champagne, and as she opened her mouth they trickled out of my mouth and into hers. For the first time all evening I felt I was the one in control. Michael might not have considered me the one for him, just one of the two for him, but I wasn't going to let my insecurities get the better of me. I would leave them both wanting more of Eva.

My Lucy moment was short-lived. Not content with being a voyeur, Michael snuggled his head between us just as our tongues began to swirl. But it didn't throw us, and the three of us enthusiastically picked up kissing each other, flicking tongues, biting lips and smacking naked bodies.

After all the messing about, this was a fantasy made real. And a lifelong memory not fit for the grandkids. I felt something fall on my head, and when I looked up I saw Michael pouring the champagne over us.

Like puppies Lucy and I scrambled to swallow the sweet nectar, our bare breasts brushing off each other in an effort to do so. Between the water and the hands, the breasts and the champagne, I almost lost sense of who was who. I was touching someone's body, but I didn't know whose it was.

And who owned the hands that were touching me? The intensity of the moment was almost unbearable. This was a pleasure overload.

Hands, breasts, tongues, bums – the Jacuzzi was almost swirling out of control . . . almost . . . almost . . . Shit. Was that a finger or a toe up my ass?

I woke to the sound of traffic.

I was stiff with the cold, yet my body was painful for reasons unknown to me.

When I cracked my eyes open I realized I was lying on a bench on the side of the road.

What the fuck?

I didn't move for a time as I tried to get my bearings. But I had to pull myself up to try and ascertain my full whereabouts.

As I sat up I saw blood. There was dried blood on my hands, across my legs and splattered across my coat.

I looked like I had been caught up in some teen slasher movie.

Looking around, I saw I was on St Stephen's Green. It was obviously still early morning as there weren't many cars around, but I was unsure how long I'd been asleep on the bench.

How did I get here?

Where was I last night?

Fuck, I was at the Hartley with Michael . . . Oh, my God, and Lucy . . .

Where were they now?

And what's with all the blood?

I repositioned my bum on the seat and got shooting pains up my back and stabbing pains across my temples.

Ouch!

Jesus, how did I get here? I gotta think . . .

As I stared down at my bare, bloodied legs, straining for inspiration, I got a flashback of the previous night's events.

I remember the Jacuzzi . . . There was champagne . . . Lucy was giving Michael a blowjob . . . And then . . . Ehhhh . . . Somebody threw a bottle.

Oh, my God, that's it. The three of us were in the Jacuzzi when some woman came out on to the balcony and flung a Heineken bottle at us which smashed a couple of glasses.

She was ranting, 'You fucking bastard, get those bitches out of here *now*!'

But how did I end up on a park bench on St Stephen's Green? And who was that madwoman?

Ohmigod, now I remember. She said she was

Michael's fiancée, in between screams that she'd cut his balls off.

My last memory was of her; she was standing over us shaking with the anger, and screaming, *'Out now!'* I then remember crawling on to the broken glass trying to clamber out of her way.

Considering the state I was in I thought it best if I got myself home before the Gardaí picked me up for soliciting, or some junkie grabbed me for his play-thing.

I opened my clutch handbag fearful of what, if anything, I would find. Thankfully I could see keys, a couple of €20 notes and my mobile.

So with my body aching like it had just run a marathon, my head pounding like I'd been hit over the head with a baseball bat, and the appearance of a hooker who'd brought her pimp home no money, I struggled towards the taxi rank down the road.

I was blessed that it was full, and that I had slipped into the first car before the driver even realized.

Although I kept our chat to a minimum he was giving me strange looks in his rearview mirror.

He finally worked up to asking 'Good night, luv?' in a sarcastic tone, to which I was able to reply, 'Just up here to the left, thanks.'

As I looked out the window trying to steady my nerves, I was hit with another flashback.

It was of Michael and Lucy whispering and laughing in the Jacuzzi. They then started telling me I wasn't brave enough to go all the way with Lucy.

Ohmigod, what had I done?

Although the journey only cost €8.50, I threw the taximan a €20 and told him to keep the change. I couldn't bear him scrutinizing me as he dragged out counting my change.

It was only when I got in the lift and saw myself in the mirrors that I discovered why he'd been giving me such strange looks.

Although the blood on my coat was out of his radar – I'd since worked out that it came from cuts on my left arm and left leg – I had massive black mascara streaks running down my face.

I was mortified. I truly looked a wreck. I even had an imprint of the bench across my face. The best thing I could do was jump into the shower, wash away the evidence and hit the hay. Sleep would be my friend. The longer I stayed awake, the more time I had to think about what I might have done.

But the second I turned the key in the latch I could hear screaming.

A nervous sounding Maddie cried, 'Eva, is that you?'

'Coming,' I answered, running in to her.

I found her on the side of her bed doubled over in pain.

When I knelt down beside her she looked up and screamed again. 'Jesus, what's up with you?'

I tried to distract her by asking, 'Listen, what's up with *you*?' But my appearance proved too intriguing.

'I'm having a baby, Sherlock. What the hell have you been at? Just come from a murder?'

She would have most likely kept barking at me only a contraction came along and shut her up. As she squealed I could nearly feel her pain from the expressions on her face.

She was squeezing the life out of my hands when Parker strolled into the room explaining, 'The taxi is going to be five minutes . . . Oh, dear God, did I miss the delivery?'

'Very funny, Parker, you're the only baby here so far . . .' My head was now having sympathy contractions with Maddie.

'OK, there's no time for cattiness, this fabulous beast here is about to have a baby. The taxi will be here any minute, so I suggest if you want to join Maddie on her journey into motherhood you get into the shower and fix yourself pronto.'

Without thinking, 'I'm wrecked' accidentally fell out of my mouth.

'*You're wrecked?*' Maddie screamed, then doubled over in pain again. 'I'm the one about to push a fuckin' basketball out of my fanny!'

'Yeah, sorry, I wasn't thinking.' My apology was lame and clearly not good enough for Maddie.

'Don't you dare start complaining, I've been having contractions since midnight. That's six and a half hours, and where the fuck have you been? You're supposed to be my birthing partner.'

'I think you better hop in the shower,' whispered

Parker, opting not to be facetious for once.

'Just hold tight,' I said, walking out the door. 'I'll be two minutes.'

Who was I kidding? I felt like death. How was I going to survive this morning?

I was in a lot of pain but Maddie needed me. This morning had to be all about her and her baby. I had to swallow some painkillers quick and try and blot out my own issues.

I was just pulling on some comfies when I heard the buzzer from downstairs.

'Taxi for Maddie,' said a voice.

'She'll be right down,' explained Parker. 'Girls, shake a leg.'

Instantly I got another flashback from the night before: Lucy sitting up out of the Jacuzzi with her legs wrapped around my shoulders.

Oh, dear God . . . Please say I didn't . . . ?

Could I have really gone down on Lucy?

I don't remember, but maybe . . . No, I couldn't have.

I'm just a social lesbian, one who occasionally kisses girls at the weekend. Yes, I can be a lesbian from the waist up, but I'm strictly hetero from the waist down.

That's it, I don't care how uncool it makes me, I am never doing coke again, no matter who bullies me into it. Parker and Maddie will freak when they hear what I've been doing.

'EVA!' Parker was screaming from the hall, 'EVA! Come on, Maddie's about to drop any second.'

'OK, I'm coming now.'

Right, it was time to concentrate. I'd just have to focus on the fanny I'd be looking at today, and forget about the fanny I can picture from last night.

'What can you see?'

'Nothing, I don't want to look.'

It was 2.42p.m. and Maddie was ten centimetres dilated and preparing herself to push.

'Eva pleeeeeease . . .' Maddie's rant was delayed by yet another contraction.

'Eh, there's nothing to tell yet, except that you're exceptionally well trimmed.'

This repetitive banter could have gone on for ever, but we were distracted by the entrance of the midwife Mary, whom we'd met when we were first admitted to Holles Street.

'Ladies,' she announced in a loud and stern voice. 'Listen up. A baby is about to be born, so we all need to concentrate.'

By now Maddie – and myself – had become extremely weak from the length of the process, and Mary's presence seemed to trigger tears in both of us.

'I can't do this,' whined Maddie.

'Of course you can, my love,' said Mary, holding Maddie's hand and stroking her hair, 'but you've got to work with me. Right then, let's do this.'

And with that I assumed the head and hand holding, and Mary along with the trainee midwife

Aoife, who'd spent all morning with us giggling at our moaning, took up their positions to welcome Maddie's baby into the world.

'OK, Maddie. On my say-so I'm going to need you to give me a big push. I need you to push from your bottom, and I need you to keep pushing until you can't push any more. OK?'

By now absolute fear had gripped Maddie, and all she could do in response was nod.

'All right, Maddie, take a deep breath in from your nose, one, two, three – now, push, push, push, push, push, push, push, push, and relax. Quickly, let's go again, breathe through your nose and push, push, push, push, push, push, push, and relax. Well done, Maddie, we've got a head. Good woman.'

She was right. I didn't want to look down, but I couldn't help myself.

It was the weirdest, most wonderful thing I'd ever seen. And although Maddie had clasped my left hand so tight that I'd lost feeling in it, and she'd even reopened the cut I'd sustained in my Jacuzzi drama, I was overwhelmed with pride.

'OK, let's get this job finished,' ordered Mary, snapping me out of my trance.

'One more time, Maddie. We need a great big push down through your bottom, you're doing great. In through your nose, one, two, three and push, push, push, push, push, push, push, push . . . Ah, we have a baby.'

The room fell silent.

Maddie and I stared at the midwife who was wrapping the baby in a little blue towel and poking about at its mouth. The two of us became statues waiting to hear the baby's cry.

We waited . . .

And waited . . .

Two other women wearing blue midwife's coats rushed in and circled around the baby, but apart from the whispers there was nothing else to be heard.

I could feel Maddie's grip tighten again. 'Eva . . .' she said, trying to fight back the tears.

'I know,' was my only response. I wasn't able to speak and I could hardly breathe for the fear that I might miss the baby's cry. But it wasn't coming and the midwives had started looking spooked too.

Although I had hoped to cut the cord, I watched as one of the women did so before whipping the baby across to a unit with loads of gadgets on it.

There they continued to fuss and began to administer oxygen to the baby. But still there were no cries to be heard. Was the baby dead?

Maddie didn't deserve this. She'd lived like a saint these last few months. Her life was a monotonous rotation of light exercise, sleep and constant grazing on fruit, vegetables and dairy products.

I was just about to start praying, which was totally hypocritical, when I heard a faint noise.

Was that a cry?

Was I imagining it?

There it was again. It was definitely a weak cry.

'Nurse,' I yelled with a newly rejuvenated energy, 'is everything OK?'

'Yes, ladies,' said Mary, 'we're out of the woods. There was a little blockage, but that has been cleared.'

'Can I hold my baby?' cried Maddie, panicked.

'Of course you can, my love. You did terrific,' said Mary, picking the baby up off the table and walking towards us. 'Congratulations, Maddie; here is your beautiful baby boy.'

As one of the ward midwives Mayia tried to convince Maddie that breast-feeding was the way to go, I made my exit to the corridor to ring all the relevant parties with the good news.

Maddie's mum was first. Despite their differences she sounded thrilled with the news and gave out stink that she wasn't allowed to call up to the hospital till six that evening. I then phoned Parker, who didn't want to hear any of the gory details but said he would dutifully call up to the hospital later and sneak in a mini bottle of champers for Maddie.

I then paused. Who else should I ring?

Parker had said he'd call Lisa and Anna, so that left no one else special enough to share this with.

It was a deflating feeling.

I wanted to scream from the rooftops that my best friend had had her baby. A gorgeous 8lb 6oz lump, perfectly pink, with a massive shock of black hair. Unfortunately he'd have to go through life with the silly name of Woody. Somewhere along the way,

Maddie had fallen out of love with Troy, and became besotted with Woody. It was just as ridiculous, but his mother would always love him regardless, and so would his special auntie.

No one else needed, or deserved to know about his arrival, I thought. This was a sacred time. All our fleeting social pals about town would find out in due course.

But seeing this child's birth had stirred something inside me.

Putting all the rock 'n' roll stuff aside I craved normality. I might have been fighting it, but I just wanted all the regular stuff in life.

Normally I would have been disappointed by the fact that neither Michael nor Lucy had left a message to ask if I was all right, but today I was glad. This was the perfect day to break contact with toxic friends. He had showed himself to be a compulsive liar and a fraud, and Lucy, well, she was just a dangerous manipulator. I wanted nothing more to do with either of them.

From now on I was going to be true to myself, and stop wasting time. I wanted babies of my own some day. I wanted to meet a good man, fall in love, get married, and then have children. It was painfully traditional but seeing the miracle of a new life being born had had a profound effect on me.

Although I hadn't talked to God in a long time, I decided now was as good a time as any to pick up contact. So I found myself a quiet step, sat down and began talking in my head.

'Hiya, God,' I started, as if we were old pals. 'It's Eva here. I haven't said hello in a while, but I wanted to check in and thank you for your help today delivering Woody safely to us. I know you're a busy guy, but I believe you had a hand in it, so thanks. Now I know it's probably a bit greedy to ask you to help out again today, but is there any chance you could do me one more favour? It's a bit of a stretch, I know, but – could you reprogram me and make me a better person?'

9

Within the space of a week, Woody Lord had turned the Bitches of Eastwick from proud doting adults, back to three highly emotional and short-tempered zombies. The sleep deprivation had hit us all bad. While Parker and I had tried ear-plugs from Boots, both soft foam and wax versions, neither worked to block out the constant crying.

Even Sister of Mercy Jeff had flown the coop and retreated to the quiet calm of his own home in Kildare, as much to escape Parker's irritability as Woody's colic.

I was literally on the verge of telling Parker that Maddie's mum had asked her to move home after falling in love with the baby at the hospital, but I knew she was happy where she was, cocooned in the Parker Hotel away from reality.

If he knew the truth he'd personally carry the two of them back to her mammy's, but aside from the hard labour, he secretly loved having them around. He just found it hard to admit.

As a dysfunctional parenting trio, we were finding it challenging. But just when you thought you'd explode with frustration, the little man would go and do something cute and you'd forgive him everything.

Sometimes it would be the simplest of bodily functions that made us laugh the most.

He'd fart, we'd praise him.

He'd burp, we'd congratulate him.

He'd wee in our face . . . we'd pass him back to his mother.

Yes, it was as if I blinked and everyone's world around me changed, but I was still stuck in my rut.

Since Parker fell in love with Jeff and Maddie became pregnant and gave birth to Woody I had felt like a gooseberry in both of their lives.

Himself no longer had the time for the heart-to-hearts we used to have. We used to spend hours just scrutinizing the minor plot-lines of *Coronation Street*, and laughing at the snotty women who ended up in corporation houses on *Wife Swap*.

But these days if he wasn't putting in extra hours on editing a glossy coffee-table book in aid of a cancer charity, a project he was introduced to by Jeff, he was hanging out with said Mr Wonderful and being a much better person for doing so.

As for Maddie, her every waking moment was consumed with being a mom, and she had no time for frivolous chats about how cute Daniel Craig was or whether Jonathan Rhys Meyers was on or off the drink again. As much as I tried to humour her, listening to the constant updates on how much cheese she had eaten that day or the benefits of swallowing strawberry and banana Innocent and probiotic vitamins to ward off thrush, she wasn't the free spirit of old.

She had outgrown me, and I hated not being able to hold her interest. Or share in the simple thrills that are support tights and Dunnes high-waisted knickers.

Both of my best friends had moved on. I felt I was the only one remaining static. My world was juvenile and vacuous compared to theirs. It was if they both decided to grow up and forgot to invite me along on the journey.

I felt it was very unfair on me. We had always done everything together.

I knew that our party lives couldn't continue for ever, I just wasn't prepared for the comedown of being the last girl standing.

After the summer drought my freelance work had finally picked up pace and I was now enjoying the privileges of occasional junket life again. Thankfully, editorial jobs at girlie magazines were just as easily changed as journalists.

Although I hadn't been asked to interview any sexy celebrities, or research any Christmas shopping trips in New York or Dubai, I was back in the saddle so to speak with a freebie murder mystery weekend at a castle in Tipperary for *Social & Personal* magazine.

The coach down was full of all the old familiar journos, looking eager to get pissed, with a splattering of newer younger faces who diligently read their welcome packs cover-to-cover. I had been hoping for a bit of male talent to hold my hand through the scary moments, but I wasn't to be given such a gift. So I teamed up with a couple of pleasant girls who were fresh to the business, and basked in their excitement as I told them old war stories of celeb interviews gone bad.

'Who was your most difficult interview?' asked one.

'Oh, the cast of *Pearl Harbor*,' I gushed. 'Josh Hartnett was so full of himself, and Kate Beckinsale was one of the most boring women I'd ever met, yet so beautiful in the flesh. She was dull as dishwater but utterly gorgeous.'

The girls hung on my every word, enthralled by my experiences.

'And who was the most famous person you ever met?'

'Emmm,' I paused for a dramatic build-up. 'Well, I've met loads of them really: Bono, Jagger, Beyoncé, Clinton, the Trousersnake, Pammie, Paris, Flatley, Leo . . .'

'DiCaprio?' the same girl butted in frantically.

'Yeah, he's not so cute in person and seriously grumpy as well.'

'Noooo.'

'Yeah, wouldn't do it for me. I had one glass of champagne in his company and left.'

'Wow. I love him. He could be rude to me all night

and I'd stand there and take it. *The Beach* is one of my all-time favourite films.'

'What about Beyoncé?' asked another now hungry for gossip.

'She's a big girl,' I retorted.

'In what way?'

'In the way I looked like a Smurf standing beside her. She's not your average teeny pop star. She's a whole lotta woman.'

Before I knew it, my tales of celebrities misbehaving had taken us the three-and-a-half-hour journey to the quaint castle.

From the outside it looked quite tatty, which I supposed helped in giving the place an eerie atmosphere, but once inside we were handed hot toddies in mock tankards and directed towards a large flamboyant limestone fireplace with heraldic arms over it, which instantly made us feel all warm and historic.

When the organizers sussed that we could be settling in for the night, after several more requests for refills, a bizarre and wizened old man appeared and asked us to follow him on a brief tour of the castle.

Of course no one jumped at the suggestion, as we were all quite happy where we were, but after a little persuasion from the hyper PR representative, we shook the lead out of our asses and followed 'Hermon' out of duty.

After a far from brief exploration of the castle, during which we learned some of its history, the people who had died there in mysterious circumstances, and that the vaults were strictly off limits, we were finally released from Hermon's grasp and allowed to check out our digs.

Since I had bonded well with the new girls Kirsty and Melanie on the drive down, we agreed to bunk together and were offered a huge Gothic room to share.

It was budget medieval, with few original features aside from the crumbling exposed beams, the damp, and the large cobwebs which seemed to stretch everywhere, but it was pretty cool, and we each got a four-poster bed to call our own.

We were just unpacking our cases when a loud knock came on the door.

Being nearest, I opened it to find a very handsome blond man standing opposite me. Kitted out in a purple velvet smoking jacket complete with a gold cravat, he looked a bit ridiculous, very Hugh Hefner, but it complemented the overall image of the castle, and I was blessed with the ability to imagine men naked from an early age anyway.

'Good evening,' he said in what seemed to be a Polish accent, 'my name is Jacub, and welcome to Castle Henry. I need to inform you about dinner. It will be served at eight o'clock sharp.'

I was shaping up for a big flirt but the words 'Thank you' had barely left my mouth when he was gone. He might have ignored my womanly wiles on this occasion but he couldn't escape me all night. Things were suddenly looking up, I thought.

I turned to my two roomies to rave about the hunky host and found them busy applying make-up and sending texts, oblivious to the in-house totty. They had missed him completely. What a stroke of luck for me!

Not wanting to miss any of the action, I bullied the girls into arriving early for dinner, which meant more red wine for us.

Wearing a midnight blue princess-style flowing dress with plunging neckline, I felt quite the part for such an ostentatious occasion.

Even some of the guys had gone to great lengths to get into the spirit of things by wearing dinner jackets. Normally hacks are a stubborn breed and wear the same smelly clothes wherever they go, but this time they'd made an effort, which suggested everyone was up for the craic.

During our starters, a very whiffy pork terrine, we were treated to musical clues for the pending murder.

It was almost painfully camp, but truly hilarious. Aongus the head waiter pranced around the long tables like a singing Poirot on acid, teasing us with details of unsolved murders which had taken place in the castle in years gone by and urging us to look out for any suspicious activity.

Unfortunately what followed was a greasy roast chicken dinner, which tasted of the pewter plates it was presented on. And despite taking extra care, I clumsily managed to splatter my lovely dress with stains.

But I wasn't overly bothered. The red wine had a strong acrid aftertaste but it was more consumable than the food, so I was happy to be out, and loving the whole spectacle.

Although Jacub had paid me little attention all evening I wasn't giving up hope, and timed a toilet break perfectly to bump into him in the corridor. Just as planned, I managed to collide with him as I walked out of the dining room. The only problem was that he was carrying a large chalice of mulled wine: before I knew what was happening I had dipped both my boobs in the hot vino bath, totally finishing off my special dress.

'Ohmigod, ohmigod!' I yelped, as the wine started to scald its way through my bra.

Mortified, Jacub quickly placed his wine on a sideboard and grabbed some cloth napkins from the dining room. Without thinking, he immediately started dabbing me down. I stopped wriggling and started smiling at him.

'My apologies,' said Jacub, as he took a large step back, even more embarrassed. 'You have beautiful breasts – I mean . . . I hope I didn't burn you. I'm so sorry. Please forgive me.'

'You are forgiven,' I said, giving him a naughty drunken pout.

'I'm so sorry again. Is there anything I can do for you?'

'You can escort me to my room, please so I can change my dress. I'm nervous of these cold corridors now, knowing of all the old souls that still haunt them.'

Without hesitation Jacub offered me his arm and we spun around and started in the direction of the bedrooms.

'You have no reason to be worried, Miss . . .'

'Valentine, but call me Eva.' Maybe it was the vinegar wine but all of a sudden his eyes seemed more sparkly, his ears looked decidedly edible and his chest, which was directly in my eyeline, looked more impressive. His jacket, I had now decided, was more Friday night Jonathan Ross than *Playboy* attire.

'Of course, Eva,' he smiled. We walked the rest of the way in silence, our arms still linked, the sexual tension building. By the time we reached my room we had shared nothing but a few lustful looks.

As I rooted for my key, Jacub stood awkwardly, probably trying to decide what to do or say.

'Would you like to come in and help me drink my welcome gifts?' Drunkenly, I stared him straight in the eye.

'Emm, er, I don't think that would be appropriate. I must get back to my service.'

Out of nowhere I sprang back into old diva mode. It was totally out of left field and I didn't see it coming. Nor did Jacub, bless him.

'Fine,' I hissed, as I hastily opened my door and slammed it shut behind me, 'thanks for nothing.'

Once inside I cursed my stupid temper. I had just

been childishly rude to an utter gentleman. Why did I never learn?

I was about to fling myself on the bed in a huff when there was a knock at the door.

I hoped it would be Jacub on the other side, and it was.

'Miss Valentine—'

'Listen, I'm really sorry,' I butted in, 'I'm just a little drunk. I get really stupid sometimes.'

'But I just wanted to say—'

'Jacub, ignore me. Honestly. I saw a come-on where there wasn't one. I had too much to drink. Go do your thing and forget about me.'

My self-pity stank, but Jacub seemed forgiving. 'You are very beautiful,' he whispered. His polite words caught me totally off guard.

'Excuse me?'

'You are very beautiful,' he repeated, 'I wanted you to know that.'

'Oh. Thank you . . .'

'I'm afraid I must go now,' explained Jacub, almost sounding regretful.

'OK.'

And before I shut the door he had walked back off down the corridor.

Why couldn't I have fancied one of the journalists? I wouldn't have to ask one of them twice to share a free bottle of wine. It would have been a wham, bam, thank you ma'am, one-night-stand that I'd regret in the morning, but at least I wouldn't feel guilty about wanting casual sex. Journos don't do guilt. It's a forbidden gene in our shallow business.

Philosophically thinking that being shunned wasn't the end of the world, I changed out of my soiled dress back into the casuals I had arrived in and texted Maddie, who I knew would be still awake with Woody. I then retouched my make-up and headed back down to the group before they started wondering if I was the surprise murder victim.

As I made my way down the grand staircase adorned with moth-eaten tapestries and portraits of tyrannical-looking men and women, I was greeted by an unfolding drama.

At first glance I could see several people pacing around frantically on their mobiles, while a couple of ambulance men wearing fluorescent jackets ran through the reception towards the dining room carrying large black cases.

It was a much bigger production than I had expected; it was very authentic.

I walked back into the dining room. All I could see were shell-shocked faces everywhere. Still drunk, I started to laugh at how seriously everyone was taking the murder mystery but all I seemed to evoke were evil glares.

On closer inspection I saw Alfie, one of the older broadsheet journos, lying on the ground looking very pale and bloated. Was he in on the gig, or had something happened to him for real?

I looked for the girls, to hear what had happened

since everyone around me seemed so panicked, but they were nowhere to be seen. Jacub was also conveniently missing. Poor bloke probably ran out of the castle crying sick to the management.

In the midst of the commotion I did manage to grab our singing waiter Aongus, but I had to walk and keep up pace with him as he wasn't prepared to slow down for a chat.

'Some sort of nut allergy,' he blurted before rushing on to the kitchen.

Nut allergy? Surely that wasn't part of the mystery weekend?

Not knowing quite what the etiquette was in such situations, I poured myself another glass of burgundy-coloured petrol and sat down in a corner. There were already too many people interfering and taking up space, the best thing I could do for Alfie was stay out of his way so the professionals could attend to him.

Poor guy, I'm sure the only drama he thought he'd be witness to was death by chocolate mud pie and a bad actress slumped over a writing table leaving a crucial clue.

Just as I emptied my glass, the situation began to calm down.

With Alfie *en route* to Nenagh hospital, our stressed-out hosts huddled in a corner for a pow-wow and then returned, suggesting we rejoined the evening where they'd left off.

'It would be a shame to spoil the fun for everyone,' explained Aongus, trying to sound upbeat.

The response, 'Yesss, Alfie's an awful selfish fucker tryin' to upstage the show. Less carry on,' echoed around the room, from an even drunker journo than me.

As a displeased rhubarb murmuring grew, Aongus asked for hush and encouraged us to move into the drawing room again for after-dinner drinks beside the fire. Clearly no one had told Aongus that the more alcohol you serve journalists, the uglier an evening gets. I reckon he was probably hoping we'd all get so drunk we wouldn't be able to remember how disastrous the venture was, and would write up our stories based on their glowing press release.

Although we were never going to restore the gaiety of the start of the evening, a level of joviality conquered. But no matter how hard I tried to get back into the groove, I had peaked too soon.

Quietly removing myself from a Cluedo moment of trying to solve whether it was the Butler or Colonel Mustard who bumped off Mrs Richardson the castle's cleaning lady, I slipped back upstairs to climb into bed. Unable to stomach any more drink, the idea of a night's sleep without the boom of a newborn's cry in the next room was most appealing.

I hoped Kirsty and Melanie would not come back till late, when I'd be in such a deep sleep that they wouldn't disturb me.

I was just slipping into an old Rolling Stones T for bed when the antique phone beside my bed rang.

I wasn't going to answer it as it couldn't possibly be for me, but out of sheer curiosity I had to.

'Hello?'

'Hello, it's Jacub.'

'Who?'

'Jacub. I walked you to your room earlier.'

'. . . Oh, Jesus, Jacub sorry, I wasn't expecting . . . I mean, hi. Sorry.'

'I didn't mean to disturb you.'

'No, not at all, I've only realized there was a phone in the room. Is everything OK?'

'I was wondering if you were OK. You left without saying goodnight.'

'Yeah, I just got tired. It's been an eventful night.'

'Oh.'

'Is there anything else?'

'I was hoping I could spend a little time to talk with you.'

'If you like, but should you not be dipping someone else's boobs in mulled wine?'

'Hemm, sorry again, no, I'm free now.'

'All right, where are you now?'

'I'm lying on my bed.'

'Where are your quarters?'

'The next floor up . . .'

'So basically you're on top of me now?'

'Ha, very good, yes I am.'

'Soooo, how does it feel?'

'Pardon me?'

'How does it feel to be on top of me?'

'Oh yes, very nice . . . Em, so what are you doing now?'

'I'm just lying on my bed, all alone.'

'Em yes, and what are you wearing?'

'Aren't you the naughty boy, what do you think I might be wearing?'

'Well, I think you would look very nice in your underwear.'

'Really? And what colour underwear would you like to see me in?'

'I think maybe red, or white – no, definitely red.'

'Well, aren't you the lucky boy, Jacub. It just so happens that I am lying on my bed with nothing else on except my red lace bra, and my small red thong.'

'Thong?'

'Panties.'

'Ohhh . . .' I could hear him starting to breathe quite heavily on the other end of the line. Without warning, my evening had once again turned around.

Was this phone sex? I'd learned from previous occasions that I wasn't very good at talking dirty. I just hoped my Polish pal was able to take the lead. As I waited for him to speak again, I could just hear some sort of disturbance, then 'Hello Eva?'

'Yes, what ya doin'?'

'Sorry, I was just making myself more comfortable.'

'Are you comfortable now?'

'Yes, very. Can I ask you to describe yourself?'

'Sorry?'

'I just thought you might be able to tell me what you are doing, or feeling.'

Feeling randy, I decided to go for broke with my

Amanda Brunker

dirty talk. I'd never see this bloke again, so if I was crap I wouldn't have to face the mortification.

'You know, it's very hot in here, Jacub. I think I might have to take my bra off.'

'How would you do that?' he asked lustfully.

'Well, I'd have to sit up on my bed, arching my back and carefully undo the delicate catch at the back. Then I'd slowly slip my two hands up over the straps and slide them down over my shoulders . . . Then with a light shaking movement I'd ease my red semi-see-through bra over my breasts and down across my nipples.'

'What do your nipples feel like?'

'They're haaaard,' I panted. 'And they're pert. And a beautiful dark brown colour – do you like dark pert nipples, Jacub?'

'Oh, very much.'

'And what about you? What are you wearing right now?'

'I'm not wearing anything.'

'And are you touching yourself?' My confidence had grown with my desire.

'I am stroking my penis. But I imagine it is with your hand.'

'And how am I doing that?'

'With long strokes, and then . . .'

'And then what? Would you like me to lick it?'

'Oh, yea'us . . .'

I was about to offer up some more words of motivation when—

314

'*Tak, tak, tak . . . O moj boze . . . Ja pierdole . . . Ja pierdole.*' He'd clearly started orgasming in Polish.

Disappointed that there was very little satisfaction in it for me, I made the swift apology that someone was coming into the room and hung up the phone. He rang back immediately, but I ignored it. Instead I lay back in my lush four-poster bed and invented a romance between myself and the Irish rugby captain Brian O'Driscoll.

Over dinner one of the girls had mentioned that she met him in a club one night and found his bulging biceps under a tight black T a real turn-on. I had never fancied him myself, but I could appreciate her anecdote of a beefy rugby player. So since I was already turned on, I thought I might as well have a happy ending like Jacub.

Although I started off picturing the BOD grabbing my breasts from behind with his meaty hands, fingering my nipples and kissing the back of my neck, by the time he had worked his way around to face me, he had miraculously morphed into Piers Morgan.

Stripped of his dark trademark suit, Piers was wearing nothing but an expensive crisp white shirt with its high collar open, exposing just a little of his tanned bare chest. And he looked very happy to see me.

But although I had always secretly fancied him, his cheeky smile wasn't working for me this time, so I pictured Gordon Ramsay, Jonny Wilkinson and even Vinny Jones before I settled on Michael; my bad-assed, cocaine-sniffing slut of a man, Michael. Well, my once upon a time Michael.

I hated the bastard for all the hurt he had caused me, but it seemed the more I cursed him in my head, the more turned on I became.

Within seconds of imagining my New Yorker being rough with me, grinding against me, and slapping my ass the way he did, I trembled with the most intense orgasm. I had built up such immense emotion that my body twisted and crumpled until I could no longer continue touching myself.

For a few moments I lay there prolonging this glorious sensation I was feeling. Why was it that someone I now harboured such venom for could manage to serve me so much pleasure?

What a typical woman I was. Treat the bitch mean, keep her forever keen . . .

The morning of Woody's christening had started off a disaster.

Everyone was in a grump to start with as Woody had spent the whole night waking up on the hour, every hour. Parker and I reckoned it was something to do with the full moon, but Maddie was convinced her child was teething.

'Babies can be born with exposed teeth,' she informed us, 'I know my baby. And he's getting teeth. The fact that he's only a month old means nothing.'

To make matters worse, the poor little fella also had a bad cough and Maddie was frantic with worry.

I'd pleaded with the local pharmacist to give me some sort of medication like a cough bottle, but was told bluntly, 'There are no cough bottles for children under twelve months.'

If that wasn't enough to be going on with, yet more annoying problems surfaced. There were the curious yellow stains that somehow magicked themselves on to Woody's christening robe, the unknown whereabouts of Parker's video camera, not to mention the issue with the melted baptismal candles.

Bright spark yours truly had foolishly left them in a bag beside a radiator, which resulted in an unholy mess and many more grey hairs for Maddie.

After much screaming and stressing, we gathered our bits and walked out of the apartment at 1.15 to make the church at two o'clock.

By then Woody's robe was pure once again, thanks to the power of Vanish.

Jeff managed to locate the video camera on top of their wardrobe, and as he looked incredibly suspicious we just said nothing and thanked him. And after an emergency call to Maddie's highly religious grand-mother, the candle situation was sorted; she'd bought several back-ups just in case.

It'll be all right on the night, we told ourselves. What could possibly go wrong now?

But our cheery optimism didn't last long, as Jeff's Porsche Cayenne Jeep decided to have a flat battery. A far from amused Maddie then drove us to the church in her tiny 3 Series.

God only knows how four adults and one Maxi Cosy car seat actually fitted into such a small motor. It was a tight squeeze, but on the plus side we got to know each other more intimately on the journey.

When we arrived not only was Maddie's family there to meet us, but so was the rain, which in fact was a good thing because it ushered us all into the church quickly and cut out the idle chit-chat.

With just minutes to spare, Parker, Maddie, myself and Woody took our places at the top of the church along with five other families who were also having their children christened. Tragically Jeff had to sit alongside some of Maddie's family, and got off to a bad start with them when his mobile phone started to ring from inside his jacket pocket.

The theme from *Fantasy Island* clearly wasn't popular with this clan, but he made his apologies and looked very cute in doing so.

With Parker as the Fairy Godfather and me as the Wicked Godmother – that's 'Wicked' in the alcoholic beverage sense – I started to fear for Woody's moral upbringing. I don't think I was alone with such concerns. While I tried my best to ignore the whispers of the extended Lord family, as I didn't think I'd benefit from their gossiping, I couldn't escape hearing from two pews down, 'He's the queer who won't let her move home', and, 'She's the adulteress. The one who slept with her married boss and then leaked it to the papers.'

I was maddened by the inaccuracies.

How dare they pontificate over Parker and me! They have no right. They don't have a clue what they're talking about.

Yes, he's the queer, but there's nicer ways to put it. But he's not stopping Maddie from moving home. She just couldn't stand to be near such bigots. And who could blame her? As for being called an adulteress, I suppose that's fair enough, but I wanted to march straight over to them and put them straight that it wasn't actually my boss that I snogged – and only snogged – and that I *never* leaked it to the papers. As if!

Sure, the running joke in my business is never let the facts get in the way of a good story, but it sure ain't funny when you're on the receiving end of mistaken hearsay.

I was building up to an evil glare when the priest turned to face us from his cup-polishing and table-laying and introduced himself. The words, 'Welcome everyone, my name is Father Neven,' had barely left the man's mouth when Parker blurted out, 'Oh good God.'

As the congregation stretched to see what the commotion was, Parker dipped his head in shame, leaving Maddie and myself also to look around in bewilderment, pretending we didn't know who was taking the Lord's name in vain.

'What's up with you?' I whispered, furious that he'd given the relations more ammunition to attack us with.

'I've shagged the priest,' laughed Parker, all the

while holding his nose trying to stop himself from snorting.

'What?'

'You heard me the first time . . . I shagged the bloody priest.'

'Are you sure it was this old wrinkly?' I asked, making sure Parker was right before I alerted a highly stressed Maddie to the fact. 'Are you sure it was Father Neven or whatever he calls himself?'

'Ha. Trust me, it was him,' sniggered Parker. 'His name on Gaydar is Neven Heaven '69. We met at a café in Dun Laoghaire and after two skinny lattes we were back at his, getting jiggy with it.'

'Fuck off.'

'Excuse me, Miss Valentine, that sort of language is not acceptable in such places as this. We are in a house of worship.'

'Listen, I can't see much worshipping going on, can you? Ohmigod that's so funny. Half the family look like they want to bash us. I'm surprised you didn't explode into a big puff of smoke as you walked through the door.'

'I was quite surprised myself.'

'I'll have to start calling *you* Eve from now on, you temptress.'

'Actually, I quite like that. Grrrr. Fancy a bite of my apple?'

I thought we had been keeping our conversation at low volume but the second I turned to inform Maddie of our news I found she was snarling at me.

'Eh, is there any chance on keeping focused for like five minutes please? I can hear my mother complaining, saying I told you so in my ear. What's so blinking funny?'

'I'm sorry, hon, just forget it. We'll behave.' I tried to sound convincing but her face remained angry.

'Tell me now so we can get it out of your system before the really important stuff kicks off.'

'You'll go mad. I don't want you to go mad. Please just forget about it.'

'Just tell me.' Her face was turning a scary beetroot colour and totally overripe.

'OK, OK, it's no biggie really, it's just Parker's shagged the priest.'

'What?'

'Calm down, I'm sure it was ages ago. It was just a one-off thing. I'm sure Neven Heaven '69 won't remember him.'

'You're kidding me?' As Maddie's jaw dropped, her sense of humour thankfully popped right back in.

'That's ma-ad. I won't be able to look him in the eye now. God, what hope has my child got? I get a randy reverend to baptize him. I give him two nymphomaniacs as godparents, and as a further insult I stick on him a stupid name like Woody. You couldn't write this stuff.'

'I'd say we've got the makings of an infamous porn star on our hands.'

'Yes, this is a very proud moment for me, Eva,'

explained Maddie, as she bounced Woody on her knee to pacify him. 'I'll be talking to the Biography Channel in years to come, and they'll ask me when I first knew Woody would become the most successful porn artist of all time. And I'll say it was his christening day. The day we wetted his head and all the sex addicts in the room prayed for him to continue their good work!'

Despite some childish chuckling from the three of us, the saving of Woody's soul went off without any further hitches. Jeff even managed to catch some of the event with the five minutes of battery time the video had left.

By the time we gathered up our coats and made it outside, the clouds had dispersed and the smokers among us had set about making new ones.

Trapped by Maddie's overly excited grandparents, who were beaming with pride, we struggled to find adjectives to compliment the service.

Parker got in early by saying what a lovely sermon it was. Maddie claimed that having the baptism 'was extremely special to both Woody and me'. Which left smarty-pants here claiming, 'Isn't it nice to see a priest so in tune with his parishioners? I really felt he touched a part of all of us today. Parker, didn't you feel touched by Father Neven?'

Putting on his grown-up face Parker concurred. 'Yes, I feel like I've been touched.' Poor Jeff could only look on in confusion.

This discussion was about to run out of legs when

it was abruptly cut short by Granny Lord screaming, 'Over here, Father!'

With no time for escape his holiness had descended upon us and insisted on shaking hands with everyone. It was one of those sturdy firm handshakes which showed strength of character and was instantly endearing.

Maddie and I held our breath as he grabbed Parker's hand. Had he recognized him? Ohmigod, he had . . .

'Oh, hello again,' smiled the Father. 'You're the chap who has just become godfather to Woody, isn't that right?'

'Yes, Father,' uttered a bewildered Parker.

'Great stuff, wonderful name and a wonderful child. Yes, a great day for everyone.'

'Indeed, Father, a great day.' Parker was now almost hyperventilating with the fear that either Maddie or I would blurt something out, and was bulging his eyes in our direction.

I was just about to make an excuse to head for the car when Neven Heaven '69 had a twinge of recollection, and asked, 'So have you been to my church before? I'm thinking you look very familiar, Parker.'

Once again Maddie and I held our breath.

'Em – mm,' stuttered Parker, 'No, I must just have one of those common faces. People think they know me all the time. I usually frequent the Glasmount parish.'

'Really?' Father Neven said, straining to figure out Parker's familiarity. 'I never forget a face.'

The voice inside my head screamed: Maybe you might recognize his arse! but I bit my lip and signalled in the direction of the car to Maddie.

Making excuses that she needed to get Woody out of the cold, Maddie told her grandmother how well she looked and asked if they were OK for getting back to her mum's for some food and drinks.

'Yes, yes, your grandad will get the car for me in a minute, but thank Father Neven again for his beautiful sermon.'

'Sorry, thank you, Father Neven, for everything,' Maddie smiled dutifully.

'Not at all, it was a pleasure. I hope to see you back to the church soon. And call me Adam, it's less stuffy . . .'

'Jaysus, would you Adam and Eve it? I mean, what were the chances?'

Back in the safety of the car, Jeff was brought up to speed about Parker's dalliance, and being the easy-going guy that he is, took it very well.

'Sure I ended up sitting behind some nutter I'd met in the George a few months back, he wouldn't stop annoying me. You know, one of those blotchy drunks. Maddie, you'd know who he was. There was a man in a dark navy suit, pale pink shirt and badger grey hair, about mid-sixties. Do you know him?'

Now it was the turn of Parker and myself to hold our breath. As Jeff spoke you could feel the tension build.

Jeff looked worried. 'What's wrong?'

'Let's just drop it,' said Parker.

'Why? Who's that guy? I'm sorry if I offended anyone, I just thought we were sharing honesty moments.'

'It's fine, Jeff. That guy you were talking about has a drinking problem, and sometimes falls off the wagon. He also suffers with depression. But your sighting kinda answers a lot of questions we had about him and explains the reason for much of his torment,' said Maddie quietly.

'Why?'

'Well, Jeff, that man you're talking about is my father . . .'

10

It was now mid–December and Maddie was still refusing to leave the security of the apartment.

Parker or myself bought any essentials, and the Tesco online service was her only other lifeline. The only fresh air she was getting was when she'd drive to the Phoenix Park to push Woody around in his buggy. 'No one will spot me there,' she confided, 'Christ, I'm so out of shape. I look like Sharon Osbourne before the surgery.'

Despite offerings of Spanx and pink wigs, Maddie declined all suggestions of camouflage and remained a constant feature in front of either the TV with Dr Phil or at the kitchen sink washing, preparing bottles or soaking soiled babygros and bibs.

I'm still personally coming to terms with the sight of a yellow mustard poo substance dripping off one of our chopping boards, after Mammy Maddie dumped a pile of clothes there in a panic.

While she claimed to be perfectly happy in her

domesticity, and yes she looked pretty contented, my once vibrant and witty pal had cut herself off from the rest of her friends, and we were all starting to worry about her.

Sure, babies were meant to change your perspective on life, but they weren't meant to spell the end of it. Life as Maddie knew it had become an endless ritual of never-ending baby chores, which was something none of us could identify with or understand.

Without complaint she would feed, burp, bath, dress, nap Woody, and then while he was restlessly dozing – which was when she was also supposed to be taking a break – she would do all of Woody's laundry, make up his bottles and then just as she was sitting down for a cuppa, Woody would start to whinge from his crib, and the whole cycle would start again.

She joked that we should call her 'iRobot', and said we didn't need to be concerned for her mental state, because 'mammies were programmed to cope'.

I wasn't convinced, though. She was due a melt-down, so I made it my number one priority to ease her back into socializing. But my master plan needed more planning. My efforts to coax her to go shopping in Dundrum failed miserably. She'd moan, 'All the glamorous yummy mummies who had tummy-tucks with their Caesareans go there to while away their maternity leave. I don't want to bump into any skinny women with younger babies than mine. It's too depressing. I can handle being fat in my own shower, not frumpy in an H&M changing room.'

Silenced by her rant I stocked up the fridge with low-fat dairy, and conveniently forgot to pick up her favourite treats such as Tayto cheese and onion crisps and Magnums whenever she requested them.

I'd starve this bitch back to a social life if that's what it would take.

Because selfishly I really missed my friend, as she had always been my rock.

I was about to give up hope of ever getting Maddie to rejoin the outside world when she agreed to let her mother babysit Woody, and join me for an early supper at Le Café. It had to be a Monday night though to keep it low key, and for no longer than two hours.

Thankfully, since the release of two new publications on the market, work had started to flood in again, but I still missed the security of my regular gig at *So Now*. I shouldn't complain though, my face was out there again for all the right reasons, and if the level of money I was earning continued, I'd soon be able to start to look for my own apartment.

But for today my new-found wealth would be spent on treating Maddie.

Happy days.

All I'd need to do was ply her with some vino and before she knew it I'd have convinced her to have 'A cheeky one' round at the Haven.

Before she had time to change her mind, I booked a table for two at eight o'clock, and requested a quiet table away from the window.

When I headed off Monday lunchtime to interview some young girl band, who were being touted as 'the next big thing' by their publicist, Maddie was extremely positive about getting out and swore blind that she wouldn't dream of cancelling on me.

I was ecstatic. It was as if I had been cooped up for forty days and forty nights, starved of all social contact.

With Lisa occupying herself with more home improvements in Austria, I was without a wingman. (She said she was skiing but we had our suspicions that she'd arrive home for Christmas sporting a sleeker nose or the 'new sticky-out nipples', which she had been coveting for some time now.) The party season was upon us, and I couldn't face it without a girlie by my side.

Speaking of all creatures feline, Parker had, believe it or not, taken to the gym in his spare time, instead of spending countless hours lounging around A-list hangouts drinking, posing and gossiping.

'I've grown up,' he boasted, all the while keeping a straight face and somehow believing the words he was speaking.

Could this be true? Could Parker have finally changed his ways?

The idea of dragging Maddie back to our nirvana after her maternity sabbatical made me giddy with excitement. She had always been the main show, and I was just her support act. Without her I was directionless. But tonight was the beginning of the end. It was the end of my ligging diet, which had resulted in too many dull nights in front of the telly because I'd no one to leave the apartment with, and almost total social starvation.

Yes, tonight was the night. I was as excited and anxious as if I was going to sleep with a boyfriend for the first time.

After I finished my interview with Death's Dolls, the tragically unimpressive and moody girl ensemble, I arrived back late to the apartment to find Maddie had already left for her mother's.

Perfect. I had enough time for a quick shower, carefully avoiding the face so I didn't have to start from scratch on my make-up.

Although it was killing Maddie not to divulge her father's secret hobby of hanging around gay bars, she thought it best that it came from him instead of her.

He agreed, but then said he very rarely hung around gay men, and it wasn't something he wanted to concern her mother with just yet.

Struggling to deal with her own emotions, she'd let it go for the moment, leaving him with the stern warning that if she heard another story she wouldn't be giving him a second lifeline.

It was extremely tough for her to deal with, and I had caught her several nights crying into her pillow over him. Which was another excellent reason for me to get her out and about: to distract her from her fighting family.

As I hurried out the door almost skipping with

joy I left a quick Post-It on the fridge for Parker saying, 'Don't wait up. Maddie's back in the saddle!!!!!'

With five minutes to spare I arrived at Le Café and was seated as asked down the back of the restaurant by the manager, who was looking unusually attractive this evening. He was wearing the same all-black uniform, but must have done something with his hair, or not. He looked less groomed than normal, and had a five o'clock shadow that made him look quite sexy.

For some bizarre reason, I always thought men looked hotter just out of bed, or out of the shower, or with a hangover. Women, on the other hand, definitely need more time to perfect the sexy look.

Talking far too much like a nervous teenager, I had filled him in on the entire build-up to the night within minutes.

Trying not to seem exhausted by my nervous energy, he gave me a generous smile and said he'd send over a glass of Pinot Grigio to settle me while I was waiting for the star of the evening.

So far everything was perfect. Le Café was a happy medium; it was kinda buzzing, but there were no people sitting close enough to earwig on our conversation. Adding atmosphere, the tea lights softly twinkled on the table, which added to the dim nighttime lighting, and as I sipped on my vino I relaxed into my chair and dreamt of Christmas, and what Santa might bring me.

In my head I requested a Ferrari, a winning Lotto ticket and a call from *Vanity Fair* to be their chief celebrity interviewer, but I settled on better luck. That's all I really needed in life. I could make my own fortune with that.

By 8.15 I had knocked back my first glass of wine, so I texted Maddie: 'Get your skates on . . . I'll be pissed if I don't eat soon.'

As I called the waiter to fetch me 'Another one of your fine Pinot Grigios pretty please, and some bread, thanks', a text beeped through from Maddie. 'Don't hate me,' it read. 'Woody's broken out in a rash. En route to Crumlin with Mam.'

Rash? How could Woody break out in a rash to-night? Of all nights? Not a blemish for weeks and this is when he chooses his moment, bloody typical . . .

Thankfully my diva preciousness lasted for just a few moments. I needed to be grown-up here. My best friend would be in a panic and would need my support, not my tantrums.

Snapping out of my selfish thoughts I rang Maddie to check if Woody's condition was serious. What if there was something critically wrong with him?

Worryingly, her phone rang out three times in suc-cession. I daren't leave a message.

As soon as the waiter dropped the second glass of wine on my table, I took a massive gulp and thought of all the conditions Woody could have. Here I was complaining that Maddie had stood me up when there was a chance that her son could have scabies, or chickenpox, or worse still, meningitis!

Shame on me. Had I cursed this pure child with my

evil karma? Was it possible that I had passed on my bad luck, just because we shared the same living space? My mood was creeping into self-loathing when a text beeped through. It was Maddie. 'Can't talk now, waiting 2 see doc. Sorry 2 let U down :(((('

I felt worse.

There I was being a spoilt bitch when she was fretting about letting me down, while sitting in casualty holding her sick baby.

I rang Parker for advice, but all I got was his voice mail.

I rang Jeff, but he was busy too.

I then rang Lisa and frustratingly got her pornographic voice message which purred something like, 'Hey youuuu, its meeee, you know what to do to please me, so do the right thing after the ahhhhhhh . . . beep.'

How could I possibly leave a serious message after that? She'd be no use to me anyway. I'd wager she was flat on her back under a surgeon's scalpel, at the end of a ski slope, or indeed just under a surgeon or a skier!

I still couldn't ring my mother for advice as she was eternally sore with me over being such an embarrassment. Not to mention the fact that I'd have to listen to her usual rant of, 'Three years of college . . . for what, freelance work? Mairead's daughter down the road got an honest child-minding job straight out of school, and now she's married five years to that rich widower.'

I had no idea what to do. Should I get a taxi and go

up to the hospital? Nah, she'd know to ask me if she wanted me there.

By this stage I was starving, as I'd had nothing but a tub of Pringles earlier. I should really have gone home, but that would take another thirty minutes and my stomach was turning somersaults. So, I finished my second glass of wine, ordered a third and chicken Caesar salad to help line my belly.

Since cos lettuce was far from good soakage the wine rapidly began to take effect, and my mood became somewhat reflective as I thought over the disastrous year I'd just had.

Without doubt it had been my most catastrophic one yet, and there were still a few weeks left before I could officially start a clean slate.

I was miles away reminiscing about the domino effect a few kisses with the wrong man could have when I noticed the café manager standing over me, smiling. 'You look utterly miserable,' he said. 'I hope it's not the salad? We've got a new commis-chef from Liverpool but I'm not sure he's the real deal.'

'What?'

'Your salad, is it OK?'

'Yeah, grand thanks, sorry, I was just lost in thought.'

'So I see. Everything all right? You don't seem your bubbly self.'

'Ah, problems. You know my friend Maddie, the model, the one I was supposed to meet tonight? Well, she's had to take her son to the hospital. I'm not sure yet if he's going to be all right.'

'Of course he'll be fine.'

'Emmm . . .'

'Listen, babies get sick all the time, it's just part of growing up. She'll spend many hours with doctors over the next few years.'

'Are you speaking from experience?'

'No, gosh, no, but I come from a large family.'

'Oh.'

There was silence as I looked back at my salad, contemplating whether I could muster up the energy to finish it. Although it looked fairly appetizing, I'd completely lost my hunger and my head was kinda dizzy.

'You won't find it in there, you know,' chuckled the manager.

'Sorry?'

'The answer to all your problems.'

'Oh, very good, no I'm just a bit down. That time of year. It's been a bit of a crappy one, and I'm not sure how to go about making it a better twelve months next year.'

The wine was quite obviously working its magic, as my loose tongue had begun to run away with itself. I was about to apologize for burdening him with my woes when he asked could he join me. 'It's a slow night. Would you like some company for a little bit?'

'You?' I asked, not thinking it might sound stand-offish.

'Well, that was the thought behind the offer. I

could ask a few of the other customers if they'd be interested, but I might be arrested for pimping.'

'Ha ha, very funny, sorry, I'm not thinking straight. Yeah, sure, sit down. I'd be honoured . . . Does that mean I get a discount?'

'Ha! Even in the depths of despair you've still got your brass neck. You're priceless.'

'Always worth a shot,' I snapped back with a slight smirk.

'I agree. Let me grab myself a drink and I'll be back to you. Try not to top yourself before I get back, all right?'

Not entirely sure if I was comfortable with the manager guy, whose name I never bothered to ask, sitting down with me, my brain went into overdrive. Should I do the sensible thing, pay my bill and leave? Or should I take his kind offer of a shoulder to cry on and see how the evening progressed?

What was I thinking?

How could I be so selfish at a time when little Woody was sick?

I'd have to excuse myself politely and go.

I was just putting on my coat when a text beeped through. It was Maddie. 'Panic over. Simple rash caused by naughty detergent powder. Hope ure OK, enjoy yourself where ever U get 2. Stayin in mam's 2nite xox.'

'Going somewhere?' asked the manager, who arrived with two glasses of wine.

'Ehhh, no, there were a couple of changes of

336

plan while you were gone. But everything's fine. Cheers.'

Now that I had Maddie's consent, I texted her back, 'Phew, love you both x x.' And settled myself back into my seat.

My manager friend seemed pleased I wasn't leaving. While I wasn't quite sure if he was glad of the company because he was bored, or if he was just happy to be with me, either way I was at a loose end and I'd always found him quite friendly.

As I embarked on my fourth glass of wine my head was getting even more fuzzy and I felt compelled to ask the question that had been bugging me for over a year, 'Sorry, but what exactly is your name?'

'You don't know my name, Miss Valentine?'

'I know I should, but it's just gone on so long now that I never felt brave enough to ask before now. Sorry.'

'It's Michael.'

'Really?'

'Last time my mother called . . . Something wrong with Michael?'

'No, just, I would have thought you more of a Denis or Daragh.' I was clutching at straws. I didn't care what his name might be. I just didn't want anyone else I'd ever meet to be called Michael.

By now I could see he was starting to look at me strangely, as if I was a bit mad. And without checking with my brain first I blurted, 'Yes, I am a bit bonkers. That's why I'm sitting here on a Monday night all on my own. You'd probably do yourself a big favour by running away now . . .'

'Wow, that's the biggest helping of self-pity I've seen all year.' He fell back into his seat as he spoke.

'It's not self-pity actually. It's honesty.'

'Well, thank you for the advice, Miss Valentine, but I think I'll take my chances. I reckon I'm safe enough in your headlights.'

'Well, you've been warned. Bad karma follows me.'

'Duly noted. Actually I think your madness is quite endearing.'

'Why?'

'Well, it shows vulnerability. And that's cute. You come across as a tough cookie a lot of the time, so it's nice to see your human characteristics.'

'Maybe I'm just drunk.' I lifted my glass to exaggerate my condition.

'Maybe a little, but I've seen you worse. I've watched you breeze in and out of here over the last fifteen months, and you've always had a cheeky flirt, a funny story and a posse of people hanging on your every word. And all this time I've been throwing you freebie desserts and bottles of wine, and you never even bothered to ask my name. Yet I still did it . . . Now that's a talent.'

'What are you trying to do? Kick a girl when she's down? Make me feel bad?'

'I'm only teasing you. How about I get you a coffee and some cheesecake, and we start this conversation again. What do you say?'

'I'd say, thank you, Michael.'

'There ya go, and a smile too. I think we could be making progress.'

As he disappeared behind the counter, a wave of comfort washed over me.

I liked this guy. He was smart, witty, had the size of me, and on reflection had an easy name to remember. He probably just seemed interesting because I was half cut. And I doubt if we had anything in common other than a taste for white wine.

But I'd give him the benefit of one coffee, a piece of cheesecake and then I was outta here. Famous last words, eh?

'A café manager who used to work as a hedge fund manager – that can't be right?'

I was sitting at the end of Parker's bed, filling him in on the evening's events but he wasn't buying my new friend's story.

'And he says he lived in New York and his name is Michael? That fella is winding you up. He must have heard something.'

'No it's true. It's just a bizarre coincidence.'

'And he says he just dropped out because his head was melted with the pressure?'

'That's what he told me. He seemed quite genuine.'

'Genuine people don't exist, pet. They're just fictitious like the Easter Bunny or Santa Claus.'

'That's rich coming from the man who met his perfect partner this year.'

'OK, so I'm an exception. I met a Michael Landon and he's too good for me, and I know that. But not everyone is as lucky as me.'

'Not even me?'

'Dear God, especially not you. Well, not this year anyway, maybe next year. If I was you I'd close your bedroom door and not poke your nose out till January the first.'

'You sure know how to rain on a girl's parade. I'm going to bed.'

'I'm just being honest . . .'

'Yeah well, sometimes honesty isn't the best policy. Goodnight.'

Gosh, what an emotional rollercoaster of a night. But up until now I'd thought it had ended on a high.

Maybe Parker was right? Anything I touched this year had turned to crap. Work and relationships had been crushed with a tsunami, and I was only just managing to hang on for dear life with the few pals I had left.

I suppose I should listen to Parker and do a Snow White till New Year. Anything that seems too good to be true normally is.

In hindsight there was no way this Michael was any less of a bullshitter than the other.

Why was it that I kept attracting blokes that live in fantasy worlds? I really needed to analyse myself and work out exactly how I kept making the same mistakes in life.

As I walked past Maddie's empty room I stopped

and switched on the light. I gazed around her clutter. It was a very different sight to what you would have seen a year ago. Before her pregnancy, her domain would have been littered with magazines and photographs of jobs she'd done, girlie smalls, maybe a vibrator and even a couple of half-opened bottles of wine. Now, that scene had been swapped for Avent bottles, nappies, musical flashing toys and plenty of comfortable flannel pyjamas.

She had coped amazingly. It was moments like this that I realized how proud I was of her. Maybe I didn't tell her enough? I would from now on.

As I turned the light off and closed her door, I pictured Maddie at home in her old bed, with her son lying beside her. It was sad and wonderful all at the same time.

She had turned out to be such a caring mother – not that I'd ever questioned her abilities, but she'd taken responsibility for her foolishness in London, and Woody was now the best thing that had ever happened to her. In time she'd find someone to share her love for her son. All she had to do was open her heart just a little wider to let that person in.

As I climbed into my own bed, I wondered where I'd be in the future. But I couldn't work out what exactly it was that I wanted. I knew that I eventually wanted a family and a steady writing career. But my confidence was totally knocked, and I didn't quite know how to pick up the pieces to rebuild the foundations. Would Maddie have been able to forecast sitting in Crumlin's

Children's Hospital with a sick child twelve months ago? Of course not. Maybe I shouldn't force fate either?

Work-wise the phone had started to ring again, and as far as dating was going, tonight showed me that there were people who could still be interested in me, even when they knew my problems. But I had yet to find out if this Michael was even more cracked than me. I was too tired to figure it all out tonight. Tomorrow was a new day, and in three weeks it would be a new year. I'll right all the world's wrongs then.

I was just about to drift off to sleep when I heard a text beeping through. It was from Michael. Michael Café. Squinting with one eye I could read, 'I really enjoyed the chat. There's a whole new Eva once you let your guard down. Talk soon x.'

What a tease he was. 'Talk soon' – how thoroughly noncommittal of him. And just one x, well, he was hardly expressing his undying love now, was he? The old Eva would have texted him back immediately and said, 'Look forward 2 it! X x' but the new me will just ignore him. I'm going to try and learn from my mistakes if it breaks me . . .

'Hi mum, how are you?'

'I'm in the middle of making a stew for your sister. She's snowed under with work. What's up? Are you in trouble again? Are you looking for money?'

I had felt inspired to ring my mother and make friends since Maddie had mended bridges with hers.

Mum never made it easy but it was nearly Christmas, and I missed her and her lectures. Maybe if I had listened to her more carefully I might not be in such a state. Mother knows best and all that!

'Eva, are you still there?'

'Sorry, hiya. No, I'm not in trouble. Everything's great, actually. I was just ringing to see if you wanted to go for lunch on Saturday. We could do a bit of shopping and catch up.'

There was silence.

'Mum, are you still there?'

'Em, yes, where did all that come from? I'm not sure if—'

'Listen, Mum, I just want everything back to normal. I hate you being disappointed in me, I just want to straighten things out between us and since it's the season of good will and all that I thought we could—'

'That would be nice, Eva. Thank you.' Her interruption was timed to save us both embarrassment. We weren't a family that told each other that we loved them, and obviously my mother didn't want to break that tradition now.

It didn't matter, though, she had agreed to lunch. It was a start and that was all the window I needed to make me feel like a worthy daughter again.

Saturday lunchtime arrived, but instead of eating humble pie with my mother, it was vino with the gang at Le Café. She'd cancelled due to a neighbour dying, and promised to reschedule next week. So our relationship was still technically on the up, I hoped.

My rationale to meet up was a Christmas get-together, but it was really an excuse for me to pester everyone to look closer at Michael. They already knew him but they'd just never had cause to take a serious interest in him before. Today they were ordered to be on high alert, to pick up on any faults the poor bloke might possess.

Not that I was thinking of dating him or anything. I just wanted their opinion on him in general.

I was halfway through telling them how I'd called a truce with my old sparring partner Caroline Higgins, after bumping into her in the tiny waiting room area of Dr Freedman, the STD specialist, when Michael appeared at the table.

Without my realizing it, he'd crept up behind me as I revealed, 'I was only there for a smear, but with the look of mortification on her face, God only knows what condition of itchy fanny she could have been in for.'

'Hello everyone.' Michael smiled, all pleased with himself. 'Are we all enjoying the festive season?'

'Yes, thanks,' rang the chorus. 'Oh, hi,' I stuttered, taken back by his arrival. 'How long have you been here?'

'Long enough,' he smirked. 'So, how did you get on with the doc?'

'Oh God, I got on grand, thanks.' My face had now turned bright red. 'Clean as a whistle, apparently.'

'Well, congratulations, Miss Valentine. Yet another reason to celebrate this Christmas. Now everyone, are we all ready to make a food order?'

And just like that an awkward situation passed. He was a slick dude, and as he departed to pass our orders to the kitchen, thumbs all around the table were raised. Everyone agreed he was a decent skin.

It would be a lot easier if he was a jerk and the gang hated him. Staying single would be a lot simpler.

'He's almost as cute as my William,' gushed Lisa as she rubbed noses with her newest recruit.

'I don't know . . . I might be better off letting him go. If I gave him a chance and then messed it up, where would we go to eat?'

It was a weak argument, and Lisa was having none of it.

'There'll be other cafés, Eva, but you gotta let the love in when it comes a-knockin'. Just look at me and Will. He was my chalet boy at Lech, and the instant I set eyes on him I knew I'd met the one.'

'Jaysus, don't hold back, princess, whatever you do. No offence, Will.'

'None taken,' he smiled.

'Look, Will walked in offering clean sheets, and I offered him the chance to dirty them. He wanted to service me, and I wanted to be serviced. It's a supply and demand thing. You have a desire to be loved, and Michael "nervous breakdown boy" wants to show you love. Life is not a rehearsal. You got to make every moment count.'

'Get her,' interrupted Parker, almost choking on a piece of brown bread. 'What movie did you stroke that line out of? Life is not a rehearsal. Who are you, Mae West?'

'She's got a point,' agreed Maddie, currently enjoying her own *carpe diem* moment, 'I sure as hell wouldn't be turning down the opportunity of love from a guy who has that much familiarity with money. Then again, lunch with you lot is the most exciting thing that's happened to me in weeks so I'm easily pleased.'

She was right. Who was I to close the window of opportunity? Despite recent events I was a survivor, and although the war wounds of age were starting to collect, I was still able to attract interest from the opposite sex, and I'd be a fool to reject a seemingly decent bloke like Michael. The fact that I'd already been left with egg on my face by a different son-of-a-bitch called Michael, who also had a New York connection, was irrelevant.

I was too young to worry about my heart getting broken. And too old to let such a bachelor get away.

Maddie was always the spontaneous one. But now I'd have to be impulsive and unrestrained for the pair of us, since her reckless days were over. God love her. She has a mean task ahead of her trying to find a good man to love her and another man's child. It wasn't an impossible mission, but her luck and outlook would need to change drastically.

I was just drifting off into a little world where I imagined how life would be as Mrs Whomever, when

Parker put his arm around me and told me how well I was looking.

'Are you feeling all right?' I asked, not used to praise coming from his direction.

'Fine, thanks,' he chirped back. 'Just thought you deserved to know you were looking particularly attractive today, that's all. No hidden agenda.'

Wow. Compliments without demands from Parker, maybe my luck had already started to change. Strike that: Parker was the one who had changed, but I was happy for him and *his* new happiness. And who knows, maybe it was time for my own reversal from such terrible qualities as selfishness, greed and an insatiable need for attention and fun. I'd love to be considerate, compassionate and less diva-like.

I might not have believed such a change possible. But Parker was living proof. And Maddie had become the definition of compassionate.

She no longer made fun at other people's expense. She now got sad when looking at TV commercials for third world charities and she listened to all our problems, even if she was double-jobbing and changing Woody's nappy at the same time. Motherhood had made her warm, gentle and sympathetic. She was a new woman, a better woman, and I hoped to get bumped on to her road of enlightenment a.s.a.p.

Realizing I was still being self-absorbed, I immersed myself in Lisa's excitement. She was beaming with delight. Was this young Will guy 'the one' for her? Who knew? Not even she knew, but it wasn't a question to be dissected today. She was capturing her moment, and she wanted us to be witness to her plans.

'He's meeting the old pair tomorrow,' cooed Lisa. 'His parents are Irish. Tell 'em, Will.'

'Yes, my Paddy blood has proved me a keeper so it seems,' he smiled.

'And they moved to London before Will was born in the seventies and built most of the major roads. So we've got builder families in common. How cool is that?'

No one at the table needed to reply. She was lost in her bliss. So we just nodded and gave her encouraging smiles and allowed her to be happy.

As I started to daydream, thinking how well Lisa was looking, and wondering could that be a new nose? And is it her new highlights or the broad smile that's making her look so well? Parker interrupted the happy couple's début. 'I've an announcement to make,' he said. 'So I would like a bit of hush.'

Announcement? Was he sick? Was he evicting Maddie and myself on to the cold city streets of Dublin to fend for ourselves?

'Jeff and I . . .' He began with a nervous twinge in his voice. 'We got engaged. There, I said it. That wasn't as difficult to say as it was in my head.'

There was a silent two-second delay as the penny dropped.

'Wow, congratulations!' screamed Maddie.

'You old romantics, when did this happen?' enquired Lisa.

Leaving me with the important question: 'Does the role of chief bridesmaid come with a fab dress?'

Bizarrely, Parker rebuffed all our questions. And once we settled, he began to speak in a very slow and calculated tone. 'Actually, I've a second announcement to make . . .'

Before he had the chance to continue I squealed, 'Please don't tell me he got you up the duff?' Which was followed by Maddie choking, 'I can lend you my maternity knickers!' But our comments were met with a fake disapproving glare.

'Children, children,' he reprimanded us: 'respect for the man centre stage.'

'Sorry, Dad,' we giggled, gesturing for him to continue his story.

'OK, now that I've got your attention, I'd like to tell you all my second piece of information. It involves my wedding . . . And wait for it – ' the table had started to erupt once again with giddiness – 'my wedding to Jeff which took place . . . last weekend.'

In unison we screamed, 'What?' A smug-looking Parker took a large mouthful of vino, kissed his beau and resumed a casual posture in his chair.

'You got married? When? Where? Why weren't we invited?' As I vocalized my questions, my heart sank a little. Why didn't he want his friends at his wedding? Had it some kinky leather bondage theme that excluded us? Did he not consider us important enough to share his special day?

'Eazzzzzy,' said Parker, realizing his good news

wasn't sitting too well with the masses, 'don't take the hump with me, Eva, it was a spur of the moment thing. Jeff, you explain it better. We just got caught up in the romance of Christmas, didn't we, hon?'

'Yeah, sort of,' whispered Jeff, looking a tad guilty. A little confused, Parker dismissed his new husband and continued, 'We just happened to be walking past the Unitarian Church on Stephen's Green as a wedding was leaving last Saturday and I happened to say to Jeff, "Do you think you'd ever like to marry me?" And with that he said, "Marry me. Marry me today?" And I said, "I'd love to!"'

'What? And you just walked in off the street and they married you? Get real, we don't live in Vegas,' I reasoned.

'Don't mention the war,' teased Lisa.

'But come on, you're not really married? Are you?'

'Actually we are,' piped up Jeff. 'I organized the paperwork about a month ago.'

'You did what?' Parker gave Jeff a stare.

'I had it all planned.' He smiled, taking Parker's hand and kissing it. 'We didn't just happen to be walking past the church, and I didn't just happen to bribe the minister with €500. It was all planned in advance, because I love you.'

Without speaking, tears welled in all our eyes, especially Parker's. It was the most romantic thing that had ever happened to any of us.

'You did that for me?' cooed Parker, a little overwhelmed.

'Of course, you're my honey.'

'But, but why didn't you tell me?'

'And ruin the surprise? No chance.'

Not entirely comfortable with being surrounded by so much love, I broke the moment with, 'I can feel a big one going down . . .'

As Maddie, Lisa, Will and Parker raised their glasses in support, Jeff halted the toast. 'You can count us two lovebirds out, I'm afraid,' he said.

'How come?' Parker's smile visibly dropped.

'Because I've a little surprise planned,' explained Jeff. 'Now leave it at that.'

As if part of a pantomime we had started to whoop and cheer at the dramatic scenes. And our joy was infectious; people at neighbouring tables were smiling over with interest.

'OK, OK, sshhhh!' Parker's excitement was reaching fever pitch. 'I need to concentrate here. There's a surprise? Tell me . . . you can't leave me hanging.'

'Noooo, it wouldn't be a surprise if I told you.' Jeff had started to squirm, but from his facial expressions it was apparent that he was about to buckle.

'Go on, Jeff, tell us,' begged Maddie, 'make us all pea-green with envy.'

As the pressure from around the table mounted, Jeff finally caved in.

'All right then,' he muttered while trying to hide his broad smile, 'I've booked us on an early morning flight to New York tomorrow. It'll be our mini honeymoon. Your bags have already been packed, though obviously a generous amount of space has been left for some shopping on Fifth Avenue.'

Once again all at the table held their chests and 'Ahhhh-ed' loudly.

'And as a treat for my honey, I've organized a fabulous personal shopper by the name of Ella Goldin to help you spend some money.'

As Maddie hugged Jeff and Parker, and Lisa started snuggling with her new man Will, I looked down the café to see a very smiley Michael staring back up at me. Through the throng of fellow lunchers, he subtly winked at me, and raised his coffee cup as if to say cheers.

I toasted him back with my wine. But I wasn't sure how I felt when I looked at him.

He didn't make me feel nervous, and I couldn't work out if that was a good or a bad thing. I suppose he was just easy to be around. I was comfortable in his company. Maybe he was my comfy slippers guy?

Waiters arrived at our table of love to drop off our starters. My phone beeped.

It was Michael Café. 'Don't look so sad. Can I cheer you up?'

Can he indeed? He'd already charmed a smile out of me with his text, so I suppose he had potential.

Lisa was right. I did want someone to love me. I was ready to let love in. I was sick of all the messing that had gone on in the last year.

I had to stop looking back at what a disaster I'd made of things. I had the ability to turn my life around, I just needed to focus. And I didn't need a man to help me do that, but it would be nice to have someone to hold my hand. OK, I've got to stop obsessing and start acting on my impulses. Doing just that, I texted Michael back asking, 'Any suggestions how you could make me Happy Eva After?'

'Plenty,' came back the immediate response. 'Meet U outside Quinn's Pub 4 quick chat in 10 mins . . . Mx'.

A secret meeting. I liked his cloak and dagger style. Slowly he was beginning to warm my stone heart that had been frozen from repeated disappointment.

After devouring my minestrone soup, I stood up and was excusing myself to the loo when my phone beeped through another text. Before I could open it, Lisa had grabbed it, complaining, 'Who could you possibly want to be talking to aside from us? Let's have a look here . . . Michael?'

'Yes, I'm meeting him outside for a chat. Now give me back my phone.'

'What the hell are you meeting him anywhere for?'

''Cause he asked, and I thought, what the hell?'

'Eva, don't do it,' pleaded Lisa with strange sincerity.

'Relax, sista, I'm not running off anywhere . . . Well, not that I know of yet.' And as Lisa sat wide-mouthed, I slipped on my jacket and snatched my phone back out of her hand.

'Parker, speak to Eva,' pleaded Lisa again, now looking disturbingly worried.

'What's up now?' beamed the newly-wed.

'She's meeting Michael. Stop her.'

Parker understandably had no interest in anyone else's affairs, but did his best supportive friend act nonetheless. 'I don't know why she's getting upset,' he sighed, 'but be a pet and do what she says.'

But I wasn't going to be told. Why should I be the last old maid left on the shelf? So without further explanation I left the table and pushed my way out into the cold.

The streets were lined with festive Christmas lights, and the women screaming from the flower stalls at the end of the road helped add to the Christmassy atmosphere.

What a perfect time to start a new relationship, I thought.

As I fixed my scarf to block the wind-chill with one hand, I opened up my text messages to see what Lisa had been so upset about.

And there it was; the ultimate reason why I shouldn't step outside the door.

There staring up at me were the words 'Michael's Cell'.

Ohmigod!

Holding my breath as I opened it, seconds seemed like minutes as I waited for my screen to flash up, 'Guess who's back begging forgiveness?'

My heart skipped a beat. The mere thought of him near me made me feel nauseous. He had some cheek. He had treated me so badly, how dare he even think about making contact?

First he makes me take cocaine, and then he abandons me on the streets of Dublin. He was a total bastard. So why was my heart beating so fast? Was it hatred or stupid dangerous lust?

I could have been dead on the street and he wouldn't have cared. Did he think I was some cheap ho? How could he have the balls to text me for a bootie call after what happened last time?

I was almost snarling with anger when I glanced up from my phone to see the other Michael waving to me from the corner of the pub. He looked so happy and kind; nothing at all like the fucker who was trying to steal his thunder.

Half-heartedly I waved back signalling, 'One minute', to gather my thoughts.

Should I ignore Michael's message? No, I needed to put that selfish fucker straight.

I could see my date was starting to get anxious, so I needed to make this text quick and precise. I was just starting to plan a message in my head, when another text beeped through. Once again it read 'Michael's Cell'.

FUCK!

I thought about deleting it, but I couldn't help myself. A part of me still craved this guy's madness; his touch; his velvet voice . . . even the sight of his name in my phone was thrilling.

I didn't want to allow him into my head space, but I couldn't resist.

Through one squinted eye I pressed OPEN to read the

words, 'Don't pass out, but TURN AROUND beautiful . . .'

It was as if I had been stabbed in the chest. Michael's
text had totally winded me. I didn't know what to do
. . . so I panicked.

Not thinking straight, I started to run directly at
Michael Café who was standing outside Keogh's. He
had a cigarette in his hand and a worried look on his
face.

I wouldn't look behind me, I couldn't look behind
me for fear that I'd be sucked back in by Mickey Blue
Eyes's bad boy sex appeal.

So I ran, and kept running past Michael, Café
Michael and the cloud of his smoke, and just as I
turned the corner I heard this loud screeching of
brakes. I turned and as I did I saw a motorcyclist go
into a skid and slam into the back of a delivery truck.
With a bone-crushing crash the bike-rider, head to
toe in black leather with a matching black helmet, was
thrown in the air. As I followed his ascent I noticed
his bike skidding towards me.

With no time to react, I stood and watched as this
large motorbike came hurtling towards me and then
BANG! It hit me and as I felt myself being flattened to
the pavement, there was first intense pain in my legs
and then crack, my head hit the ground.

Shut down.

★   ★   ★

I woke up to darkness; total darkness and pain. I didn't know the cause of either, I just understood that I had been gripped by both.

As I lay flat on my back I could feel every muscle in my body ache. My legs were so painful that I almost couldn't feel them, they were that numb. As for my head, it was stinging with pain, with a piercing stabbing on the right side.

I tried to lift my hand to my head but I couldn't move it. I then tried to open my eyes to see where I was, but I couldn't open them.

What was going on? I tried again and again, but I only succeeded in working myself up into a panic. I wanted to scream for help but I couldn't open my mouth either.

I don't know where I am, I'm unable to move, or speak or see; could I be dead?

Is this what death is like?

Fuck. Is this my hell?

With no concept of time I didn't know how long I'd been alone, but it seemed like a lifetime.

With nothing active except my brain, and no one to talk to, I had driven myself to the brink of insanity trying to analyse my situation.

I remembered everything. I remembered running away from my problems, Michael Café's concerned face, getting knocked down by the motorbike. But I didn't recall anything after that.

I didn't know what injuries I'd received, or even if the motorcyclist survived.

I was so scared, so alone – but wait . . . I can hear someone's voice. It's very faint but I can work out that it's a woman. Hold on, there's actually two voices. Two women are speaking.

I'm obviously not dead. I can't be if I am hearing people talk.

I just need to concentrate really hard to work out what they're saying.

I was tuning in and out, only catching snippets of their conversation when I heard my name.

They definitely said my name.

And then it was as if someone turned up the volume. I was listening to their entire conversation of boy-friend chat. What times they were taking their breaks, and how my poor legs had taken a hammering.

'I hope for her sake she doesn't get drop-foot. There'll be bad scarring there,' said one.

'Yeah, but her Glasgow coma scale is improving. She's tolerating her NG feed now.'

Drop-foot? Scars? How bad am I?

I wasn't enjoying this Snow White status.

Somebody come wake me up, please . . .

I still wasn't able to open my eyes, or move, or speak, but I woke to the sound of a tearful Parker calling me a silly cow.

'I could have been shopping in Barneys, or having cocktails at the Rose Bar, or dinner at the Waverly.

How dare you ruin my honeymoon? When you wake up out of this coma, I'll bloody well kill ya.'

I wished I could have told him how sorry I was for destroying his surprise trip.

There were a lot of things I wanted to tell him. Thank him for.

I didn't thank him enough for all the support, financial and friendship-wise, he gave me. He was my rock when the good times got rough, even if he was often a pain in the arse.

Without him, I would have been living in a gutter somewhere. When I woke up I'd make sure to tell him that. Well, if he hadn't managed to strangle me first.

Over what seemed like weeks everyone I ever knew had passed by my bedside, with all of them crying.

Keeping a protective vigil, my parents must have etched their backsides into the chairs they banged about beside me.

As my mum fussed about, washing my face and brushing 'the little bit of hair left sticking out from under the bandages', my father did his usual moaning, and God knows what untold damage to my right hand as he continued to squeeze the life out of it.

It was such a comfort knowing they were with me. It was the closest I had felt to them in years.

Why did it have to take such an accident for my mum and dad to show their love for me?

My emotions would bounce from frustration with

them to an overpowering sense of contentment.

Of course on my bad days I'd blame my mum's eccentricities for all my difficulties in life, but on my good days it was a totally different story. I loved her and my dad no matter what our differences, and deep down I rationalized that without their stance on my lifestyle I might have been lost in transit for a very long time indeed.

Maddie being Maddie checked in with me every day, had her little cry, sprayed me with perfume and filled me in on all of Woody's latest antics. Today he woke himself with a massive fart, apparently, and managed to scrape stripes across his nose with his razor sharp fingernails, leaving him looking like a mini Adam Ant.

Lisa keeps bringing in tropical bouquets of flowers, which my sister constantly complains 'makes the place look like the bloody Botanic Gardens'.

But it's the late-night calls from Michael, Café Michael, that give me the most pleasure.

He told me he bribed the night doorman, and that it didn't take much, only a twenty, but then teased that he woulda stretched to €23, maybe €24, but nothing higher. Anything over €24 was far too rich for his blood.

We've talked for hours. Obviously he's never heard my side of the conversation, but I definitely hear his. Each evening he brings me a red rose. 'Which is kinda tacky,' he mused, 'but I'm a traditionalist at heart.' Like on any other dates, he talks about his family and friends, his hopes and dreams, and lavishes me with compliments such as, 'You're looking very attractive this evening in pink PJs' and, 'You are by far the best-looking coma patient on the ward.'

Amid the pain and the frustration of not being able to be myself, he has me smiling on the inside. When I hear sadness creep into his voice, he makes silly jokes like, 'In bed already? You really are a cheeky minx.' But my favourite part of our 'dates' is when he steals a kiss from me.

Before he leaves he leans in over me, smelling all manly, and gently presses his lips against mine. They're soft and warm, and even though I can't kiss him back, I imagine I do.

Then he whispers, 'Don't give up the fight, Eva. I think we could have a lot of fun together. I'll be waiting for you when you wake up. Sweet dreams, my dear.'

It is just a matter of time before my body heals itself.

The doctors and nurses are doing their best to fix me. And going to great lengths to reassure my mother, but it's getting easier for them to stay positive as apparently I've started to respond to stimulus.

With so much time to think, I've had time to sort out my head, and really get a grasp of what it was that I want out of life.

I want to write, I want success, and all that other 2.4 kids crap too.

Obviously I need to wake up from my coma

first, but it's coming. I can feel it, just like I can feel Michael's kisses and his honesty. It's a nice trait in a man, a novelty compared with the men that I was used to meeting.

I no longer hanker after my wild lifestyle of forgotten drunken nights and sordid one-night-stands. That's not who I want to be any more.

Sharing champagne kisses with him is a while off yet though, but I'm not letting go. I've someone to fight for, and someone fighting for me.

Maybe this accident was the best thing that ever happened. It may have been the bang on the head that I needed to knock a bit of sense into me.

Yes, my mind is made up once and for all. It has taken some time, but now I'm definite about the happiness in my life.

Because I've hope on my side, an army of good friends behind me, and a bright future with Michael, Café Michael, in front of me.

THE END

Acknowledgements

Wow. Finally it's time to say thank you to all the people who helped me along my journey.

Writing this novel was as lengthy a process as making a baby for me, but while any plans to 'Go for the girl' are definitely shelved, this experience has only ignited my passion for writing. I've loved every late night and long weekend creating it.

And while my name, in especially large print, graces the cover, I unfortunately can't take all the credit for this baby.

So here goes.

To the man I interrogated on a long four-hour car journey to Milan airport and from whom I learnt all there is to know about writing a novel, thank you Eoin Corry. You undoubtedly equipped me with the knowledge to do this.

To Ita O'Driscoll my agent, and Aine McCarthy at Font International, you have both been invaluable. Ita, you had to endure endless phone calls from me, so thank you sincerely for all your support.

As for my editor Francesca Liversidge, thank you from the bottom of my heart for seeing the potential in *CK*. You had the belief in me to make this happen and for that I will be eternally grateful. Thank you, of course, to the rest of the Transworld team, Lucie Jordan, Eoin McHugh and Lauren Hadden.

Special thanks go to the two men who claim to have created Amanda Brunker – I use the word create in a very loose form – John Sheils and Robbie Fox. Thank you for everything.

To the *Sunday World*, who have been the best employers a lost directionless former Miss Ireland could have ever imagined, thank you. Especially my editor Colm MacGinty.

Thank you to Alan Boyce and his creative team at Toni&Guy for always giving me fabulous hair.

And thanks to everyone on the social scene for inspiring me – and just in case you're vain enough to think that there is a character based on you, get over yourself. This is not an autobiography – it's fiction darhling!

Special thanks go to my great mates Joan, Ciaran, Cindy, Richard, Anna and Blathnaid. You're all a pain at times, but I love ya's.

I'd like to thank all my readers for buying

Champagne Kisses, I hope you enjoyed it as much as I wanted you to.

And lastly I'd like to thank my family – again – for everything. Norman, I told you I'd get here eventually! To Dad and Linda for following your dreams and encouraging me to follow mine. To my fabulous mum, Betty, you're a legend. Without your support (and babysitting) none of this would have been possible. I love you loads.

To Mrs McLaughlin, thank you for nurturing Edward and listening to my moaning. And to Carol for listening to Philip's.

And lastly to Philip, my partner in life. Thank you for taking the kids all those afternoons to Dundrum for me to get some peace. Thank you for rescuing me and helping me build a home and a family. And also to believing in me 110 per cent. I love our little family.

CHAMPAGNE BABES
by Amanda Brunker

Eva Valentine is back! Following on from *Champagne Kisses*, the spoilt diva finds that 'Trouble' is still her middle name.

After a near-death experience which left her in a deep coma, Eva survives against all odds and quickly marries the man who nursed her back to health. Boozing her way through the wedding and three-week honeymoon in Mauritius, Eva is shocked to learn that she is already three months pregnant.

She doesn't want a baby yet – and neither does her husband, Michael. And when Daisy is born, life is far from perfect. Weight issues, guilt about her daughter, and the struggle to keep alive a marriage to a man she hardly knows ensue. Thankfully, her hilarious best friends, Parker, Maddie and Lisa, drag her away for naughty weekends of fun and lust to Paris and New York.

Eva has been feeling like a desperate housewife, but with so much forbidden sex on offer she'll soon be feeling a whole lot more!

Praise for Amanda Brunker:

'Fresh, funny, frothy and fabulous.' Claudia Carroll

'Amanda Brunker stirs up a saucy, steaming pot-boiler spiced up with racks of totty hot enough to self-combust.' *Sunday Independent*

9781848270497

Coming in July 2009 from Transworld Ireland . . .

DO YOU WANT TO KNOW A SECRET?
by Claudia Carroll

Vicky Harper is still hopelessly single and having to face up to the unpalatable fact that the last time she had a relationship with that highly elusive species, the decent single man, was *well* before *Phantom of the Opera* hit Broadway.

So, having discovered an ancient book which says you can have anything you want from the Universe . . . and that all you need to do is ask, she decides to give it a whirl. Turns out all she has to do is focus on *thinking* her wildest fantasies into reality. Kind of like Pollyanna, except with a Magic 8 Ball, a mortgage and a lot of vodka.

So, along with her two beyond-fabulous best friends, Vicky decides to put 'The Law of Attraction' into action. Trouble is, 'The Law of Attraction' doesn't come with an instruction manual and Vicky soon realizes that you have to be very, very careful what you wish for . . .

97818482702445

FORGIVE AND FORGET
by Patricia Scanlan

*There's nothing like a good wedding . . . to
start world war three!*

And that's exactly what's going to happen if Connie
Adams, the mother of the bride, can't smooth
things over between Debbie and her dad.

He's hell bent on bringing his stuck-up second
wife and their sulky teenage daughter to the big
day, but Debbie would rather walk up the aisle of a
supermarket than have *them* at her wedding.

It's the last thing Debbie needs right now – her boss
is making her life hell and she's starting to suspect
that her fiancé's getting cold feet . . .

*So will they all live happily ever after, or are the
whole family heading for divorce?*

Reasons to love Patricia Scanlan . . .

'The ultimate comfort read' *Glamour*

'More fizzy fun from the Irish bestseller'
You magazine

9781848270152